THE DISRUPTORS

Thanks for reading!

THE DISRUPTORS

COLLEEN WINTER

The Disruptors
Copyright © 2021 by Colleen Winter

All rights reserved. Except for use in any review, the reproduction or utilization of this work in whole or in part in any form by any electronic, mechanical or other means, now known or hereafter invented, including xerography, photocopying and recording, or in any information storage or retrieval system, is forbidden without the written permission of the publisher.

This is a work of fiction. Names, characters, places, and incidents either are a product of the author's imagination or are used fictitiously, and any resemblance to actual persons living or dead, business establishment, events, or locales is entirely coincidental.

Cover design by Design for Writers

Electronic Edition: July 2021
ISBN-13: 978-1-7776132-4-2(ebook)

Print Edition: July 2021
ISBN-13: 978-1-7776132-6-6

Hard Cover Edition: July 2021
ISBN-13: 978-1-7776132-5-9

To Bella and Elise,
for teaching me the important things in life.

"In a crystal we have the clear evidence of the existence of a formative life-principle, and though we cannot understand the life of a crystal, it is none the less a living thing."

—Nikola Tesla

ONE

THE PORCH LIGHT WAS out, the space beneath the canopy dark, and the glow of the moon on the house turned the windows darker. Compared to the brightness of the streets and the blazing storefronts Maria had travelled past, it was a welcome haven. And yet she would have liked to be able to see further into its shadows. She crossed the road, her face tucked into her collar, grateful for the cover of the porch.

The rows of painted wood boards were neat and swept clean. A welcome mat lay at the door and Maria wondered if she had gotten the right place. She had been watching it for over an hour and there had been no signs of life from within the dark house. A window looked out onto the porch, double hung. She could have jimmied it, but the noise would attract unwanted attention inside and out.

She knocked three times, the door vibrating dully. It was metal that had been made to look like wood. Amanda could be watching her from inside the house even now. As kids she had always liked to play games, usually several steps ahead of Maria and everyone else. Maria turned her head to check for movement on the street. The pools from the streetlights rose up the fronts of the houses on either side.

She felt the door open, an awareness of space where there hadn't been any before.

"Look who's here."

Amanda was thin and wiry, as she had always been, her black hair pushed back from her face like an afterthought. She was fully clothed in the middle of the night, as if she had been waiting.

"Can I come in?"

Amanda ignored the entirely inadequate greeting and tilted her head to the side in invitation. Maria stepped over the threshold.

A staircase led straight up against one wall, and a dim hallway ran beside it to the back of the house, the glow of a computer screen at its end. The tension in Maria's shoulders eased as Amanda closed the door behind her, her chest loosening enough to allow a deeper breath.

She heard four deadbolts slide into place and spun back. She pulled at the handle, fear flooding into that brief release of tension, certain she had walked into a trap. It didn't move.

"Relax. They aren't for you."

"Then who are they for?"

Maria heard the panic in her own voice, a knee-jerk reaction to her fear. Amanda's silhouette moved into the shadows of the living room.

"It will be getting light soon," said Amanda, her voice cool and remote, as if they were teenagers again and Maria was overreacting. "You can't be out on the street anyways."

Maria turned her back to the door and leaned against it, forcing herself to breathe and take stock of what was really there.

Amanda sat on a high-backed couch and the red burn of a cigarette end glowed at her lips.

"You knew I was coming."

There was the flick of her cigarette into an ashtray as Amanda leaned forward. In the spill off from the streetlight, she looked older than she should, with lines around the corner of her eyes and a mouth that aged her far beyond her thirty-something years.

"Actually, I thought this was the last place you would come."

There was a ticking sound down the hall. Four taps and then it stopped.

"Is someone here?"

She could imagine her unit waiting at the back of the house, knowing she would come here. Yet how could they when she had never once mentioned Amanda's name?

Amanda tilted her head. Exhaled smoke.

"It's just me."

There was a challenge in her answer. Defiant like she had always been, but there was also something protective. New.

"Mind if I check?"

Amanda ground out her cigarette and gestured for Maria to go ahead of her.

"Be my guest."

The carpet was thick and deep. The dimness hid the details but she got the feeling there was wealth here, a level of comfort and quality that came with money. The blue cast of a screen grew brighter, its glow defining the edges of a sheer, formal kitchen.

Amanda hung back, watching with amusement more than trepidation. Maria could feel her calculating the changes in her, assessing who she had become.

"Did you kill that guy on the train?"

Maria had the memory of dead weight on her shoulders, the metal of the handcuff digging into her wrist as she had dragged Coulter across the floor. She hadn't killed him, but the media had made it look that way, his death providing an easy way to label her as a rogue soldier operating outside of the established command. She peered into the room with the source of the glow and faltered. The room was empty but for nine large screens mounted on one wall in front of a single desk and chair.

"What is this?"

Amanda moved past her and sat in the chair.

"I saw you on this one first."

She pointed to a screen showing the view of a street.

With a single key tap, an image of Maria appeared, not doing a good job of staying out of sight two streets over. She looked ragged and peaked and more than a little paranoid as she cased the street.

"Why do you have all this?"

Amanda leaned back in her plush office chair, her gaze moving from screen to screen. She looked calm. This was a place of comfort for her, no longer the fearless rebel she had once been.

"I like to know who comes to the neighbourhood."

One of the views showed aerial footage of the neighbourhood slowly lightening.

"Is that a drone?"

"I only run it at night. After the neighbours complained."

Amanda ran her hands down her thighs, frowning up at the monitors before she switched the view to a close up of Maria's face when she had stood on the porch. She smirked.

"I never expected to see that at my door."

Maria looked worse up close. Gaunt, blonde hair in tangles, an agitation in every movement that Maria hadn't been aware of but felt now in this quiet, controlled place. Every moment of the past weeks echoed in her. The journey to the Yukon to find Storm Freeman, the inventor of the Gatherer; their escape … and the moment when she had been forced to leave her behind.

The feed next to it showed a live stream of a lone figure strolling down the back lane.

"That's Marcus. Off to work. He lives three doors down."

Marcus laid a finger against one nostril and leaned over to blow the mucus into the weeds at the side of the lane. On the next step he did the other side.

"Does that every morning too."

Amanda sounded indifferent, as if she had watched this routine too many times.

A tall, broad-shouldered man appeared on the screen showing the street in front of the house. Maria stiffened. Amanda looked up at her.

"You know him?"

"He was a guard at the warehouse where they held Storm and me." His energy had been unsettling, an intensity to it that felt broken. He strode casually down the centre of the street. A stocky figure she didn't recognize appeared on a different street, accessing the alley from the opposite end.

"What about him?"

Maria leaned in closer but shook her head.

"They think you're still in the alley," said Amanda.

"What?"

She struggled against the feeling of being trapped, too much of this place not making sense.

"I let them hack into my cameras, so I know when they're looking. This morning I changed the recorded footage, so they think you're still in there. I'm part of a network that the police can tap into."

She felt for the door frame, needing something solid to hold onto against the screens, the bolts on the doors and the cameras that prevented her from leaving without being seen.

The two men spoke briefly into their shoulders and entered the alley at once.

"I need to leave."

She walked into the cool, hardness of the kitchen, its sharp corners taking shape in the growing light. Patio doors led out onto a dim, well-tended back yard with the ghost of a Gatherer installed along the fence.

"I never should have come."

The doors didn't move. They were as solidly locked as if they had been sealed shut. Her panic rose at her own stupidity. How had she thought this place would be safe? She yanked on the handle.

Amanda sat down at a small breakfast table set next to the door and tapped a cigarette out of the pack. She lit it from an electric lighter and spoke as she exhaled.

"Where are you going to go?"

Maria leaned closer to the door, trying to see an escape route, only noticing the distortion from the glass when she looked to the back of the yard.

"How thick is this glass?"

She pressed her hands against the coolness, as if she could test it.

Amanda reached out and gently touched it.

"Took me forever to find it."

Amanda's gaze followed the frame of the door, as if seeing the installation for the first time.

"Why do you have this?"

Maria's voice had risen, the fortifications here speaking too much of fear and danger.

Amanda shrugged, tucked a strand of hair behind her ear. The headlights of a car bounced down the lane, the light refracting oddly through the glass.

"Is it one-way?"

Maria looked back towards the front door and the deadbolts that had slid into place, the awareness of her confinement a prickling on her skin.

Amanda stood, came to stand beside her.

"Yes. And you need to calm yourself."

Her features were still delicate, her beauty always that of a fragile doll. She had used it many times to deflect blame, transforming into a wide-eyed innocent when it suited her, the oscillations between light and dark intoxicating.

And now she was telling Maria to get her shit together, like she had so many times before. Maria bristled at her presumption that she still had any right to do it.

Maria returned to the computer room. She watched the screens as the guard and the other man emerged from the alley. They checked up and down the street. They would only have to knock on a few doors before they found her. She moved back to the solid quiet of the kitchen where Amanda sat at the breakfast table.

"What is this place?"

There were no personal notes on the fridge, no discarded clothing, nothing giving the appearance that anyone lived there at all. It was only the artwork that showed any sign of the person Maria had known. A huge painting of a seventeenth century battlefield with all its blood, gore and suffering. A small framed painting of a spotlighted woman, her expression one of either fear, pain or ecstasy. Another showed a woman in a library, the sunlight that highlighted her only making the shadows in the corners darker as if they would consume her.

"This is my home."

"Not for the Amanda I knew."

Amanda leaned back in the chair, and rested her hands carefully on the table.

"I'm not that person anymore."

"Then who are you?"

Amanda looked up at her and Maria saw the protectiveness again, only now recognizing it as fear.

"The security is for me. It's to keep people out, not you in."

"Then let me go."

Amanda looked down at the table and nodded as if an argument she had been having with herself had been decided. She moved to face a panel set into the wall beside the door. The small display flashed on to the word "authenticating." When the word "verified" appeared, she heard the smallest of thuds. Amanda slid the door open a crack and cold air flowed into the closed stagnant kitchen.

A ping sounded from the computer room. Amanda pulled the door shut and pushed a button on the panel, moving faster than she had since Maria arrived. Maria followed, stopping at the centre of the screens. More alarms sounded, the warnings turning into a blaring alert. Amanda silenced them with a single touch on the keyboard as a screen showed the first guard climbing the steps to the porch. His stride was cocky, knocking on people's doors at this early hour without a care.

His face loomed in another camera. Amanda pressed keys, his frozen image with an empty box beside it as the computer accessed data to fill in the empty fields for name, organization, and defining characteristics. They heard the distant rap on the door as he knocked on the screen.

Amanda stood.

"Don't answer it."

"Why?" Amanda turned, frowning at her concern.

"He's armed."

Amanda touched a key once again and another screen turned on, showing the man's torso and legs. The man's elbows splayed out from his sides which could be weapons under his arms or too much upper bodybuilding. One elbow splayed out further.

"Under his right arm."

Which would mean he was left-handed.

In the camera view, he leaned down, pulled up his pant leg and released a buckle that was holding a knife to his leg.

Amanda rose and flicked a switch on her way out of the room.

"Armed and stupid. My favourite kind."

"I said don't answer it."

"He's not going to just go away."

She shook out her hair as she glanced back over her shoulder. The light in her eyes that had been missing since Maria's arrival had returned, her mouth twisted in a playful smirk.

Maria caught her in one stride.

"Relax," said Amanda. "He won't know you're here."

"He has a weapon."

There was the roll of her eyes again as she stepped towards the door.

"Go upstairs."

Amanda lifted her chin towards the long steep staircase.

There was a second more insistent knock that echoed between the door and the computer room.

Maria paused. Looked to the light of the back door.

Choose.

She took the stairs two at a time, her steps soundless in the dense carpet. She had turned into the upper hallway when the deadbolts retracted in unison, a sound she hadn't heard from the outside.

She forced herself to retreat as muted voices rose up to her, the tone and content muffled by the fortress. Halfway down the hall she stopped. The man's voice was short and clipped. Amanda's responses relaxed, friendly. Chill.

"... a photo of her?"

Amanda's curious words rose above the low murmur. There was a snatch of conversation. A pause. The smell of damp, morning air flowed up the stairwell from the open door. Had she let him into the house? Maria's body vibrated with the need to flee as her attention locked on the conversation below.

The outside air brought no movement or voices with it. She felt the draw and excitement of whatever it was Amanda was doing accompanied by a paralyzing fear. It was as it had always been with Amanda. Always wanting that next adventure, needing it until your life became nothing else. One thrill-seeking day after the next.

"... my husband is still asleep. I wouldn't want to wake him."

Maria checked the hall behind her.

"Okay. I will."

There was the sound of the door closing, that brief opening to the outside world gone.

Maria listened for the sounds of his boots retreating but nothing penetrated through. A beep sounded from the computer room. She moved towards the back of the house, past a painting of a woman sitting on a long tree branch, her toes dipped into the surface of a murky swamp, the painting leaving no question as to the woman's fate.

A window looked out over the alleyway and the houses opposite, the scene one of a normal neighbourhood waking for a new day. Had they really passed her by?

She tried to see further down the row of backyards, her cheek touching the glass when she heard a floorboard creak.

Amanda stood at the top of the stairs, watching her with an unreadable calm that didn't fit with the fortifications that surrounded them. What had she been through that would make the armed, unsettled man at the door an amusing game rather than a threat?

"What is it going to take for you to calm down?"

Amanda's exasperation irritated Maria, the feeling familiar, if rusty.

"They won't give up that easily."

Amanda came to stand beside her, looking beyond the backyards to the split clouds on the horizon.

"Why would they?"

A darker band lay close to the horizon, the clouds dispersing higher up.

Maria was suddenly desperately tired. The enormity of what lay beyond the window was too much to take in. She rested her fingers on the sill, shifting some of the weight onto her hands.

"I can't let them find me."

She could still feel the others with her: her commander, Havernal, who had first sent her on this mission; Storm, who she had left behind in the hands of the rebel group, and Storm's team that had created the Gatherer, who watched her from beyond the grave. How long could she keep carrying them?

Amanda was nodding, for once not arguing.

"Do you have a plan?"

The white outline of the Gatherers in the opposite yards were taking shape as the daylight grew. A carefully installed row of deadly abundance.

"I need to find Ari Chaudhary."

Amanda seemed to pause, as surprised as Maria that she had spoken the truth about needing to find the only member of Storm's team still alive. Yet why else would she have come here, after all this time?

Amanda watched the horizon as if she could see the clouds change shape and offer a different view.

"Okay."

There was confidence in Amanda's voice, despite what lay beyond the window, and what was trying to get in. She was grateful for it, allowing herself to think, for a least a moment, that this may have been the right place after all.

TWO

MARIA STOOD BEHIND AMANDA'S chair as the screens above her displayed views of the surrounding streets. The guards hadn't reappeared—nor anyone else—yet she felt as if they were waiting for her, beyond the reach of Amanda's network.

"How far can you see?"

Amanda changed the view and every screen divided into multiple shots, showing live footage from all over Rima: the empty early morning streets of the downtown, a handful of vehicles on a freeway, what looked like a government building, and ocean waves rolling onto a vacant beach.

"The whole city except for a few small patches."

The network looked continuous and sophisticated, a grid of areas matching together like Tetris blocks across the city. A screen in the top corner changed to show the front gate of the compound that housed the Gatherer corporation. A half dozen guards stood behind it.

A cold sweat crept along her torso. She didn't breathe as Amanda pulled up a different angle of the gate on a separate monitor. It gave a closer view of the half dozen soldiers—not guards—and the shack that had once housed only two private security guards.

"The military is at the compound?"

She had tried to keep her voice flat but Amanda looked up at her, sensing her alarm. Maria had imagined slipping into the compound to find Ari, or waiting for him outside the gate.

"They've been there for weeks."

Maria couldn't take her eyes off their coiled strength and the subtle turn of their heads as they scanned outside the gate.

"Can you see the whole compound?"

The view changed again, so that every screen showed a different angle of the perimeter. The soldiers covered the front and side gates, and had set up posts at regular intervals. The obstacles to her succeeding were solidifying into a solid wall, the number of soldiers in the compound filling in the few gaps she thought she might have been able to slip through.

"What about the interior?"

Amanda circled the mouse on its pad, the pointer on her terminal spinning in abrupt, uneven loops.

"I can't get in. They have a firewall that no one has been able to break."

Her frustration was obvious and familiar, Amanda having never liked when anything got in her way.

Maria moved closer to the screen, the images growing pixelated and the details harder to make out. The attack on the headquarters by a group of protesters warranted more security, but this didn't make sense. There was more security here than they had had at the outpost in Afghanistan.

Amanda's fingers were on the keys again, a flurry of touches and minute pauses that seemed more dance than function.

Ari's photo appeared, out of date, probably from sometime around when the Gatherer had been released. His dark hair was swept back, his eyes black. A second screen scrolled through an endless series of code. A third showed files being added one by one to a growing list.

When the scrolling stopped, Amanda opened the first item on the list, and there he was, checking in with a security guard at the side gate from the driver's seat of a silver sports car. The next showed him checking out and rolling slowly to the first stop sign outside the gate. Every clip showed him either checking in during the late morning or out well into the night. The final one was dated three weeks ago, around the time when Storm had destroyed the Gatherer in Three Rocks. It followed Ari as he checked in with a soldier this time, his tail lights flashing briefly as he disappeared into the well-manicured path of the compound.

"Is that the last one?"

While Amanda searched for more footage, Maria studied Ari's photo. He was young, distracted, as if the photographer had only barely been able to catch his image. It had been Ari that had rivalled Storm's intelligence, his more analytical approach complimenting her intuitive understanding. It was that powerful combination that had probably allowed them to create the Gatherer in the first place.

"There's nothing showing him leaving again."

"Could you have missed it?"

Amanda frowned.

"I don't see anything but he could have left in another vehicle."

Maria moved back, the images from the cameras resolving into focus. There could be another way out, or he had been inside the most protected area in the city for three weeks.

She rubbed at her eyes, no amount of blinking able to relieve the burn of fatigue.

"Can you get me there?"

Amanda pushed off lightly with her toes and spun to face her. Her gaze roamed over Maria's tangled hair, filthy clothes and the lines of hardened dirt on her socks.

"You won't get there looking like that. If we change how you look. And I alter the footage. You might have a chance."

"Might?"

Some of the screens had flipped back to showing mostly empty cityscapes. It reminded her of a city at dawn with its lack of activity —except they were well into mid-morning.

"Might is the best I can do," said Amanda. "The rest is up to you."

She needed better than *might* to banish the images that no amount of eye-rubbing would make go away: the turn of Storm's head when

Maria had left her and Daniel's final stillness when she had rested her hands on his chest.

"It won't be enough."

Amanda was acting like failure was an option, that if it didn't work out, they could try again.

"Then what will?"

Amanda's hands were draped over the arm rests, her feet planted on the floor. The relaxed pose belied the sheer intensity of her gaze.

Maria opened her mouth to speak and felt as if anything she could say would betray Storm, or Daniel, or everyone that depended on her. She had set out to find Storm and a cure for the plague the Gatherer was creating. After finding Storm, the goal had changed to stopping the operation of the device completely. When she had left Storm in that warehouse, weak and close to death, she had let everyone down.

"I don't even know if I can trust you," said Maria.

Amanda pulled in her feet, pushing a hand through her hair in a poor attempt to conceal her irritation.

"You don't know if you can trust me?"

Amanda stood close enough that Maria could see the deep creases of her scowl and feel her agitation.

"You show up in the middle of the night like some feral animal," said Amanda. "Bring thugs to my front door, ask for my help and then suddenly you don't know if you can trust *me*?" The gray of her pupils had gotten darker, the deep purple smudges beneath her eyes close to black. "You won't say whether you killed that guy, like it's none of my business—"

"It is none of your business."

" —and now you want me to manipulate my entire network for you without an explanation?"

"Yes."

Amanda's eyes widened in disbelief, her mouth open mid-word.

"And why should I do that? You're bullheaded and presumptuous— as if I was just waiting here for you—and you have the nerve to ask whether I'm trustworthy?"

"Are you?"

Amanda had stopped, her words and the screens behind her paused.

"If you need to ask that, you've come to the wrong place."

Maria could feel the old wounds opening, the rift that had separated them still fresh after all these years.

"Maybe I have." Her weariness was deep and complete, her disappointment inseparable from it. She didn't look at Amanda as she turned away, instead gathering her strength to go back out into the world.

Amanda followed her back to the kitchen, neither of them finding any words.

"Can you open this?" Maria gestured to the glass door.

Amanda silently stood in front of the panel, the authentication process scrolling on the display. When it finished, she slid the door open a crack, then paused, her gaze fixed on something at the end of the garden.

The guard that had stood outside the conference room where she and Storm were held captive, peered up and over the back fence into the yard. He was in his twenties, untrained, and making no effort at all to stay out of sight. The last time she had seen him, she had stepped over him on her way out the door with Storm.

Maria stepped back, her heart in her throat.

"Lock it."

Amanda let her hand drop, the cold air streaming in. She waved a hand at him as he lifted himself up to see into every corner of the yard.

"He can't see you," Amanda said.

He was hovering above the fence, scanning the backs of the houses, his attention returning more than once to where they stood.

"Are you sure?"

She could feel the net tightening, her options for escape almost gone.

He dropped down and moved onto the next yard.

Maria's her heart pounded, cold air swirling around her feet.

Amanda leaned against the table. Arms crossed.

"Looks like you're going to have to trust me."

Maria's hand closed around the door handle and she pulled it shut. The locks clicked. The air had been sucked out of the room and her lungs, whatever pretense she had been standing on ripped out from under her and she could finally feel the ground beneath her feet.

Amanda let out a long slow breath.

"How did you even get caught up in this?"

The breakfast chair scraped on the floor, heavier than Maria expected, as she pulled it towards her. The guard was already out of sight, likely checking the yards beyond her view. The house, with its many fortifications, waited.

"How much do you know?" said Maria.

She sat down and rubbed the heels of her hands into the burn of her eyes. The tired muscles on the back of her legs eased, and the tension in her hips and lower back released.

"Storm Freeman, the notorious inventor of the Gatherer, disappears." Amanda tilted back her head, watching the scene she described play out on the white stucco ceiling. "Somehow, you are with her when she comes out of hiding and destroys a Gatherer. You are both caught on video, and shortly after that you are on the run and you are considered armed and dangerous because of some guy on a train you are accused of killing."

She looked to Maria for approval. Maria didn't respond. So many of the details were missing, yet from the outside, that's what it would have looked like.

"Somewhere along the way, the headquarters is attacked, and Storm is captured by the rebels. You may or may not be with her. They take a video of her looking close to death and post it online. All hell breaks loose, and you show up here in the middle of the night, alone and as wired as a hunted animal."

She lowered her gaze from the ceiling, the show over.

"Is that it?"

Maria nodded but it wasn't all of it. It didn't include that she had left Storm behind and that it still felt like a mistake.

"The headquarters wasn't us," said Maria.

Amanda's eyes narrowed as she stepped towards the computer room as if to verify Maria's claim and then thought better of it.

"Were you with her?"

Maria tried not to think of the last moments with Storm.

"I had to leave her behind."

Amanda settled back against the counter, watching Maria intently.

"But at least you got out."

She felt the need to go back for her, its urgency not fading since she had left the warehouse.

"I don't even know if she's alive."

She had promised Storm she would help her stop the Gatherer. And yet she'd been unable to keep her safe. Another failure to add to her list.

"Oh, she's alive."

Maria sat up, alert to the certainty in Amanda's voice.

"Have you heard something?"

She had an image of Storm at a press conference, having miraculously reached the compound on her own.

"If she was dead, there isn't a person on earth who wouldn't know about it."

Maria leaned back, seeing the logic, and latching on to the small hope.

Was Storm still locked in the conference room, unprotected from the electromagnetic fields that would kill her?

"I told Storm I would find Ari." Maria ran a hand down her face, to wipe away the dullness of fatigue. She drew in more air, willing her body to find a second—or fourth—wind. "And finish what we started."

Amanda stood and offered Maria a hand up. Her skin was cold, her natural wiry strength still there in her grip.

"Where are we going?"

Amanda linked her arm through hers and spun her around, leading her through the kitchen and into the more formal, sophisticated dining room. A crystal chandelier dangled above the wide, polished wood table. Amanda lightly touched the table and a hidden door opened along the inner wall. A staircase led down, a lace bra and underwear lying on one of the steps next to stacks of books and paper.

Maria let go of a breath she hadn't known she was holding.

Amanda rolled her eyes. "You think I could have changed that much?"

She picked up the bra and tossed it further down the stairs, clicking on an LDC display panel that flashed to *Alarm: On.*

The smell of cooked food rose up and Maria's stomach rose to meet it.

"I thought something really bad must have happened to you," said Maria.

Amanda ushered her in ahead of her and closed the door behind them. There was a faint thud of a lock sliding into pace.

"It did." Amanda nudged her to start moving. "But I'm still me."

Amanda's hideout consisted of three rooms that were as large as the main floor. Discarded clothes lay on the floor, dirty dishes filled the sink, breadcrumbs covered the counter, and an empty bag of chips sat on the couch that faced the colossal big screen mounted on the farthest wall. Several overflowing ash trays dotted the end tables and the corner of an expensive looking dark wooden dining table. Above the table, several screens continued their vigil, monitoring the surrounding streets. The dishevelled queen bed visible through the open door had a single pillow in the tangle of sheets.

"How long have you been here?"

Amanda offered a shrug as she wove her way through the chaotic mess of furniture and clothes that led to her bedroom door. She sauntered more than walked, a hint of the old cockiness in her stride before she stopped in front of a long open closet. The contents of her wardrobe were almost entirely black and a jumble of exclusively black shoes covered the bottom of the closet. Maria's shoulders relaxed, the messy normalcy of the place grounding her in a way the upstairs never could.

"You should shower." Amanda nodded to another open door. "And you look thin. Have you changed size?"

Maria looked down at herself. She didn't remember the last time she had given any thought to clothes. Or when she had last taken these ones off.

"Never mind." Amanda pushed her towards the bathroom door. "I'll find you something."

The light in the bathroom hurt Maria's eyes. Her harried reflection was an even harsher affront. It was the same animal she had seen in the video footage. There was a peaked, rabid look around the eyes, dirt ground into her face, the same way it had into her jeans and coat. It was a wonder Amanda had even opened the door.

She unzipped her coat slowly, her arms heavy, the silent quiet of the space siphoning off her energy. She let the coat fall to the tiles the way Amanda would. She added her filthy pants and muddy socks, the stench from her body growing stronger with each layer she peeled off. The threads of her stitches showed as black crosses on her calf with the surrounding bruised purple flesh beginning to turn brown at the edges. She had a memory of Storm's hand pressed over hers as they had tried to staunch the blood.

When she got to her bra and underwear, her thinness shocked her. She had been aware of her hunger and ongoing exertion but she was thinner than she was even after a mission. She ran her hands over her bones, touching the hard leanness of her abdomen, remembering the first sight of Storm in her bra and underwear, when the fabric had hung on pointed hips.

She stood in the shower for a long time, the water streaming down her back. She gave into it, the fatigue and failures of the trip hitting the hard tiles before being swept into the drain. She emerged pink-fleshed, her scalded skin tingling, her pile of clothes gone from the floor. A heat lamp warmed her shoulders. Her feet absorbed the heat from the tiles.

There was surprisingly little damage from the journey. Several blisters on her heels, a bruise on her forearm where the guard had briefly tried to fight back, and the neat row of stitches. It was like she had been wearing a protective shell and she momentarily regretted the loss of her dirty clothes.

She towel-dried her hair and pushed it back from her face. Her cheeks bones were more prominent, her eyes like raccoons – that part of the journey she at least still carried with her. She slipped on a satiny robe as Amanda appeared in the doorway with scissors, dragging a chair behind her.

"Just like old times."

Amanda grinned, her face lighting up as she snipped the scissors twice in the air.

"Don't make it too crazy."

Amanda pointed her at the chair.

"It has to be as far from your normal as possible."

"That's what I'm afraid of."

The hair came off in big chunks, falling to the tiles like everything else. On one side, the soft curve of her skull emerged from beneath the hair along with the white line of a scar above her ear.

Amanda's movements were easy, self-contained, the certainty she had always had more evident now they were downstairs. Occasionally, she met Maria's gaze in the mirror, but it was brief, her focus on the clipping and changing of how Maria looked.

"Do you know the Agri-foods warehouse? South of the city?" asked Maria.

The scissors momentarily stopped. Amanda held her gaze longer, before she shook her head. "The network doesn't extend much beyond the city."

Amanda began cutting again, the cool metal of the blades touching against the back of Maria's neck.

"It's where we were being held. It's one of the headquarters for the rebels."

Amanda had cut the sides close and left a row of bangs hanging in her eyes. She combed the bangs straight in front of Maria's eyes and clipped carefully on an angle.

"There's more than one?"

Maria shrugged and Amanda put her fingers on top of her head to hold it still.

"It's not well-protected. None of the guards have any training."

Amanda paused mid-clip. A lock of hair had stuck to one blade, tiny clipped ends fanned out along the edge.

She moved around in front of Maria, pulling the bangs so that they tickled the bridge of Maria's nose. She snipped an escaped hair, the tips flashing in front of Maria's eye.

"You can't go back for her," said Amanda.

"I know that."

Maria's response was sharp. Amanda paid no attention as she moved back behind her.

But did Maria know that? There had been an excitement when she had thought of the warehouse. A desire to move in that direction that Amanda had heard too.

"You're right," said Maria. "I just—"

Amanda brushed clipped hair off her neck.

"I get it. You want to go back to her. You wouldn't be you if you didn't."

A comb slid against the back of her neck before she heard the final snip of scissors.

Maria half smiled. To think after all her training, her time overseas, and she hadn't really changed.

Amanda laid the scissors on the sink and stood behind Maria, lightly touching her forehead as she arranged her hair.

"I can't see."

Her bangs were an inverted triangle, the tip touching the middle of her nose, the base the breadth of her forehead, like an alt-rock hair style gone wrong.

Amanda ran her hands down the edges, smoothing it into perfect lines.

"This—" She pointed to the section that covered from her eyebrows to her nose. "Will confuse the face recognition software. Officially it's illegal but it is still out there."

Maria saw her own mouth open, reflecting her surprise. Amanda had been far ahead of her, thinking of consequences long before Maria got there. Maybe neither of them had changed after all.

"I didn't kill that guy."

Amanda smiled and cocked her head, a gesture that said she had already known that.

Maria moved to stand up and Amanda rested a hand on her shoulder. "I'm not done yet."

* * * *

The chemicals in the hair dye made Maria dizzy, and she had the strange feeling of being nauseous and hungry at the same time. While Maria sat with a towel on her head, Amanda disappeared and returned with a warm macaroni and cheese microwave dinner.

She ate ravenously, only realizing when she came up for air and saw Amanda watching her, how primal she had been. Amanda took the empty container from her and laid it next to the sink.

"So what's next?" asked Amanda.

Maria exhaled, the warmth of the food spreading into her arms and legs.

"Storm and Daniel were working on something they believe can disable the Gatherers."

Amanda's eyebrows rose and there was the slightest opening of her eyes. The closest she got to showing surprise.

"You mean remotely like some kind of firmware?"

The food had triggered an overwhelming fatigue, making it hard to focus.

"It has to do with the crystal structure and imperfections." Her legs and arms were heavy, and her thoughts were drifting towards a thick, welcoming haze. "I think Ari is the only one who can do it."

Her eyes burned and she closed them for an instant, confused and disoriented when she jolted out of a sudden sleep.

"Come on."

Amanda left the bathroom, leaving the discarded container and chunks of hair where they were. Maria rubbed her face and pushed the bangs out of the way.

Amanda had laid her outfit on the bed. Shivering, and moving slowly, she clipped the bra strap and slid her arms into the straps before tugging an exquisite pair of lace panties over her hips.

"God, you're skinny."

Maria pulled on a pair of black jeans that hung loosely from her hips and slipped into a silky, fitted top. The body was tight around her while the sleeves ballooned softly, and lightly touched on her skin. Totally impractical, and the touch made her skin itch. She tied up a pair of shiny black boots that had no support and felt like a pair of slippers.

"Something more fashionable would be better but you'll need to be able to walk. Maybe run."

When she was done, the woman reflected in the full-length mirror was a leaner, scrappier version of Amanda.

"Black suits you."

Maria rolled her eyes as Amanda laid a towel over her pillow. She hated the loose fit of the boots, the silky flow of the blouse. She would have preferred the rough practicality of her uniform.

"We'll do your make-up once your hair sets. You can sleep while I figure out the cameras."

"I can help."

"You'll only get in the way."

Amanda moved a tablet off the bed.

Maria frowned. She had the skills, training, knew who would be looking for her. Amanda wouldn't know any of it.

Amanda laughed, as if she had read her mind.

"This is my world, not yours. And besides, you're already barely functioning. I'm surprised you're still standing."

Her words seemed to push aside Maria's resistance – Amanda and the fatigue were a formidable team. She didn't move as Amanda climbed the dimness of the stairs and the alarm beeped. There was a quick opening before the door shut.

The quiet was absolute, nothing from the world upstairs reaching down the steps. She lay carefully on the towel so as not to get dye on the sheets. The mattress curved around her body and she smiled as she floated in the soft cloud. Count on Amanda to have found an amazingly comfortable bed.

THREE

SHE STARTED AWAKE AT Amanda's touch, not knowing the time of day or how long she had been asleep. Amanda loomed above her, her hair tied back in a bun and impatient for Maria to get moving.

"You have to see this."

Maria's head was thick with fog and she struggled to take stock of the room. Her legs responded slowly, and it wasn't until they were in the lower kitchen that she was fully conscious. The smell of toast and old dishes nauseated her even as she craved food. She grabbed a half bag of chips off the counter.

"Did you find a route?" Maria asked.

She felt as if she hadn't slept, her mind and body craving a return to the comfort of Amanda's bed.

"Better."

The lock slid back and they stepped through the emptiness of the formal dining room and into the spare, unused kitchen. By the light in the garden it looked to be late afternoon.

Amanda closed the door to the basement behind them, and locked it before almost skipping into the computer room. Three of the screens were blank. A fourth showed the layout of a surveillance network across the city.

"We are here."

Amanda pointed to the lower right on the screen and the end of a path of highlighted cameras.

"I've set up a sequence that will give you enough time to traverse each section with an average walking speed of three kilometres per hour."

"How will I know the cameras are blocked?"

Amanda's gaze lifted to Maria's hair and Maria instinctively lifted her hand. Her hair would be black now and there was barely enough to run her fingers through.

"You won't. You'll just have to trust it."

Amanda placed the slightest emphasis on the word trust, a reminder to her that there was no going back.

Maria scanned the route, aware of the countless ways that this plan wouldn't work.

Amanda was pointing to where the route reached the blockade of military personnel at its end.

"There are two possibilities." She flipped between views, landing on one of the perimeter fence where it entered a stand of trees. "There's a break in the fence in the middle of these trees."

"They'll know it's there by now."

Amanda didn't respond immediately, her gaze flicking between the various feeds.

"Right." She paused. "Well, you can go in here."

The view was of the rocky shore, bursts of water splashing up between the boulders where the waves struck shore.

"You want me to swim?"

"They won't be expecting it."

"Yeah, they will."

The route would be easy enough if nothing went wrong. She just had to hope it got her close enough that she would be able to take it from there.

Amanda slid a small black square off the desk, about the size of a SIM card and concealed it in her palm.

"I need you to do something for me."

She was jiggling the hand holding the card, in time with her leg, and if Maria didn't know better she would have thought she was nervous.

"When you get inside the compound—"

"If I get inside."

Amanda shrugged, dismissive of the possibility of failure and Maria was surprised by her faith in her.

"I need you to find a computer on their network, and put this in it."

She extended her hand, the small device at its centre. She lifted the tiny slice of technology.

"It will give me access to their internal network, their cameras and processes."

It would be like Amanda was still with her, embodied in the technology, her physical self still safely here. At one time, Amanda would have been beside her, embracing whatever danger they could find.

Maria folded her fingers over the black square.

"So you'll be with me?"

Amanda nodded, the explanation for why she wouldn't come with her, instead staying behind in her lonely fortress, sitting between them.

"It's not perfect," said Amanda. "But I may be able to help."

Maria waited for Amanda to explain what had happened, but she simply held Maria's eyes, her refusal solid and unyielding.

"And it will fill a hole in your network."

Amanda flashed a wicked smile. Unapologetic.

"Definitely."

Maria knew countless soldiers who refused to talk about what haunted them. She had learned to accept it. Understood that some pain was too deep to share.

Maria went to put the card in her pocket and Amanda stopped her.

"There's a place in your bra where you can carry it. So they won't find it if you get caught."

It still surprised her that this was part of Amanda's life. A life that Maria had known nothing about.

Amanda took the square from her and slid it into a tiny plastic sleeve that fit its shape exactly.

Maria lifted the blousy material, cringing when Amanda's cold fingers touched her skin. Amanda lifted an eyebrow and half-smirked.

"I'll be quick."

Gently, she lifted the bottom edge of her bra strap at the base of her cleavage and slid the square into the strap. A small opening lay on the back of the strap, invisible once the device was inside.

Amanda flipped the strap back into place.

Maria ran her fingers along the strap, feeling only the slightest increase in hardness where the card sat.

* * * *

The city hung in a strange twilight, the daylight faded and the brilliance of the artificial lights not yet asserting their dominance. They had chosen dusk as the best time to leave, enough daylight for Maria to see the alleyway, and enough darkness to camouflage the details of her disguise. She couldn't get used to the flimsiness of Amanda's boots, the low heels adding an instability to her step and feeling as if she would tear the thin leather with each step.

"Here."

Amanda handed her an old flip phone, that hadn't been current in over a decade.

"I've put in a new SIM card and the only number is mine."

She dropped her hands quickly once Maria took it, her fists clenching and unclenching at her sides.

"So if you need anything…"

The phone was small, compact and functional, nothing like the slick tablets people carried with them now.

"Does it still work?" asked Maria.

She ran her finger across the raised Motorola emblem.

"For calling, they're still the most reliable. And if you drop it you'll be fine."

Maria slipped the phone inside her coat.

"Thanks."

"Do you remember the route?"

Maria nodded. A thin sweat had formed on her palms as she had watched the daylight fade. There were people out there looking for her.

"If you run into trouble, you can always come back. I'll be here."

Maria tried not to notice the raised pitch of Amanda's voice, and the nervous pushing of her hair back from her face.

"You never told me what happened to you," said Maria.

Amanda shook her head

"You need to get going."

They stood for a few moments.

"Once this is over we should—"

What should they do? Get together? She didn't even know what the world would look like. Or whether it would ever be over.

"It's been really good to see you."

Amanda breathed in, a shake to to her breath that hadn't been there before.

"You too."

She drew a cigarette from the pack on the counter. Her hands shook when she tried to light it. Maria drew the lighter from her hand and stopped.

It was the lighter she had given Amanda before she left, a square silver Zippo with the words "Never Look Back" inscribed on the side. It had been their mantras as teenagers, helping them move past, or at least away from, events out of their control. The edges were worn, most of the texture on the silver rubbed away.

She held the flame to the tip of Amanda's cigarette as she inhaled. She blew a long stream of smoke away from Maria.

"You always hated when I smoked."

Maria handed her the lighter.

"Still do."

The daylight had faded further and the distant lights above the houses had started to gain strength. Energy gathered in Maria's legs.

The locks snapped when Amanda released them. She eased open the glass door. The damp evening cold slid in, circling their ankles, the hum of the city crowding in.

"Thank you."

Amanda waved her cigarette dismissively, the smell of smoke warm in the cold air.

Maria's boots thudded softly on the wood deck and the three steps down, the sound vanishing as soon as she reached the manicured lawn. It felt different than when she had left before, recognizing the friendship that was still there, and the comfort and support they had once provided for each other.

A breeze blew across the tops of the fences, playing across her newly exposed scalp and the understanding of how much she had missed her. Halfway to the back fence, she turned. Amanda had backed into the shadow of the kitchen, the slow burn of her cigarette tip the only sign she was still there.

FOUR

MARIA'S SKIN CRAWLED AS she forced herself to stroll casually, every part of her wanting to lean forward and charge down the street. Streetlights were coming on, turning every street into a brilliant runway, with Maria, the not-so-glamorous model, working hard to look casual. She tried not to think about the cameras recording her, trusting Amanda had done her job.

She wrapped Amanda's coat tighter around her. There were people looking for her and likely citizens hoping to spot her. Her anxiety rose with a panic across her chest that would only be relieved by running.

At an intersection, a young man crossed the adjacent street and stood beside her as they waited for the light.

Early twenties. Ear buds in. A hunched stance that didn't scream military.

But that didn't mean he wasn't.

An overhead heater blasted warm air as they waited, creating an oasis amidst the cold, a pointless luxury brought in by the access to limitless electricity.

When the light changed she pretended to pick something off the sidewalk, only crossing when he was well ahead of her.

Halfway across the crosswalk, she felt a vibration under her feet. The sound of an explosion rippled through the night. The boy with the earbuds kept moving as she turned towards the source. To the south, a mile away, maybe two. Loud enough that the city had paused, waiting for a second detonation or whatever would happen next.

A car honked, her stance in the centre of the road blocking its path, the crosswalk sign a solid red. She hurried out of the way, cursing herself for drawing attention as she curled her shoulders and tried to pretend she was an ordinary citizen who hadn't just recognized the sound of a contained explosion where there shouldn't be one.

She ached to let her legs drive her fast down the street. A dead giveaway for anyone who had seen her run.

There were more people on the streets as she grew closer to downtown, rushing past with their chins tucked in their collars, faces averted. Huge electronic billboards flashed from buildings above the street; a glimmering, frenzied display that the hurrying people barely seemed to notice. They didn't notice her either.

The few restaurants she passed were closed, or only had a few patrons. The silhouettes of idle wait-staff shifted in front of the lighted display of bottles behind the bar, talking and waiting for diners that wouldn't come. She walked over a grate, momentarily encased by a blast of heat. Cars rolled by, silent but for the pulsing vibrations of their stereos. She saw a flash of young, indifferent faces before they were gone.

She dug her fists into her pockets and walked faster, her face lowered, the thud of her boots on concrete marking her path.

Many of the windows in the small apartment buildings were brightly lighted with the curtains closed. Gatherers sat next to many buildings, their white gleam already faded.

She turned onto a street leading to a large square and her steps faltered. Angry shouting came from an agitated crowd in front of the gleaming white curved roof of one of the largest Gatherers Maria had ever seen. A ring of armed guards in full riot gear kept the rioters at bay. A tree turned entirely white stood beside it, the visible damage from the Gatherer likely why they had chosen this device to target. Why had Amanda brought her here?

She considered back-tracking, taking another route, but she couldn't risk being recognized on camera. She stuck close to the wall. Six guards that looked like cops surrounded the Gatherer. She checked the rooftops for a sniper team but the incessant scrolling signs left them in deep shadows against a featureless sky. At least two hundred protesters occupied the perimeter, an indication of the public's growing certainty of the connection between the Gatherer and the plague. The video of Storm, showing her near death as a result of her work with the device, had probably been the final straw to confirm what people had already feared.

An alleyway led off the square twenty paces on the right. She made her way towards it and away from the two camera crews that had set up at the back of the crowd. The protesters were calm and subdued and she wondered if the protest had yet to start. They didn't look armed, their only aggression so far the act of forming a ring around the Gatherer and its guards.

Ten more paces.

A single voice rose, female and shrill, and the rest of the crowd grew quiet. The guard closest to her adjusted his stance. Ready.

Even with their shields and use of force tools, the guards were totally outnumbered. Were their orders to protect? Or attack? Were they even trained for this kind of confrontation?

Five more paces. She could already feel the freedom of the alleyway.

A balding guy with the stocky frame of middle age stared down one of the guards. Their noses were close enough to taste each other's breath.

Two more steps.

She ducked into the opening and was stopped short by a group of young women, their hair in messy ponytails, with glowing healthy cheeks and eyes bright with adrenaline and determination. They blocked the alley, and she stopped, aware of the rising pitch of the woman's voice behind her in the square.

Each of the young women held a rifle in their hands, with no idea how to use it properly. An open crate lay beside them filled with explosives, another with rifles. Maria checked for the Agri-food label, the name of the warehouse where she and Storm had been held, but it wasn't there.

"Whoa! Whoa! Whoa!" said Maria, holding up her hands. One of the girls held the rifle horizontally, its barrel pointed at the girl next to her. Maria carefully eased the end of the barrel towards the ground. "Do you know how to use these?"

A shorter girl with dark brown hair and heavy eyebrows pulled the rifle towards her protectively.

"They showed us how."

"Who are you?"

The question was from a taller girl, skinny with narrow eyes.

"John sent me to help," said Maria.

Was the leader of the rebels even named John? She'd gotten very few details about the group's organizers when she was being held. This might not even be the same group.

"We're having trouble with the safeties," said the dark-haired girl. She held up her rifle, again unwittingly pointing it at her friend.

Maria guided it to point down.

"First rule. Don't point it at anyone unless you mean it."

Shouts of encouragement now joined the woman's speech in the square and Maria felt ill. Who would give these weapons to young women who were little more than children? If these women went out there with these rifles, they would be seen as armed protesters and would activate a level of response they weren't prepared for.

"John wants me to look after these and for you to be on the other side of the square," said Maria.

Would it be any safer for them on the other side?

The dark-haired girl's grip on the rifle loosened, the tall girl was already placing hers back in the crate.

The third one, athletic and with the intensity of a zealot, lifted the rifle across her chest.

"That wasn't the plan."

Maria checked whether the weapons in the crate were loaded.

"We need more support on the other side. Dorian will meet you there."

She cringed at how far she was digging herself in. Was Dorian, the disturbed woman who had been with the rebels, even here?

"Come on, Brayden." The dark-haired girl was already turning away. "We have to go where we're needed."

Brayden didn't move as the two girls—young women, except they were so far out of their depths Maria couldn't help but think of them as girls—turned away from the square towards the end of the alley. Brayden's safety was off and she adjusted her grip on the barrel.

"Who's Dorian?"

Maria felt the cool calmness slide down her spine. The readiness, knowing what she needed to do. She had to be careful. Brayden was young, strong, and there was a fierceness in her eyes that reminded her of her younger self.

"John's partner," said Maria. "Have you not met her?"

Dorian had looked after Maria when the rebels had held her, healing the wound on her leg, for which she should be grateful. She'd also stolen the jewellery off Daniel's dead body and Maria's response to that had been the catalyst that had allowed Maria and Storm to escape. If this protest was led by different rebels, the girl wouldn't know Dorian or John. Maria adjusted her stance, checked that the other two had made it to the end of the alley and leaned her rifle against the brick wall.

A roar came from the square.

She dared not look behind her.

Brayden slowly tilted her head to the side, her eyes narrowing. At the end of the alley the other two had given up waiting.

"Are you that—"

Maria stripped Brayden of the rifle and dropped her unconscious with a single strike. She caught her before she hit the ground.

There was the sound of footsteps running towards them from the square and a face, a boy of around fifteen, appeared around the corner, reaching for a rifle. Maria handed him one, the pit in her gut opening up. She left the safety on.

The man who had been staring down the guard appeared next and he looked at her in confusion before she placed an unloaded rifle in his hands.

"Go! Go!" she said.

At the sound of shots, the man turned away.

Maria grabbed a rifle and ran away from the square. There were more shots, followed by screaming. Her stride faltered.

She gritted her teeth. Bore down on her legs. That wasn't her fight. She couldn't fix it. She reached the end of the alley, couldn't help but look back. Brayden lay next to the crate, the only one Maria had managed to save.

Slinging the rifle over her shoulder she headed deeper into the city. She was far off of Amanda's route and fully exposed to anyone that was watching. She cut across the intersection, the signal lights changing from green to red above the empty street. The noise of the protest had fallen behind her and she still ran as if pursued.

She chose a smaller street going west, briefly checking for cameras. A pointless activity. They could easily be hidden and what would she do if she saw one anyway? Any meddling with it would only draw more attention.

She tried not to think of those young women. A rifle wouldn't do anything against what those guards were carrying. There would have been injuries when those shots were fired, possibly deaths. And it was all because the corporation and the government were refusing to acknowledge that the Gatherer was the cause of the plague. Forcing unequipped civilians to be the ones to take up arms to get it stopped. And forcing Storm to come out of hiding and risk her own health. It was irresponsible and cowardly and it made her want to hunt down whoever was making these stupid decisions.

Her anger pushed her faster towards the headquarters, and she did her best to keep her rifle hidden inside her coat. It would be obvious she was carrying *something*, but not the specifics.

Her injured leg throbbed and the wind grew colder as night fell. She wished she had her own clothes instead of Amanda's thin, flimsy outfit. She felt the presence of those watching her along the back of her neck, the awareness of the forces gathering behind her, and of her need to get out of sight.

She ran through the brightly lit, abandoned city, the fear of the plague keeping everyone indoors. Her footsteps echoed back at her from brick walls. She needed to slow down. Think. Tearing through the streets was only going to get her caught.

She slowed and chose the side of the street with more shadows. She was passing a series of small houses. Between two with darkened windows, she slid down the alley and through the wilted remains of a garden. A broken wooden fence separated the small yard with the one behind it. She straddled it and landed softly in the next yard.

As soon as her feet landed, a dog started barking in the house, the pitch growing frantic as she silently opened the gate and escaped out the driveway. She passed quickly through another yard, the dog's barking fading behind her, the lights on the next street brighter.

Some of the houses had been turned into businesses, the signs glowing above refurbished doors. She kept her distance, wary of potential cameras, and started at the sight of a figure silhouetted down the street, before she recognized it as a woman walking away from her, in as much of a hurry as she was.

Behind a rundown garage, she took a moment to re-adjust her rifle and listen. Beyond her own rapid breathing the street was quiet, except for the low purr of an electric vehicle as it passed. The stillness unsettled her and she moved faster. She came out on a street where almost all the houses were businesses.

She was completely lost, her general knowledge of the larger arteries not helping her in these smaller veins. She seethed with frustration and a growing sense of panic. The rank scent of the ocean blew over her and her confusion increased.

She started jogging, the hell with whoever was watching. She jolted forward at the sound of footsteps keeping pace behind her. At a corner, she snuck a glance. A man in casual clothes, his movements precise and controlled, strode behind her.

Long hair. Definitely military.

She turned into a driveway that led into the paved yard of an automobile junk yard. There were rows of gasoline-fed vehicles lined up in neat rows next to an abandoned bucket truck they had used to maintain hydro lines parked at its end. Had there been something familiar about her pursuer? More than his training?

A bent chain link fence separated her from the next lot and she crawled through a torn opening at its base. The footsteps had stopped but that didn't mean good news.

The lot was mostly empty, a single car parked behind the low-slung building and a security light above the door. The building was unusual in that all of its lights were out, and it made her feel exposed, whoever might be watching hidden inside that darkness. The next building looked abandoned, boards over the windows. No lights at all now.

Ducking into a dark entrance way she pulled the rifle from her jacket, wishing she had something other than a dated Winchester. There was no movement and only black emptiness in the building behind her.

She clung close to the wall, feeling like an easy target if anyone wanted to shoot. The mortar between the bricks was cracked, and chunks crunched under her feet as she ran, the larger pieces threatening to turn her ankle in the flimsy boots. The row of blank windows on the second floor offered no escape or encouragement and everything smelled of dirt and decay. She bolted for a narrow alleyway that ran along a fence at the back, avoiding the lights that blazed at the front of the building. Had she seen movement along the side wall? She ran for the alley, feeling increasingly like a rat in a trap.

The space behind the brick building was narrow and smelled of piss. Every step echoed, blaring her location. She ran faster, scanning the shadows for a way out but the alley ran straight and long.

Anger flared at her pursuer's cockiness and she stopped, turned, prepared to face him down. The alley was empty, her ragged breathing filling the small space. Was he messing with her? She tried to quell her panic. The fences at the back were eight feet high, solid wood. Was he keeping pace with her on the other side?

She ran for the end of the building, hoping for something other than another long confined space where there was no escape. She stopped at the sight of a three-metre-high chain link fence that ran in both directions along a narrow path. Three rows of barbed wire slanted towards the other side. The hum of electricity ran through the thinnest wire along the top. The fence angled around buildings, with lights brightening it every twenty meters.

Beneath the closest light stood the man, his neatly clipped goatee a contrast to his mane of long hair. He hadn't even bothered with a weapon. She heard a footstep behind her as a second man stepped beneath a different light, his skin darker than the first and his smooth competence more than threatening. The third blocked the way she had come, and at the sight of his wide eyes and baby face, she shook her head.

She lowered the rifle. Almost embarrassed she had it. She couldn't see their smiles but she knew they were there. Amused like this was just another one of her screw ups.

The long-haired one approached, strolling. Instinctively she shifted her left foot forward and her right foot back, though she wouldn't fight. These guys were some of the few she couldn't beat. She hadn't recognized him because of the long hair. A goatee he had never had before.

"I didn't think I'd be worth coming after," she said.

Adams smiled. Picked up the Winchester to examine it.

Benoit Adams. The second in command of their unit when Havernal had still been active. The fastest. The strongest. His combat skills so flawless no one had ever bested him. Jones and Hamel weren't far behind him.

"Why not? You're famous now." He shook his head. His mouth twisted into a smile at the almost useless weapon. "What are you doing, Kowalski?"

It was a friendly razz, as if they had caught her adding a scope to her rifle. The air was solid around her, the tension giving it a rigid structure too thick to move.

"How's Havernal?" she asked.

Havernal had been the commander of their unit, before the plague had weakened him so completely he had been medically released.

There was a flicker of something across Adams' face at the mention of Havernal. Concern? Or was it anger?

He nodded to Hamel and she felt the quick brush of hands down her legs and along her sides, and Amanda's phone taken away.

"Let's get out of here boys." Adams held the rifle loosely in one hand, ushered her ahead of him with the other. "After you."

Part of her railed against it. Wanted her to fight the men who wanted to take her off course, even stop her. The rest of her, the part that could think, knew this wasn't the time.

FIVE

Amanda jumped between screens, searching for a camera that would show where Maria had gone. She saw the parking lot where Maria had been, the chain link fence she had crawled under, yet when she tried to connect to the adjoining network, she got a blank screen.

She swore under her breath, and backed up, trying to approach the blank area from a different access point.

She could see the dim inactivity of the streets Maria had passed through, the spaces empty, no one active in the industrial area as the night approached. The streets in front of Maria's last position were a swath of dead signals and unresponsive networks.

There were no assets worth protecting, the area mostly warehouses, and it didn't make sense that the entire area would be blocked out.

She slowed down, moving through the different access points methodically so that there would be no chance she would miss anything. Someone had been there before her, cutting off access to the area, and she felt the combined excitement and apprehension of finding something she wasn't supposed to see.

Eventually, she found a single camera on its own. She zoomed in and what she saw didn't make sense. It showed the shadowed line of a fence with barbed wire on its top, slanting inwards. Its path cut across a yard that should have held vehicles and discarded packing material. Instead it was stripped clean, the only disturbance the cracks in the pavement.

She had been to this part of the city with Simon, before things had fallen apart. The fence hadn't been there, the area still busy with commercial life. She tapped the keys, coming up repeatedly against blank screens and cameras that didn't respond.

As she searched farther, the blocked-out area took shape. It was a large section of town, centered around the old, reeking canal. It extended all the way to the shoreline of the river, a semi-circle zone of darkness far wider than she had known.

A man with long hair and a goatee followed part of Maria's path. His casual stroll was fake, the loping gait not having any of the looseness required to make it real.

She stood, trying to ignore the anxiety that was running along her veins, even as she reveled in how good it felt to feel alive again.

Two other men showed on a different street, one short and powerful with darker skin, the other thin and wiry. Their movements were equally casual, neither of them relaxed.

She took screen shots of their faces and let the database do its work. They weren't the same men that had come to the house. These men looked far more capable, and dangerous. Was Maria good enough to best them? The woman who had stood in her kitchen seemed capable of almost anything. The wild, impulsive creature she had been, sharpened and tuned into something far more deadly.

Her apprehension grew as the results from the database popped up. *Unidentified. Unidentified. Unidentified.*

The first man went into the alley where she had last seen Maria. The other two disappeared into a lane that would cut her off.

"Shit!"

Amanda moved around searching for another angle.

It was pointless – what could she do anyways? Call Maria and tell her she was being followed by three men? Watch while they caught her, or she got away?

Her pulse thrummed in her veins, returning to a frequency she hadn't felt in months. She hated the feeling of helplessness, blinded, with no information.

THE GATHERER

She paced away from the desk, walking in a full circle only to return to the same spot. She waited, watching the larger blacked-out area of the city, as if her vigilance would somehow save Maria from what was coming.

SIX

"Where are you taking me?"

There had been a short ride in the back of a van through streets that curled in on themselves, twisting and bending around the curves of the foothills so that she lost complete track of where they were. The glimpse of a mountain through the windshield was the only indication of what direction they faced before they were down another street, buildings rising on either side. Wedged between Jones and Hamel, the windows blacked-out, she saw only glimpses of brightly lighted streets or the dimness of crossroads. The sky above was unknowable, any distinctions obliterated by the flood of lights.

She sat in the silence of their response, her heart pounding even as part of her relaxed to be back in the security of her unit. Part of her yearned to be in that place again, knowing someone had your back and that if you didn't have the answer someone else would.

"Did Havernal send you?" she asked.

Neither Jones' nor Hamel's expression changed, their gazes forward. Adams, driving, didn't acknowledge her.

"Is he alive?"

Jones shifted his feet. He had always been the easiest to read.

"He's alive."

Adams gave him a hard look in the mirror, the message clear. She was grateful for the moment of connection, their concern for Havernal still in common.

They turned onto a long, narrow street. Blank industrial buildings on one side and a spiked wrought-iron fence lining the other. A dense hedge blocked any view through the fence. It was the perimeter fence along the side of the Gatherer compound, the gate less than a block ahead of them. She had the knee-jerk thought that Havernal had sent them to help her before she realized there was no way he could have known. It would have been something he would have done when he was still in command, before he got sick.

Adams slowed the van, though there was no obvious entrance, the opening in the fence emerging suddenly out of the hedge. The van bumped into the drive and six soldiers in full combat gear and activated rifles stepped out of the dusk to stand in front of the metal barrier that blocked the entrance. Another unit from the hill, also known as CANSOFCOM, the special forces unit of the Canadian military.

Was Amanda seeing this?

Adams lowered the window and a soldier she didn't recognize approached.

"You should be expecting us," said Adams.

The soldier scanned the interior, noting each passenger, his gaze resting longer on Maria. Amanda's disguise wasn't stopping anyone from recognizing her. She held his blank stare until his gaze moved on.

"Go ahead."

The gate slowly lifted, the long arm rising into the sky as the soldiers crowded in behind the van.

The road passed through well-manicured grounds, the walking trails marked by low level lights. They wound towards the front entrance where the new buildings towered beside vast parking lots. The number of structures had doubled since she and Havernal had visited over two years before.

They passed a large matte-black warehouse, difficult to see its full size in the dark, the shining production facility beside it more delicate and finer-boned, a reflection of the delicacy of the Gatherer process that drew energy from the air through a series of crystals.

The trees pulled back to reveal the gleaming front of the Gatherer headquarters and the statue of the open hands in the center of the circular stairs. Maria experienced the intended awe and the sense of entering an exclusive, privileged world. The illusion caved in at the sight of the blackened hole where the entrance used to be, evidence of the rebel's earlier attack.

They didn't touch her. Hadn't yet, opening a metal side door of the headquarters and following her in. Adams led, his tight butt and broad shoulders ahead of her.

They fell into order as if they were back on patrol, following a service corridor, several doors marked as restricted access. An open door revealed the disorganized jumble of a cleaning room, and she got a whiff of acrid cleaning products as they passed. Was this their command center? It was an odd place for it, restricted with too few exits.

They boarded an elevator, Hamel and Jones standing on either side with Adams in front. They faced forwards, the floors blinking by. She took a long, low breath, tuning into the men's breathing.

The elevator decelerated at the top floor, the doors opening to the curved line of an empty desk. It was a small reception area painted in the brilliant white of the Gatherer. The upturned hands of the open hands symbol was etched in the wall behind the desk.

A guard taller and broader than Adams stood next to a set of double doors. He nodded to Adams as they approached and pointedly ignored her. Stubbs. The final member of their unit; fierce, loyal, and the strongest person she had ever met.

Adams opened the door, letting her enter first.

The room was in darkness with a wide expanse of windows overlooking the dizzying brilliance of the era of light. Screens cycled on the sides of buildings, streetlights traced the maze of streets and the flash of a new electric jet crossed the sky. Every nook and cranny, alley and storefront crammed with electricity.

She caught a movement to the left. A shadow in front of the sea of light. Her first thought was that it was Storm, miraculously healed, before logic re-aligned the tall, willowy woman into Alicia, her back stiffer and an indifference that spoke of good health.

Light levels in the office rose, a desk lamp and several lamps in a small sitting area growing to full brightness. The contours of Alicia's face defined in the light. The resemblance to Storm was there, the auburn hair, the line of the cheek bones, the defiant set of the shoulders. Yet Alicia's beauty had hardened, her unrelenting gaze leaving no room for humour or compassion.

"We meet again, Ms. Kowalski."

A sleek minimalist desk separated them, Alicia's body still half-turned towards the city beyond the window.

"Yes."

Alicia made a short impatient gesture to Adams who had remained inside the door.

"We're fine."

He hesitated, understanding more than Alicia the harm that Maria could do if she chose.

"My instructions are to stay with the prisoner."

It took a moment to realize Adams was referring to her, the term not one that she ever thought would ever apply to her.

"I'll be fine," said Alicia.

It was a dismissal, Alicia's edges as sharp as when Maria had first met her.

The door beside Adams was the only entrance to the room, any exit out the window was limited by the unbreakable glass and the ten stories to the ground.

There would be nothing to gain by harming Alicia. Nowhere for her to hide. In the end he must have seen that, for he slipped out the door, likely taking his position next to Stubbs.

Alicia turned to face her. "Where is she?"

It was a demand, though the undercurrent of worry in Alicia's voice surprised her.

"I have no idea."

And she wouldn't have told her even if she'd known.

The windows looked over the grounds ten stories below with its lighted pathways and spotlighted gardens. In the distance, beyond a parking lot, was the outline of the newest warehouse. No spotlights, no signs, the entire building in shadows. Maria moved closer to the window and Alicia adjusted her position away from her. As if that few feet would save her.

"Is she alive?"

Maria scanned the edges of the city wondering if one of the lights was from the Agri-foods warehouse where she had left Storm, the small brightness showing where Storm's heart still beat.

It was wrong to be here without Storm. She should be the one answering these questions.

Alicia's heels clicked on the hardwood floor as she retreated to the far end of the window.

"I need to know if she's okay."

There was a fierceness and impatience to Alicia's voice and Maria responded with plain truth.

"You know she's not."

"Were you there when they took that video?"

"No."

Maria had been locked in the same conference room shortly after the video was taken. Storm had been barely conscious, and Daniel already gone.

"She should have stayed in the Yukon," said Alicia.

"How could she? The plague was spreading, people were getting sick, and you weren't acknowledging it."

Maria could see the rise and fall of Alicia's chest. Her fear close to the surface.

"You knew there would be cameras when she destroyed the Gatherer in Three Rocks," said Alicia. "That the whole world would see her do it."

"I arrived as she attacked it. I had been tracking her and only just found her."

"Was it your idea to attack? To force our hand?"

Maria didn't respond. Alicia wasn't listening, seeming intent only on laying blame.

"You knew what that would have done to Storm," said Alicia. "The risk she put herself in. She should have left it alone."

Alicia's gaze had returned outside the window, locked on the dark shape of the new warehouse.

"She felt like she had to do something."

"Her job was to stay in the Yukon. And get better. I told her I would look after it."

"But you aren't."

Alicia pulled her attention from the warehouse, her calm so absolute Maria felt a sudden uneasiness. Alicia stepped back from the window and circled away from Maria through the sitting area to her desk.

"Are you going to tell me where she is?"

A small framed photo sat on the corner of her desk, showing the team at a press conference shortly after the release. Storm, Daniel, Callan, Jana and Ari, young and on top of the world. Alicia briefly adjusted its position, turning it away from the window.

"I don't know."

"I don't believe you," said Alicia.

A silver Gatherer symbol pinned to Alicia's lapel caught the light.

"That is not my problem."

Alicia's expression turned to pity, and apprehension fluttered in Maria's chest.

"Do you know what it took to get them to bring you here? I could have let them take you off to whatever they plan to do with you but instead I got them to bring you here. If you care about Storm at all you will tell me where she is, while you have the chance."

"Is any of the team left?"

It was Ari she cared about, not the team, but Alicia couldn't know that.

"You know the answer to that already."

"Do I? Officially Daniel's been dead for years and yet I watched him die the other day. So are the others out there? Are they able to help fix this?"

Alicia lifted the photo, frowned at the small figures. What did she expect to see? After a moment, she lowered it, still holding it in both hands.

"Did Storm and Daniel have any time together?"

"Not very long."

Alicia placed the photo back on the desk. Other than a closed laptop, it was the only object on the shining surface.

"I need to know where she is. There is a safe room for her here. There have been advances in treatment. I can help her."

The city shimmered behind her, the incessant spin of a Ferris wheel curving over it all.

"Then why did you leave her in the Yukon?"

"It was the safest place for her."

"Safe from what?"

She had a long, candid stare into the cool depths of Alicia's blue eyes. A momentary opening, gone as quickly as it came.

"From the fields?" said Maria. "The plague? The truth?"

"You have no idea what you're talking about."

Maria took a step towards Alicia, her body trying to do what words couldn't.

"There are thousands of people out there who may not survive this, and Storm is one of them," she said.

She didn't see Alicia move or make any kind of signal but suddenly Adams was behind her, his arm on her elbow, her body tensing in reaction to his coiled energy.

"You can take her," said Alicia.

Maria was too surprised to speak.

"What should I tell Stanton?" asked Adams.

Maria's surprise changed to alarm. Adams' fingers pressed into her arm, pulling her into him. She reacted instinctively, slamming her heel into his foot, slipping away to the right. And he was there, unphased, gripping harder, and yanking her arm behind her back.

She gasped, her face hot with humiliation as he bent her forward.

Was Stanton here? Havernal's superior who had shut down the investigation into the plague?

There was the sound of the wheels of Alicia's chair on the wood floor, the creak of leather as she sat. She spoke as if she were dismissing a servant.

"She didn't tell me anything. If that's what you mean."

She felt a deep burning as Adams twisted higher. No malice, only effective neutralization. He steered her towards the door. Stubbs pulled it shut behind them. She had the briefest of glimpses of the etched figure of the open hands and she was in the elevator, arm released, surrounded by her unit, plunging back to ground level.

SEVEN

MARIA SAT IN THE back seat of an electric mini-van wedged between Hamel and Jones, trying not to freak out that they were en route to see Stanton, the man whose orders she had disobeyed when she set out to find Storm. The orders that had prohibited them from investigating the plague and its connection to the Gatherer.

They had slipped through the compound gates, the van winding further into the brightly lighted maze of night-time streets. The glare felt too bright, leaving too much exposed, the van fully visible.

"If you help me," she said, "we could stop this."

Adams drove and Stubbs sat in the passenger's seat, their response an affronted silence, their judgement hardening the air.

"Didn't we always talk about that?"

It had been their final words to each other when they would head out on patrol or to take down a target.

Let's go save the world.

A way to justify or compartmentalize whatever happened next.

"This is a chance to do that. Simple and straightforward, with none of the usual bullshit."

They passed a boarded-up gas station with the gasoline pumps removed.

"There's still plenty of bullshit."

Adams's words were clipped as he turned onto a curbless street, the houses old and run down.

A man stood at the center of the brown grass of his front yard, following their progress as they passed. His expression was vacant, lost and when she turned her head, he still watched the van as if waiting for its presence to tell him something. He was deadly thin, and wore his house slippers, the outline of a Gatherer visible behind a shrub.

She would never see the light of day if they took her to Stanton, the inevitable outcome of that meeting bad for both her and Storm.

"We won't get another chance at this."

She was talking to a blank wall, none of the men's expressions flickering as they scanned the empty yards.

A garbage can had overturned at the end of a driveway, the lid a black mound in the center of the street. Adams steered around it, swerving into the opposite lane. There were no other vehicles on the road.

She wouldn't have been any different if she were still part of the unit. Yet the loyalty she had once had felt misplaced, a shadow of the purpose and clarity she had now.

They stopped at an intersection with a larger street. The day struggled to arrive, only the faintest of light in the sky. The street was a series of fast food places, motels, and charging stations. Large green signs that signaled the freeway dominated the street further down, the lights creating a strip of brilliant emptiness above the dull gray overpass. The shift in the men was subtle, a straightening and new alertness. The drop location must be close, the anonymity of the strip hiding all kinds of sins.

Half a block down, Adams turned the van into a motel parking lot. He parked next to one of the small, toy-like electric vehicles. Dirty white stucco and uneven shutters made the place look abandoned, as if the era of light had passed it by. Ten rooms were lined up in a row, with the office at its end. Concrete flowerpots with dead flowers marked each room with bug-filled lights mounted above the door. A two-story industrial office building filled the next lot and a boarded-up fast food kiosk with a cracked sign for *Happy Burgers* encroached on the other side.

"What are we doing here?"

They should be housed at a local armory or have borrowed a room from law enforcement.

Stubbs got out first and she tried to prepare herself for Stanton's wrath, expecting him to stride out the door. Stubbs unlocked the door to room number seven and gave Adams the all clear.

She caught Adams' eye in the rear-view mirror, his expression unreadable. He held her gaze for what felt like a beat too long.

Hamel and Jones flanked her on either side as they escorted her to the motel room.

She had two escape routes: one through the piles of trash cans and discarded chairs behind the burger place, the other through the concrete pillars at the front of the office building. Hamel and Jones would have identified them too and kept themselves positioned between her and any opportunity for escape. Just a happy gang of four guys and a single woman entering a seedy hotel room. Nothing that anyone in this neighbourhood would blink an eye at.

Adams stepped out of the way to let her enter first. Each of the men was going overboard to maintain their professional distance, denying a connection had ever existed.

Two sagging, double beds filled the drab room with four bags neatly lined up along the wall. A kitchenette had clean dishes drying on a towel. The television screen had been pushed aside on the top of the dresser.

"Cozy," said Maria.

"Have a seat."

Adams indicated one of the scruffy breakfast chairs. She sat dutifully, waiting for handcuffs or some kind of restraint. Thankful, for the moment, that Stanton wasn't there. Stubbs stood guard at the door, Hamel and Jones sat on the edge of the second bed, and Adams sat in front of her, close enough she could see the stress lines around his eyes and the stubble of his beard, surprised that some of it showed gray.

Her gaze dropped to his hands, clasped in front of him. There was no sign of any tremors.

"What the hell happened?" said Adams.

She drew back. Did he know the mission Havernal had sent her on? Did Stanton know? Or was he bluffing?

"I don't know what you mean."

The bed creaked as Jones shifted, his awareness of her lie obvious. Adams didn't move.

"One day we're heading out to the unrest along the border. The next you've disappeared and Havernal takes a leave," said Adams.

"You knew he was sick."

They had witnessed his growing weakness, the tremors in his hand as it rested on the desk. Now. they would recognize it as the Gatherer-induced plague. Back then, they hadn't known.

"We thought you went with him."

"I'm not sick."

In fact, she felt more alive than ever, the closeness of Stanton making her grateful for the life and freedom she still had.

"Yeah. We noticed."

His focus never left her. He would see the weight loss, Amanda's hair and make-up likely accentuating her thinness and the toll of being on the run.

"Did Havernal send you or was this something you thought up on your own?"

Adams's question surprised her. She hadn't thought what Havernal would have told them. It had been between her and him, and the blatant contradiction of orders was why she had traveled alone.

"I did what I had to do."

"On whose orders?"

"You know I can't answer that."

Adams shook his head once, a darkness to his expression that was new.

"The shit show you created didn't come down from the top brass," Adams said. "That much I know. They might have sent you out here but not for this circus."

His derision rankled. He thought he could have done it better. Brought Storm back in a tidy box.

"What do you care what I do?"

Any comfort at being back with them had gone, replaced by an agitation that made her want to run.

"You're still one of us."

"I was discharged."

Jones didn't hold back his snicker. Even Stubbs allowed himself a grin. She looked from one to the next. It had been on the news. That Dishonourable Discharge stamp printed across her face.

"You should be so lucky," said Stubbs.

Adams was watching her with that look he had when he was way ahead of her.

"You're not free until they say so."

There had been no written missives for her discharge or directions to report to a certain place at a certain time. She had assumed they were in her email inbox somewhere, or at her desk. All that judgement and reckoning she had walked away from hadn't been gone after all. They still owned her and could pluck her out of the world and away from her ability to do anything about the Gatherer. It explained the out of the way hotel room. The nondescript van. She would simply vanish, drawn back into the claws of the military, leaving Storm and the Gatherer to fend for themselves.

"Why are so many units deployed at the compound?" she asked. "Since when do special forces play security guard?"

At her question, the darkness in Adams's expression returned. Stubbs looked above their heads, his expression closed. His two hundred and fifty pounds blocked the door, the only other escape the faint light from the bathroom window.

"Who gave you the order?" asked Adams. "Did anyone?"

"You've got no authority to ask that."

Adams had a sudden look of frustration before it cleared. This wasn't his usual cool.

"We're trying to understand what happened." It was Jones, a normalcy to his voice that made her pause. Had they taken this detour on their own?

What could she say? This was her unit. Her team. They had worked flawlessly together. A team at the top of their game.

"So you acted alone," said Adams.

"Yes."

Adams watched carefully and Stubbs gaze had never left her. They would be looking for signs of lying and she intentionally stiffened her spine, lifted her head in belligerence. It was an easy sell, a stance that had once been her natural state. It made her think of Amanda and wonder how much she had seen of Maria's capture.

"Havernal won't be able to save you from this one," said Stubbs.

She had become damaged goods. But why bring her here? She sat rigid and unmoving as the agitation rose. All of them knew her too well to be able to hide from them.

She stood and Stubbs' bulk shifted. Adams held up a hand and Stubbs heeled. She paced to the small bathroom. It was cramped and stained, the window impassable. Stubbs and the three men were unbreakable. Which left her with nothing. She moved back to the main room.

"If you don't let me go, the damage of the Gatherer will be on your head."

They had intentionally put her in a small room, trapped.

"No," said Adams. "It will be on yours."

She had been charged with stopping the Gatherer before it was released, Storm having played her and released the Gatherer under her nose. Her reputation had never recovered, her need to right that wrong part of why Havernal had chosen her for the mission. She paced to the large picture window, peaked through the curtains. There was no sign of Stanton, the lot as dead as when they arrived. The row of cars solidified in the rising sun.

"What are we waiting for?"

The window was double-paned and discoloured. Probably installed in the 1970s when they made glass thick and strong. The glass would barely be broken before they were on her.

Adams had his elbows on his knees, head bent. Jones and Hamel looked at their hands. There had been no easing of tension, their body language implying that they were mid-mission.

She walked up to Stubbs. He had once been protective of her, Havernal having to step in to get him to treat her like any other soldier. The door handle was within arm's reach. He would probably break her wrist if she reached for it.

The buzzing of a cell phone broke the room and Adams was on his feet, moving towards the door as he took the call outside. She felt the change of tension in the room, though it may have only been her. Three to one was better than four.

She sat on the closest bed, opposite Jones and Hamel.

"How are things?"

Hamel turned away. Jones shook his head with only the briefest flick of his gaze to her.

"I'm just asking," she said.

They all knew she wasn't. In her shoes, they would have done the same, looked for help anywhere they could.

"I made my own choices. You guys have your orders."

She moved down the bed, breaching the space between them. "It doesn't have to be personal."

It was like feeling along a solid wall in the dark, searching for the light switch.

Jones gave her a longer look, absent of the connection they had once had. Hamel was younger, less hardened, but he still refused to meet her eyes.

"Are we waiting for Stanton?"

She got an exasperated glare from Jones before he stood and moved to the window. He briefly opened the curtains, a slice of light breaking into the dimness of the room.

"What is she like?" asked Hamel.

She almost smiled, Hamel's curiosity getting the better of him. She took her time answering.

"Brilliant. Though that is probably a given. And tougher than you'd think. The making the world a better place line, it isn't an act. She's still trying to make the world better, only this time from a different starting point."

She had an image of Storm hacking away at the side of the Gatherer and bent low over the boat's steering wheel in the cold, hard rain.

"The protests are only going to get people killed." It was Jones who spoke this time.

"Was anyone hurt today?"

The brash naivety of those young women still made her stomach turn.

"Was that you?" Stubbs eyes were accusing, always searching for proof of her guilt. "Did you start that protest?"

"It had already begun when I found it," she said.

"By accident."

Stubbs believed she was capable of everything the news had said, as if the person who had trained beside him and provided cover on missions, had suddenly vanished, erased by whatever he heard in the news.

"Three casualties. Uncounted injuries."

Hamel had always been their details guy, able to draw information from the air. Much like the Gatherer but with fewer lethal consequences.

The casualties could have been one of the young women or the older man with the bald head.

They heard the muffled words of Adams outside the door, the final goodbye understandable by its clipped tone. Adams opened the door.

"We're moving."

They rose in unison, and Maria felt again the ache of regret that she was no longer part of this. Their relief to be moving filled the room, their movements fluid, unified.

"Hamel and Jones, you take Kowalski," said Adams. "Stubbs, you're in the front with me."

The full sun had risen above the buildings to the east, a weak, watery light not yet broken free from the dawn.

The alley behind the burger joint.

The space behind the building next door.

The laneway next to the boarded up laundromat across the street.

She scanned for another choice. There had to be something better.

Hamel opened the van door for her and Jones followed. She swallowed a swell of regret and swung her elbow up and back to Jones' jaw, feeling the solid impact as Jones grunted. She kicked out at Hamel's chest.

She felt the fleeting clasp of Jones's hand on her arm and she was running, every part of her funneled into getting away. She was at the end of the parking lot, jumping over the concrete barrier when boots sounded too close behind. She surged forward, the air sharp in her lungs, as arms grabbed her waist and slammed her to the ground. The impact tore her breath away.

Adams' weight was on her back, his knee digging between her shoulder blades. Tiny rocks on the pavement dug into her cheek, and the toes of polished boots crowded around them.

"That was a stupid thing to do," said Adams.

Finally, she gasped a gulp of air as she was hauled to her feet for a shameful walk back to the van. She was pushed in front of the others and their silence hurt more than the angle of her arms.

The windows, the lot, the street, it was all empty, no one to witness any of it. They shoved her into the back seat with Jones and Hamel on either side. Her cheek throbbed and there was a intense kind of pain coming from her elbow.

Adams and Stubbs got in and Adams paused with his hands on the wheel, the vehicle not yet started. Her fear rose higher than the pain, filling out into the silence. This no longer felt like a team but like something broken. Each solitary man equally adrift.

The deep whir of the engine vibrated beneath them as the wheels engaged, and they bumped out of the parking lot. The empty abandoned street stretched ahead of them. Far in the distance, the dark mass of the forest rose up the mountain before the van turned, the walls of the alley close against the sides, the dimness of the night clinging in the corners.

EIGHT

THE SILENCE IN THE car was different now, whatever trace of goodwill her unit might have had for her obliterated as soon as her elbow had connected with Jones' jaw. She had been lucky to even make contact. If it had been anyone else, he would have been expecting it.

Her elbow throbbed and shoots of pain ran into her fingertips, her knees smarting where the pavement had torn the skin. Blood ran from the cut on her cheek and dripped onto her sleeve. No one offered a towel or tissue to stop the flow and she let the dark patch grow. Jones hadn't touched his jaw and Hamel sat rigid beside her.

They felt closer against her, the city an interminable maze as she marked each turn Adams made, trying to anticipate their destination. Every second she was being drawn away from where she needed to be, the fate of Storm and the Gatherer falling through her fingers. She had pleaded with them, failed miserably at an escape, and the military's claws were firmly lodged in her skin and her future.

"You're making a mistake," she said.

A quick flash of Adams's gaze in the rear-view mirror before he looked back to the road. There hadn't even been anger, no recognition of the relationship they had once had. She leaned forward to ease the feeling of being trapped and hands clamped down on either shoulder, pulling her back against the seat.

They waited at a stop light; a single vehicle beside them. An older woman sat in the driver's seat, her head barely above the window. She wouldn't hear her if she shouted and would be able to do nothing to help. They accelerated slowly off the line, Adams driving like the old woman at the speed of traffic. The pressure grew tighter.

They had entered an older residential area with one-and-a-half-storied houses built sometime after the Second World War. Driveways held old gas cars with an air of having been parked permanently; others had sleeker, smaller electric vehicles. If she looked hard enough the white shadow of a Gatherer could be found at each one, installed next to an air-conditioning unit, under the defunct meter or glowing dimly from the back of a garage. This late in the year it was impossible to tell whether the bleached grasses surrounding them had given in to the approaching winter or had been destroyed by the machine itself.

The neighbourhood hung in limbo as they bumped slowly along the uneven road. It would have been why Adams had chosen this route, a generic beige van easily passing unobserved through the empty streets. Otherwise it made no sense, this route and their destination still frustratingly unknowable.

A railway bridge crossed the road ahead of them and an electric train streaked across it, an instant of light and speed in the muted neighbourhood.

Jones and Hamel shifted beside her, an indication of their continued alertness despite the seemingly subdued street. She dabbed at the blood on her cheek, the flow having slowed. She closed her eyes for a second as the damaged flesh throbbed beneath her fingers.

They sloped down under the bridge, the space darker in that moment of adjustment from light to shadow. The faded yellow line ran down the center, the sloped curve of the ceiling patched with lighter splashes of concrete. A car entered the opposite end, its lights glaring, and she turned her head, the beams whitewashing Hamel's face. She saw the half-formed word on his lips an instant before a bone jarring jolt slammed her into her seat. Her head snapped back and she was flung forward as a second, stronger impact struck them from behind. She slammed into the back of Adams's seat and rebounded towards the side door, hitting Hamel's knees and the front passenger seat. She landed wedged between the two seats, gaining her bearings in time to see the doors on both sides yanked open and a taser shot into Jones's thigh. He stiffened, the current freezing him in place. Her hand fell to her hip and grasped nothing, her brain taking a second to remember she wasn't armed.

"Out of the car!"

It was an order screamed from outside the vehicle. Jones teetered in the open door, held rigid by the current running through him, Hamel equally immobile on the other side. She grabbed the pistol from his holster, lifted, and fired at the torso of the man outside Hamel's door. There was a satisfying grunt from her target. At the same time, Hamel toppled onto the pavement. She spun, pistol in front of her, the barrel coming to rest on the forehead of the man coming in from the other side. He froze.

Wide face. Flat blue eyes. Shaggy black hair. His shoulders filled the back seat, his hands the size of plates.

"Get back," said Maria.

Jones lay immobile on the ground behind him and there were sounds of a struggle from Adams's direction. The man's gaze didn't leave hers, a smirk playing on his lips as he backed out, light filling the space as he retreated.

"Step back from the car!" yelled Maria.

The man was huge. At least six and a half feet tall, and four times her size. She kept the pistol trained on him as she scrambled out of the back seat. The electric ticking of several tasers reverberated inside the tunnel, like a swarm of deadly insects.

Jones lay stricken on the ground where he had fallen and she had the briefest of glimpses of his face contorted in agony. She stepped over him and let her foot drag against one of the prongs, all her focus on the giant man. The prong fell from Jones' thigh and he collapsed onto the ground.

"Don't move," she said.

Hamel's assailant had come around the vehicle and Maria leveled her pistol at the thin, pasty rail of a man before bringing it back to her larger problem. With her back to the vehicle she inched her way along the bumper. The back end was pushed in where the second vehicle had struck it, a narrow space left between it and the monstrous black Predator SUV they had used for the attack. She squeezed between the vehicles, halfway through when the taser on Hamel timed out behind her. He gave a ragged gasp as his muscles released.

She had her back to the Predator now, with too many potential assailants. The man who had attacked Hamel now focused on her. The beast had moved to the other side of the gap.

"What are you going to do now, little girl?"

She fired a single bullet into his thigh, dashing for the Predator's driver's side door before she heard his scream. There was a flash of movement out of the corner of her eye and she spun to face Hamel's attacker. She lifted the pistol to fire as Adams tackled him to the ground.

Blood ran down Adams' face and one of his arms hung loosely at his side.

"Go."

It was a hiss, pushed out between gritted teeth as he grappled single-handedly with her attacker.

She bolted for the driver's door. Now not the time to understand.

She kept the pistol in her left hand as she shifted into gear. A fast, powerful reverse and she was pulling out and around the big man roiling on the ground. Stubbs's attacker was making a dash for the vehicle that had slammed the front of the van as Stubbs struggled to his knees. *You can't run fast enough*, she thought.

She checked in her rear-view mirror as Adams hauled Hamel's attacker to his feet and Stubbs reached the second vehicle's door. She burst from the tunnel's dimness into the gray brightness of the day. She pushed hard on the accelerator, feeling the deep pull of the engine's power, and flew over the potholed pavement. She blew through a stop sign, a driver on the cross street looking up at her in alarm. Only then did she remember the pistol held tight in her hand.

She lowered it to her lap, unwilling to let it go, and gripped the wheel harder with a single hand.

She swung onto a side street, turned when it seemed like a good idea, and after several corners made it to a wider commercial street. Early morning traffic filled the lanes and she was forced to halt at a stop light. The cars behind her were mostly single commuters on the way to work, and the drivers on the adjacent street stared straight ahead in their early morning stupor.

Her panting and heartbeat filled the cab and she forced herself to loosen her hand on the steering wheel. She adjusted the pistol in her lap. Jones loved his SIG P226 and had always kept it in top shape. He would be pissed she had taken it, but it gave her comfort to have it with her. The light turned green and she checked the rear-view mirror as she pulled forward. Stubbs could have reached the other vehicle in time. Or the attacker had gotten away and was too busy running for cover to come after her. Either way, the road was empty behind her.

Anyone could have sent those men after her, except not many of them had known where she was. Had Adams arranged it? Why else had he let her go? Except he would never put his unit at risk. Their attackers had been undisciplined, the large man who had come after her acting like it was a game he was sure to win. He hadn't even been armed.

She checked the rear-view mirror again before turning south into a residential area. She swerved hard around a little boy with a dog on a leash and had a glimpse of wide rounded eyes before she left him behind.

How many other eyes were tracking her as she fled, with no idea where to go where they wouldn't be watching?

NINE

MARIA SAT WITHIN THE silent metal frame of the SUV. Her heart resisted the slower pace, unwilling to step down from high alert. She peeled her hands off the wheel and adjusted the pistol a few inches closer on the console beside her. She had chosen a narrow residential street, wedging the attacker's massive vehicle into one of the parking spots along the broken curb. A search of the vehicle had revealed a gym bag of workout clothes in the back seat, a tablet still charged (its facial recognition software not recognizing her image), an extra magazine that didn't fit the SIG and a cigarette pack with a single cigarette missing.

She reached beneath the driver's seat and smiled as her hand closed around the barrel of a pistol. A Glock that matched the magazine in the console. Who left their weapon in the vehicle? She stared down at the gleaming, well-maintained weapon, her mind answering her own question. Someone that doesn't want to kill anyone. Or raise the stakes high enough to get killed.

She slipped the SIG and the Glock inside her coat.

There was no wallet in the vehicle. No receipts. The only identification was the reek of the guy's sweat from the gym bag. She took the tablet with her and laid her hand on the metal door handle. The morning street was empty, the line of cars parked behind and in front of her still plugged into the line of charging stations. There were no visible cameras, but it didn't mean they weren't there. Even if Amanda had been able to keep track of her, there was no way she could have covered up that trail.

She slipped out of the car, leaving the key in the console in hopes that some kid would steal it, and then disappeared into an alley between the tall narrow houses. She passed a neat row of garbage cans and a wire gate that lead to a backyard. The intoxicating smell of bacon and toast floated past. She followed the scent, walking carefully through the backyard cluttered with children's plastic toys. She quietly drew back the bolt on the back gate and stepped into the laneway between streets. The back of businesses lined the opposite side of the laneway, empty skids and discarded plastic pails spilling into the lane around the bulks of two smaller Gatherers. No noise, no hum, just the silent drawing off of energy.

The smell of food came from a business further down, the steel door propped open to the morning air. She crept down the lane until she could see inside. There were sounds of food frying, fans blowing, and voices calling orders from the front. She checked for anything close inside the door that she might be able to grab and run. Nothing but empty egg cartons and the smooth face of a walk-in cooler. She inched closer considering the insanity of forcing them to give her breakfast at gunpoint. There was a sudden opening of the cooler door and a teenage boy, long hair, all arms and legs, stopped in the open door. He held a tray of eggs in front of him.

"You can't come in here," he said.

She smiled, doing her best to act like she had arrived here by accident.

"Do you do take out?"

"Yeah. But you have to go around front."

"Can I do it here? I'm kind of in a hurry."

The boy frowned, taking in her rumpled clothes and asymmetric hair, still unsure what side of weirdness she would fall on. He shook his head.

"I'll get in trouble."

"I don't want you to get in trouble, but I'd rather order it here if I could."

His mouth pressed into a line, his frown deepening.

"I'll go check."

She held up her hand to stop him, the busyness and light of the café shining behind him.

"I'd rather it was just you. Please."

It could have been the urgency in her voice or the pleading she had let slip but his eyes narrowed and he tilted his head to the side.

"Why?"

She shrugged, unable to come up with anything that sounded believable.

"I don't want to be found."

He looked to the ground and then back up again, taking a long moment to search her face. She waited, letting him see what he needed to and counting on him to not recognize her. His jaw tightened and he nodded once. She had a sudden vision of the man he would come to be, if he had the chance.

"Okay."

Her stomach growled as he returned the eggs to the cooler. He wiped his hands on his apron.

"What do you want?"

"Whatever you've got."

He retreated into the warmth and light and she instantly questioned whether she had made the right choice. She stepped behind the skids, partially hidden and with an escape route down the laneway if he came back with anyone. Minutes passed and her agitation grew. People moved in the windows in the houses across the lane, a couple eating a hurried breakfast at a counter, an older woman letting her cat out the back door. Four separate Gatherers were installed in alternate yards. The cold bit through her jacket and she shifted her feet.

Was she really this stupid? She should have covered as much ground as she could before the day got busy. She took a final look at the empty door of the café. Had he called the police? Or worse?

She pulled up her collar and turned away, half running towards the end of the lane.

"Hey!"

He stood in the center of the lane, a take-out container held in his hands. She walked slowly back, wary of any movement in the shadows or silhouettes waiting inside the door.

"Sorry I took so long. I didn't want my Dad to see."

"This is your Dad's place?"

He handed her the container.

"It will be mine eventually."

It was heavy in her hands and the bottom deliciously warm.

"How much do I owe you?"

"It's on me."

"No, really."

She reached for the cash Amanda had given her and handed him a twenty.

He refused to take it. "We don't take cash anyways."

She folded the bill back into her hand.

"Of course." The government was encouraging everyone to go completely digital and *Embrace the Future*. "Thanks again."

He nodded with a stern, self-important air.

"Stay safe."

She was already turning, the words landing lightly on her shoulders.

"You too."

She walked on the edges, giving each Gatherer she passed a wide berth along the way. Closer to the end of the lane, she ducked into an alcove. She opened the lid to a buffet of breakfast items: eggs, sausages, bacon, tomatoes, toast, butter, jam. More than she would eat in an entire day but probably about right for a breakfast if you were a tall, fifteen-year-old boy.

When she had eaten all she could, she dropped the remains into a garbage bin and wiped her hands down her thighs. The food sat warm in her belly and she could feel her body coming alive at the welcome fuel.

She looked up and behind her, wondering if she was looking up into one of Amanda's screens. The street was starting to wake, an advertisement for an electric coffee mug scrolling brightly above the convenience store, the diner spilling light and warmth into the street a few doors back. She turned away from it and the traffic it drew, the street curving in a long arch through rows of parked vehicles, the windows of the apartments above the shops lit as people began their day. She didn't like the idea of them being able to look down at her through cracks in curtains any better than she liked the scrutiny of the people in the vehicles that drove past. The military would be after her, trying to contain her again, though she couldn't forget Adams's hiss to "Go." So whose side was anyone on? The risk he had taken and the faith he had put in her shocked and confused her.

A city bus came into view at the end of the street, rolling smoothly towards her. There was no driver where one should be, the logo of the Gatherer plastered on its side welcoming her to a free, driverless ride courtesy of the corporation. She turned away from it, in the opposite direction of the diner and the people it would draw.

A tall young man in a turban waited at a bus stop half a block away. She felt a vibration against her chest. The tablet, vibrating with an incoming call. She hesitated before pulling it out, her suspicions solidifying as she looked at the screen.

The device indicated a call from "Mandy."

Amanda didn't bother to say hello.

"You know there are cameras on the street."

There was an edge of anxiety in her voice, a shaking that Maria hadn't heard before. A man sleeping in an alley briefly woke as he adjusted his position before closing his eyes again.

"Did you send those men after me?"

There was a pause and the sound of keys clicking.

"I've blocked the feed. Made it look like a malfunction."

Maria craned her neck to search for cameras as Amanda's fingers slipped through firewalls and encryption to access the small device.

The bus glided to a stop at a light beside her. She paused, uncertain whether she would be more or less exposed on the bus.

"That bus would take you past the compound," said Amanda.

The boy climbed on the bus, a platform lowered to level with the curb. The line of shops stretched ahead of it with the subdued brown openness of a park across the street.

"In about five kilometres," said Amanda, "you'll be driving through the protesters at the front, or close to them. A whole slew of them arrived this morning."

A young woman with dreadlocks clomped down the back steps of the bus.

"Will they stop the bus?"

"They're quiet now, but I can't guarantee they won't. There are more guards all around the perimeter with at least a dozen at the gate. It looks more like a military installation than an industrial complex."

The young man who had boarded the bus watched her from the window as it glided away. Was there recognition there? Or was it simply the oddness of standing at the stop and not getting on. She turned away, facing the closed shops, pretending to search for an address. The young woman was already half a block away.

"Maria?" The voice of Amanda came from the tablet. "Maria?"

There was a rising panic in her voice.

"I'm here."

"What happened?"

She jay-walked between an extended van and a white pick-up that honked at her before he and the simulated rumble of his electric truck slid past. She passed an empty park bench, the gravel crunching beneath her feet.

"How did you know to call me on this tablet?" said Maria.

"I saw you take Simon's truck. I know he keeps it in the console."

"Simon?"

She stopped next to a circular fountain drained of water, dead leaves and dirt caught in the crevasses.

"I'll explain later," said Amanda.

"You sent them in? That was my unit. I worked with those guys."

A long pause.

"You looked like you needed help."

She had a long ago memory of Amanda always being there, anticipating what she would need whether she wanted her to or not.

"I shot your guy."

"I know."

"Is that going to be a problem?"

Blank walls bordered the sides of the park, a wood fence along the back.

"Shouldn't be."

Was Amanda telling the truth? There was that flippancy in her voice she used when she wanted to look tough.

"Are you in danger?" asked Maria.

A laugh. Was that the inhale of a cigarette?

"I've looked after myself this far."

"That doesn't answer the question."

Maria walked behind a stripped bush, taking what cover she could from the bare branches.

"You've got bigger things to worry about right now."

Behind the bush, a narrow path squeezed between the corner of the stone wall and the fence.

"Can you see me?" asked Maria.

A man in a tweed coat moved slowly towards the bench with a white terrier on a leash.

"I can see the guy with the dog. Not into the park."

"Where were they going to take me?"

Another pause. The exhale of cigarette smoke.

"Wherever you needed to go."

"What happened after I left the tunnel?"

There was a pause, no tapping keys or smoke.

"I don't know. The tunnel is a dead spot. I saw everyone go in and then you speeding out in Simon's vehicle. I didn't know right away it was just you."

"Have you seen Ari?"

The terrier peed on the leg of the bench before settling in front of the old man.

Maria waited, silence on the end of the call. The apartment wall on the side of the park blocked her view of the street.

"Amanda?"

"Three guys just arrived on the alley behind the diner. They're moving in your direction."

Maria felt the world shift, the air, the building, the old man all coming alive.

"Are they military?"

"I can't tell."

Maria was moving, reached the back corner of the park in two strides.

"There's a path out the back of the park. Tell me where to go."

There was nothing from Amanda, the sound of rapid typing doing nothing to help her.

She ran, the edge of the stone wall scraping her jacket as she followed the dirt path. A chain link fence enclosed the backs of shops, the other side of the fence people's back yards. Wrappers and empty plastic bottles lay tangled in the dead grasses, the only escape route over the fence.

Dull gray clouds hung above her, flattening the light and the day into something two-dimensional. A direction forward. A direction back. A clear, uncluttered choice.

"They're at the park," said Amanda.

Maria ran faster, the dead grasses tearing at her legs. Amanda's voice was distant, hard to hear above the pound of her feet.

"Lose the tablet!"

Amanda's panic came through loud and clear.

"Now!"

Maria threw the tablet ahead of her and adjusted her stride to slam her heel into the screen without missing a step. The path ended at a parking lot behind an apartment building, each space filled with an electric vehicle charging at a station and a Gatherer installed close to the building. An overweight businessman stood next to a sleek new vehicle, keys in his hands. She reached him before he even looked up.

It was quick and easy, his skin greasy and soft, and she half caught him as she guided his unconscious body to the ground.

A whole dashboard of lights powered on when the car started, the seat moving forward and up as it automatically adjusted to her height. She checked for her pursuers as a woman's husky voice asked if she wanted to engage the autopilot.

"No!"

She reversed hard, praying the vehicle wasn't geared to the man's voice and was relieved when the vehicle responded.

"Manual navigation active."

The vehicle was solid and heavy and it moved like an armored vehicle until she touched the accelerator and its response was quick and powerful. She was on the road, merging with a half dozen similar vehicles before anyone reached the parking lot.

A map appeared on the dashboard screen, showing her location.

"What is your destination?"

"None of your business."

She passed a car that had slowed to turn.

"Sorry, I didn't catch that."

"Audio off."

She pronounced the words clearly, speaking louder than she needed.

"Okay. Turning audio off."

A muffled silence settled around her, broken only by the deep whir of the electric drive. A sign ahead showed the universal open hands symbol of the Gatherer with an arrow pointing left. It helped that her destination was a tourist attraction, though it wasn't tourists that were parked at its gate. She blew past the sign, aware of the cameras watching her back and wondering whether Amanda would be able to do anything about it.

TEN

STORM LAY STILL ON the narrow bed, her arms and head too heavy to lift. There was no sound and no hint of fields, the inert air on her cheeks almost soothing.

She rolled onto her side noticing the IV as it tugged at the skin on the back of her hand. She pulled at the tube, easing the tension, the bag and the stand it was attached to rolling towards her. The room was white as was the door with its round silver knob. She could easily be inside a Gatherer, with the white clean walls. She had a flicker of panic at the idea, except she would be dead if she was, there being no way back from that encounter.

She rested for a moment, feeling the dull throb of her heart reluctantly beating, amazed at some level that it still did. She closed her eyes to gather her strength and fell back into the depth of fatigue.

There was a click of the door handle and a darkness opened along the door frame, a sliver that grew wider, a man in army fatigues stepping out of the darkness. He had brown, cropped hair above a narrow face. The door closed behind him, and he stayed standing, a tablet in his hand. There were no chairs in the room or tables or anything other than her and her bed and her stand for the IV. Four lights provided the illumination from fixtures recessed deep in the ceiling; the holes cut with jagged lines. The whole room was newly formed, the chemical smell of construction thick in the air.

"I'm glad to see you're awake."

The man pushed something on the side of the bed and her torso was suddenly rising to a sitting position, the complete bareness of the room coming into focus. He circled the bed and checked the liquid in her IV.

"How are you feeling?" he asked.

He reached for her wrist, his cool fingers pressing to her pulse as he kept his gaze on the tablet's screen.

She closed her eyes again, struck by another tidal wave of fatigue. She forced them open in time to see him plunge a syringe into the IV bag. She tried to pull the other end out of the back of her hand but he stopped her, his hand encompassing her wrist as a searing burn ran up the back of her hand and into her arm. The drowsiness cleared like a fog in a brisk wind. The lights brightened, the walls whitened, and she was surprised by the sudden clarity of her thoughts and an all-too-vivid well-being that seemed to flow out of the IV.

"Where am I?"

Her voice was weak, rusty, the words hardly formed. She had a memory of being in the back of a truck and the smell of farm animals. Brief, distant memories before the endless sleeping and waking in the bare room.

He withdrew the IV from the back of her hand and draped the tube on the stand. He handled the apparatus easily, his movements tidy and precise.

"What did you give me?" she asked.

"Put this on."

He tossed a bunched piece of black material across her legs.

"It will be more effective than that flimsy silver thing you arrived with."

She lifted the material, its supple thinness falling out into the shape of a body suit and a separate piece that looked like a thin balaclava.

"Do you need me to do it for you?"

She was weary beyond measure, the days of sleeping and waking blurred together so she had no idea how long she had been in the room. Her body hurt and her head ached yet her thoughts were clearer than they had been since they had reached the city.

He reached for the suit to take it from her and she gripped it tighter. "I'll do it."

She pushed the blanket carefully off her legs, having no recollection of when she had been dressed in the short briefs and t-shirt she now wore.

She slid one leg into the suit, the material soft against her skin. There was a smoothness to her muscles that hadn't been there in months. He watched her carefully and she felt vulnerable, protective of this new strength.

She pulled the suit up her thighs, a faint sheen visible in the material. "What's in this?" she asked.

She shifted to try to pull it over her hips but the effort was too great. He reached in and helped her tilt to the side as he tugged the material over each hip.

"It's a base of wool with an interwoven mesh of aluminum and—"

He hesitated.

"—straw."

She paused, a sleeve halfway up her arm and examined the material more closely. There was no sign of straw but the aluminum explained the sheen.

"Why straw?"

The sleeve slid smoothly on her arm and she fastened the Velcro that closed the front.

He handed her the balaclava as he shrugged. A gesture that made him suddenly self-conscious. She understood that vulnerability and the exposure of being judged.

"It gives something for the carbon and aluminum to ground to."

She lifted her forearm to look closer.

"There's carbon?"

He gave no response as he watched her examine his creation.

"Does it work?"

His expression withdrew, whatever emotion she had seen gone before she could understand it.

"You'll find out."

She tried to move away from him, the bed leaving her nowhere to go. He rolled the IV stand out of the way and in a quick, sudden motion lifted her behind her shoulders and knees. She tried to squirm out of his grip and his hands held her harder, the pressure hurting her still-tender skin.

"Hold still."

He carried her to the door, her bare feet dragging against the frame as they passed. They were at the bottom of a staircase with over thirty steps, the construction the same rough concrete as the room. He climbed as if she weighed nothing at all, and she instinctively wrapped her arms around his neck as the bottom fell away. He smelled of anti-bacterial soap and a deeper mustiness.

"Where are you taking me?"

They were halfway up the stairs and his breathing was heavier, his body taut. The fingers that pressed through the thin fabric under her knees felt as if they touched bone and his other hand dug into her ribs.

"You're hurting me."

His grip eased and he re-adjusted.

"Is that better?"

The pressure was still firm yet the pain of it had withdrawn. By the top of the staircase, he was out of breath. He dropped her into a wheelchair.

They were at the end of a long, dim corridor, closed doors marking the distance, the polished floor reflecting the light from a distant window. She had a wave of dizziness at the overpowering smell of chemicals, so strong she expected the painted walls to be wet to her touch.

He leaned in front of her to tighten a strap around her legs. His sideburns ended in a clean, neat line, the shadow of a darker beard emerging below it. There was a pressure as he braced against the wheelchair and pulled a plastic sheet from beneath it. A sudden heavy weight pinned her to the chair as he draped an old x-ray blanket from her chest to her feet, the two wings wrapping around her back.

"Fields will kill me."

She tried to rise, struggling futilely beneath the weight. She could barely move her arms and had no hope of ever lifting her legs.

The wheelchair made no sound as it rolled over the tiles, the squeak of his boots the only noise as they passed dark windows of doors that looked like they had never been used.

"I'm well aware of what the dangers are," he said. "Probably more than anyone else."

There was a certainty in his voice that sent a chill through her, as if it was something he held over her. She longed for Maria who had understood her needs without using it against her. Had she found Ari? Or was she locked away somewhere the same as Storm?

They passed a series of numbers on the doors, 0129, 0132, 0137. No names to indicate where she was or what this place might be. It felt more like an office building than a hospital, and the silence prevented it from being either. She detected no fields in the small area of skin exposed around her eyes, the rest of her feeling like it was clamped in a tight, enclosed space.

Her apprehension grew as they traveled towards the lighter end of the corridor. The weight on her chest made it hard to breathe and she took shallow breaths, the fumes of the chemicals sparking nausea. A set of double doors blocked the hallway and she pushed back into the chair as they approached. Several strides away, he swung her back in the opposite direction and rolled her backwards through the door, ignoring the button that would have energized the electric motor to swing the doors open. She glanced up at him as they swung forwards again. His face remained impassive, but he at least did seem to have an understanding of where the hazards lay for her. More than any of her previous captors.

Before she could see clearly out the large window, they turned a corner down a narrow hall and backed through a second set of doors. A long ramp descended deeper into the earth, the smell of new construction catching in her throat. At the bottom, a corridor stretched straight and bare, the weight of the earth above it making it feel narrower.

One of the walls had turned to a gray, dull metal, rising to the ceiling and extending as far as she could see down the corridor. She tried to lift her hand to touch it but was too weak to fight the blanket's weight. He responded as if he had seen the movement of her hand.

"It's a composite material. Nickel, copper, some aluminum."

The response surprised her, that technical questions were in the realm of things he would answer.

"Does it work?"

"There is virtually no penetration of signals through it. It's military grade, the composite originally designed to protect communication equipment."

"Is this a military base?"

They circumvented the metal wall, following its long arc, blocked after over one hundred metres by another set of doors with a guard standing outside, his combat gear and a heavy vest answering her question.

The guard nodded. Not at her, though she must look like a freak out of a horror film with her balaclava and x-ray blanket.

The doors opened to at least a dozen people in an expansive computer room, several sitting at the terminals of the numerous desks. Most watched a screen that covered the entire side wall. Some of them looked military, others reminded her of the geeks she had gone to school with. They turned as she rolled in, a soldier with broad shoulders and silver hair breaking away from the group.

"Ms. Freeman! Welcome!"

The others stepped out of the way to let him pass and the multiple markings on his uniform likely meant he was important.

"I'm Colonel Stanton. I see Wesley has been testing his inventions on you."

She felt a sudden apprehension, trying to remember where she had heard his name when he abruptly pulled off the balaclava. She felt the burn from the computer terminals and a tingling rush across her scalp. She was flustered and panicked, aware of every current in the room.

He handed the face mask to Wesley as he turned back to the group who regarded her with a hostile curiosity.

"Welcome to the group. We're glad to have you here at such an important moment."

The large screen showed a wide-open expanse that could have been a football field except that a herd of cows grazed in the wide space on a patchy cover of white and green grass. The largest Gatherer Storm had yet seen, larger than the one in Three Rocks, sat in the middle of the herd. People moved back to let her through as Wesley pushed her forwards. Each cow was chained in position, their locations forming a series of rings that spiralled out from the Gatherer.

If the Gatherer in Three Rocks had been capable of collecting hundreds of kilowatts out of the air before she destroyed it, would this be capable of gathering megawatts? Or gigawatts? One of the cows closest to the front of the screen chewed calmly at the grass. Stanton was talking. Thanking everyone for being there to help and witness their success as fear gathered in her chest. The resulting damage from a Gatherer of that size would be powerful and unpredictable. She tried to rise, couldn't overcome the weight of the blanket.

How far away was that Gatherer? Its frequency would be wrong, the process corrupted so that it stripped life and energy from everything around it. They had chained the cows in an even pattern around it, a crude way of tracking the harm it would cause.

She felt ill, far beyond the plague and its devastation. The knowledge of what that thing was lay hard and rotten in her gut.

"You don't know what you're doing," she said.

Stanton paused, turned back to face her with a strange smile.

"That's where you're wrong, Ms. Freeman. This group—" he waved his arm to encompass the room, "—knows more about the Gatherer than any others on earth. They, in fact, know *exactly* what they're doing."

Many of the group nodded, acknowledging the compliment. She looked to each of the them individually, trying to gauge in them the malice and cruelty that would be needed to make this kind of Gatherer. She saw only pride, accomplishment, and a dismissal of her objection.

Had they found the inconsistencies? A chill of dread pooled in her gut. Studied long enough, the Gatherer would have given up its secrets, allowed this deadly version to be created.

"The damage is too much," she said. "You won't be able to control it."

She slipped her feet to the floor and tried to slide out from beneath the blanket.

"But we have."

There was an excitement in Stanton's voice, matching the restlessness of the others. It wasn't the energy they were after, it was about the damage, a grand, calculated map of how far out the damage would reach.

"Take me back," said Storm.

She couldn't watch this. The suffering of all those animals added to the burden of the afflicted. Would the ability of the Gatherer to do harm ever stop?

"Colonel Stanton wanted you to see this," said Wesley.

He carefully lowered the balaclava over her head, adjusting the hole so she could still see, when she remembered where she had heard Stanton's name.

He was the commander Maria had disobeyed and the one who had pursued them when they had fled the Yukon.

Stanton nodded as he met her gaze, as if affirming her recognition.

"Wesley's team has made significant inroads," said Stanton. "And with your input we'll be able to fully realize its potential."

She swallowed against the dryness and lifted her chin away from the pressure of the blanket.

"The only potential you're going to harness is more death and sickness."

His smile broadened; his certainty unwavering.

"That's where you're wrong."

Several of the group moved forward to the computer terminals and punched keys. She searched for Ari among the faces, appalled that he could be part of this. Fingers stopped tapping and the technicians stood back, all eyes on the screen. She couldn't watch and couldn't look away.

The cows munched, tails swished, a still pastoral scene until the faintest ripple spread across the closest cow's back.

It lifted its head as if it had sensed a predator and tried to bolt, the chain cutting into its neck. Its skin rippled, alive with a thousand signals, froth gathered at its mouth, and it went rigid.

She was horrified and grateful for the speed, the cow's eyes dead as it toppled to the ground. She imagined she could smell the rancid scent of charred meat.

Some of the techs were smiling, others simply stared at the screen. A young woman swallowed before her expression cleared and she was turning to the others, joining in the celebration.

A perfect ring of fallen animals surrounded the Gatherer on the field, only the ones in the end zones left standing. The Colonel was silhouetted in front of the carnage, beaming in satisfaction. He was speaking to her, coming closer.

"—did you ever imagine this?"

The room was watching her, the shocked adrenaline of success mixed with the first inklings of the power they had unleashed. It was hard to breathe, the weight of the blanket crushing her, the balaclava tight on her throat.

"Don't do this."

The response was a croak, and some of the crowd frowned. She searched for strength, tried to find the will she had when she had first defied these people. It had been a game for her then, but this was far beyond that.

Stanton was jubilant, his voice bristling with confidence.

"No. This is the future. You've all worked hard, put in the long hours and created something the world has never seen before. When Ms. Freeman has fully recovered, she will understand what we have created and understand its potential as we do. For now, I want to acknowledge the hard work you've done, and the sacrifices you've made."

The room's attention was on him, people nodding and a few smiles returning. The cow's dead eyes stared wide-eyed out of the screen.

Stanton nodded to Wesley, dismissing them. Wesley spun the wheelchair and they were pushing through the double doors, the guard in the same stance as when they arrived as if the world hadn't changed. They moved fast down the corridor, along the rigid curve of the metal wall. Was that Gatherer on the other side? Her skin tightened in response, anticipating the damage it would do.

"You've created a weapon," said Storm.

They slowed as they reached the ramp, Wesley's raised breathing audible as they climbed the steep incline. She couldn't begin to describe the wrongness of pushing The Gatherer into a range they didn't understand.

They entered the first building again, rolling silently down the empty hall, the natural light putting what had happened in that room in a harsher context. She needed to shout, scream, convince someone to listen.

They stopped at the top of the rough stairs, the descent steep and dim, the steps not visible beyond the first dozen, the landing at the end not visible at all.

ELEVEN

MARIA GROPED FOR THE final kernel of popcorn at the bottom of her bag, biting into the crunchy saltiness as she scanned the foyer. The only people in the cavernous space were the teen boy at the concession and the barista wiping tables behind her. Movie patrons had come and gone while she had been waiting, and not one had caught her interest or looked even remotely like Adams. For some soldiers it was gaming, for others gambling, but in her experience all of them needed something to shut off the noise. For Adams it was movies, the more immersive the better, and this was the only theatre in town with the four-dimensional experience. Yet he hadn't come.

She had come in, tagged to the back of a group of teens, hoping the black clothes would help her blend in. She had hung back once inside, taking shelter behind a life-size cut-out of some action star, and waited for the kid sweeping the floors to come close enough to ask him about surveillance.

"There isn't any." He'd been irritated, like it wasn't the first time he had answered the question. "Our privacy policy has been in effect for six months now." He said it by rote, an explanation given many times. "In response to customer complaints, we have implemented a full private zone in the theatre. No surveillance, no recording."

He moved away without looking at her, his job done.

She had scanned the roofline and the high walls, convinced she would find a telltale blackened dome or the old school wall-mounted camera. The outlets where they would have been were covered over by metal plates. Her shoulders had relaxed, the sense of someone watching her easing, if not disappearing.

Did Amanda know private zones were happening? The first sign of a movement that would eat away at her network?

She checked the clock mounted above the blinking arcade. There was only one movie left to start and it was unlikely Adams would choose it as an escape. *Freeing the World* was a documentary on Storm Freeman that had come out shortly after the Gatherer had been released. It had been re-released as a result of Storm's new profile in the news.

She scanned the parking lot, hoping to see Adams' powerful stride crossing the empty lot. She still wasn't sure why he had let her go and whether he would help her again. Only a handful of vehicles filled the grid work of faded yellow lines.

"Sorry, the coffee shop is closing."

The barista wiped the table next to Maria, a large coffee stain down the front of her apron.

Maria stood, the expectation that had kept her wired while she waited unwilling to release.

Posters lined the walls, advertising the current movies, and she stopped in front of the poster for *Freeing the World: a documentary of Storm Freeman, the woman who saved the world*. An airbrushed version of a young, healthy Storm stared intently out at her. Photoshopped versions of Daniel, Jana, Callan, Ari and Alicia formed a halo of secondary characters behind her, the designer showing them less distinctly than Storm.

She stepped closer, the sound of the barista stacking chairs echoing through the foyer. Each of the people flanking Storm had contributed to the Gatherer's success. All of them exceptional in their own way. It showed Ari looking dreamily into the distance, a luxurious mane of black hair pushed back from his forehead. Storm believed they could trust him. That he would know what to do.

"Last call for tickets."

The teen's voice rang through the empty foyer. Maria was walking towards the counter before she realized she had made a decision.

"One please."

He was surprised when she handed him cash and after a pause, he rang it through and counted out her change.

"The previews have already started so you should hurry."

She scanned again for Adams, stopping her search only when she reached the corridor to the theatres. The flashing tunnel was empty, the lights around displays and on railings moving in the dim light.

Inside the cinema, rows and rows of seats faced the massive screen with only a few people scattered among the chairs. She stopped at the bottom of the staircase, overwhelmed by the gigantic image of Storm on the screen.

"Energy is what connects everything. It connects us to each other, the earth, the solar system. Which is why I always believed it was so important to understand more about it."

Her hair was to her shoulders, her eyes a brilliant blue and she leaned into the camera when she spoke. It took Maria's breath away to see her so young and alive. The energy that had drawn people to Storm reaching out of the screen.

She gripped the railing behind her back. It was like seeing a beautiful statue before it was destroyed.

A person loomed at her shoulder with another close behind. She staggered backwards, up two steps, her mind calculating where and how to strike. Her response was stopped only by the sudden brightness of the screen illuminating the startled face of a heavy-set man carrying a carton of popcorn. The woman behind him held the drinks.

He mumbled a "sorry" as he veered around her, her heart pounding as they haltingly climbed the stairs, deciding where to sit. She needed to relax and remember where she was, at least act like a regular civilian even if she didn't feel like one.

She climbed the stairs slowly, careful of where she placed her feet, the erratic light and Storm's haunting voice leaving her unsteady. Part of her wanted to turn and watch every second of this other Storm, yet the injustice of her destruction and the sorrow at that lost young woman weighed so heavily on her she hardly wanted to lift her eyes to the screen.

"As soon as I realized the possibility of what we had found I knew we had to give it to the world."

Maria chose a seat at the end of a row, at the back of the theatre, and lifted her eyes to a close-up of Storm's face. The pores on her skin were visible and an excited flush brightened her cheeks.

"What about the money you could have made?"

Maria had seen this segment of video before. The male interviewer was out of sight but his voice asking this question had been replayed thousands of times online and on the news. Storm looked off to the side, her lips slightly curved as she lifted a single shoulder.

"Sure, I could have made a lot of money. But so what? That happens every day. How often does a person get to save the world?"

If she hadn't known Storm she would have believed she had rehearsed it, planned the optimistic, humble response. It was no wonder the world had been drawn to her.

Her eyelashes showed as a light row of red, the faintest line of freckles across her nose. Storm's image froze, her hands uplifted in what had to be an intentional replica of the Gatherer's upward hands symbol. It faded out, the words *Freeing the World* coming on the screen as the opening sequence began.

The music that accompanied the outline of a single Gatherer soared so high it was close to causing pain. She didn't need to see the movie, she had been there, known Storm and the team. Yet she couldn't walk away from the Storm on the screen, caught in a moment of time when it could have all gone differently.

The Gatherer was replaced by old photographs showing Storm as a young child. A skinny, grinning, red-headed kid that always had something in her hand and seemed to be in the midst of doing something. She was alone in all the photos. It could have been an intentional choice by the director or a reflection of a child too busy for other kids. The photos were interrupted by the sudden appearance of Alicia on the screen, the coiffed slick version that headed the corporation.

"Storm was interested in everything. Even from the very beginning I had a hard time keeping up with her. And stubborn! Once she set her mind to something, there was no changing it."

Alicia was trying to play the proud mother exasperated with her exceptional child, yet it fell flat. Like she was reading from a script.

"Did you know then that she was destined for great things?"

Maria rolled her eyes and loosened her grip on the armrests.

"Her father, Robin, and I are both academics, so while we expected her to be smart, there was no way to predict all of this."

Alicia lifted her hands to indicate the room around her. Maria recognized the windows overlooking the compound, the desk facing away from the window. Instinctively, she felt along the line of her bra for the hard outline of the SD card Amanda had given her.

"Did Storm ever ask you to be involved in the development? Come to you for help?"

A laugh and a shake of her head, all of it forced.

"We would have been happy to help, of course. But we wanted to let this be Storm's. For her to have ownership of it."

This was propaganda, disguised as a documentary, likely put out by the corporation. Storm and Alicia had been estranged when Storm discovered the Gatherer; their reconciliation only taking place after the prototype had been produced.

The screen changed to footage of the original lab and Maria leaned forward. It was rough and shaky, taken with an older cell phone. Storm and Daniel sat close together on two stools, smiling at whoever was behind the camera; likely Jana, given her absence from the scene.

Callan tossed a football from one hand to the other and faked a pass towards the camera. Ari was the only one who faced away. The camera panned along the brightly coloured fish tank before zooming in on him at his terminal. He smiled, shook his head, and pushed her away, more interested in whatever was on his screen.

There was a close up of Callan that caused Maria to half stand, reaching forward as if she could press the pause button. For she thought she had seen it, though it was barely there, the twitch of Callan's cheek below his right eye. He hadn't tried to hide it, had barely seemed aware of it, yet the evidence of harm had already been there. Before it had even gone into production. It was like watching the tests of the atom bombs in the 1940s, or surveillance video of a busy street before a suicide bomber attacked, the cloud of death hanging over the people seen only by those who watched from the future.

It didn't make sense that they would put this in the documentary. Had they not seen it? Or was it intentional? A warning from a director with their hands tied?

She desperately wanted to go back and watch it again, but the camera had swung away to a slow pan of the test area, the original Gatherer sitting at its center.

She realized she was standing, the stadium seating feeling steeper and vaster below her, the screen overwhelming. Her instinct was to turn away from the sanitized inspirational slop they had made this story into. But the style of the film with its intense close-ups and intimate shooting was like watching the team with a magnifying glass. She lowered herself back into her seat.

The screen had changed to a scene inside what looked like an academic office. Books and papers and general disorder surrounded a man with a fringe of gray hair around his bald scalp.

Erik van Helsing, Professor of Electrical Engineering, University of California at Berkeley read the text at the bottom of the screen.

"What makes the Gatherer different than any energy technology we've seen before is that it taps into an energy we didn't know existed. A kind of layer of energy or life that surrounds and protects every living thing. It's in humans, animals, plants, even the rocks beneath our feet."

Maria had never heard of Dr. van Helsing and she wondered where they had dug him up from. Had Berkeley been the site where they had donated the Gatherer, for research? Had this interview been part of the deal?

"And by drawing off the smallest part of it, we've been able to supply all our needs. Some of the futuristic versions of our worlds we've seen in films and television are attainable now that we have this infinite source of energy."

He gave a pleased, smug smile like he had invented it himself.

"Is there any danger of upsetting this energy by accessing it?"

He laughed, pleased, dismissive, absolutely confident in his point of view. "Of course not! It's infinite! Which means that it is a never-ending supply. Historically, we've been chasing the wrong source to fuel our needs, generating electricity through laborious and environmentally damaging techniques like coal, hydroelectric, and nuclear. Even renewables aren't without costs. All of these sources, while necessary at the time, took us down a path that was unsustainable. The Gatherer—"

He puffed up his chest and leaned forward, speaking slowly, as if the audience were too slow to understand this. His tone of voice and his self-satisfaction reminded Maria of Alicia when they had first met.

"—has launched humanity into a whole new era. The amount we're drawing off is like drops of water from a bucket. Less than that. Like the mist overtop of the water."

Maria wished she were in the room with him, could do something to shut him up. She was grateful when the scene shifted to a tour through the Gatherer production facility, with Alicia describing the process. Maria watched intently searching for information about the facility, but the camera person was too skilled, the view too restricted for her to learn anything at all.

Alicia stopped in front of a metal enclosure the size of a storage container, the outside smooth and clear.

"This is the final stage of the process where every Gatherer is verified and tested to meet our stringent standards."

She turned as the camera panned over the smooth surface.

"We've refined the original process so that we were able to develop larger models and higher collection rates. Everyone has different energy needs and we have met those needs through a continual process of renewal and innovation."

Was this where the imperfections Storm had told her about were put into the crystal structure? Is that why the process was hidden? The crystals and the current that activated the structure allowed the Gatherer to collect its elusive energy, and the imperfections were what made it possible. If what Storm had told her was true, only a select few would know what happened inside the final container.

Maria's eyes burned with a growing fatigue, the darkness of the theatre working against her. She shook it off as the scene changed and they were back in the past, showing a clip of the team receiving the Order of Canada, in recognition of their contribution to humanity. The reward had seemed inconsequential in comparison to their achievement. It showed the five of them onstage, and as each received their award, their awkwardness was more evident. Callan was the size of a football player but was stilted as he moved; Daniel was hunched and furtive like he was being hunted; and Jana's normal aloofness had turned almost to stone. Ari was the only one who equalled Storm in the way he responded to the crowd, smiling, waving, accepting the recognition as if it were his due. And then a frozen image of the five of them – the one that had made them famous around the world.

They were a group of young people who had achieved the impossible, Storm at the center, one hand lifted to the crowd, the other wrapped around Daniel's waist. Maria couldn't help but picture the photo as it would be now. Storm alone in the middle, her arm around a Daniel who was no longer there, and Ari the only other survivor, standing apart at the end, his hand raised in a mirror to Storm's. He held onto no one with his other hand, his face towards the camera, yet his focus looking beyond it, at something at a greater distance.

Had he seen what was coming? Or had he been as certain in their destiny as the others?

Maria leaned back, resting her head against the chair, her neck tired. Her limbs were heavy, almost numb in their fatigue. If anyone arrived, she would be slow off the mark. She scanned the exits. She and the few patrons were as forgotten as the hope the Gatherer had delivered.

She closed her eyes against the tired burn as the film returned to Alicia on the floor of the manufacturing facility.

She woke from a dream where she couldn't get to training on time, leaving her confused and panicked as the credits rolled on the screen. The theater was empty and she stood, feeling strangely threatened without the other viewers. She held tight to the railing, still shaky and distracted from the dream, and was grateful to step back into the cycling lights of the corridor.

The glare hurt her eyes, her exhaustion more pressing in the light.

"Have a good night."

The young man who had sold her the ticket held the door for her as she stepped from the warm dimness of the theater into the cold, barrenness of the parking lot. The click of the lock behind her jolted her out of her reverie, and she shook off the raw dullness, alert to the dangers in the real world.

Headlights wound out of the lot as the other patrons headed for home and Maria made her way towards the vehicle she had parked behind the children's daycare in the next lot. She checked behind her. The teen had retreated back into the foyer but there would be cameras tucked in the eaves or below the marquee. Was Amanda out there? Or would it be someone else watching her through that lens?

She kept close to the wall before she turned the corner, alert for any movement or anything that had changed since she had left the vehicle. Scraps of colored paper still plastered the base of the dumpster, the yellow lines of the parking lot marking the spot for her car alone. Another building backed onto this one, the lot equally abandoned, a rusted trailer with flat tires parked along the chain link fence that separated them.

She was relieved to slide into the protection of the luxury vehicle, eager to get out of the city and find somewhere to take cover. She shifted into gear but didn't lift her foot from the brake. She had no destination, all her bets laid on her certainty that Adams would be at the theater. She couldn't stay here. The car already too much of a target.

She eased forward, slowly turning the wheel, following the line of pavement between buildings that would lead her to the road.

She drew past the corner of the first building and an open space appeared beside her. A stack of wooden skids and the sleek enduring glow of a Gatherer were tucked up against the back of the daycare. She braked. Light reflected off its surface, defining the darker outline of the upturned hands, a solid, wondrous presence that now felt like a threat. Was it even operating? Storm would have been able to tell.

She wanted to damage it enough that it would never operate again. The need to do it was overpowering, a quick dismantling to prove to herself they could be stopped.

A check in the rear-view mirror showed the straight emptiness of the lane, the brick walls and asphalt red in the glow of her tail lights. She breathed and clenched her hands on the wheel as she lifted her foot off the brake. She rolled forward, the ghost of the Gatherer sliding away behind her. She was in a narrow alley, the light from the headlights forced high and bright by the blank walls. A bad place to be if she were being followed, trapped if she were attacked.

She almost didn't see him. The sudden shadow on her right, stepping in front of her in a short, dark section between blank walls. She stopped, the bumper inches from Adams's knee, his appearance making total sense, the temptation of the Gatherer somehow providing the opportunity for him to appear.

He wore a hoody beneath a down vest, jeans, and running shoes. A typical civilian, if not for the coiled stance, ready to spring depending on her response. He arrived with a burst of energy and movement, crashing into her shoulder as he twisted and climbed into the narrow back seat. He tucked his head down, a shapeless mass of torso, arms and legs. She was surprised he fit in the small space, though she shouldn't be. He had done more remarkable things in the field.

She kept rolling forward, as if two hundred pounds of soldier hadn't just crammed himself in the back seat. She was alone, isolated, and she forced her body language to reflect that reality. She turned down a wider alley, the brightness of the main street at its end.

"How did you find me?" she asked.

He shifted in the back seat as if his re-adjustments would make the space bigger.

"I saw you at the theater."

They reached the end of a brick wall, the last one before they would be out on the road, exposed on all sides.

"Was anyone else with you?"

He gave a muffled grunt that sounded like a no, before he swore and a thud sounded from the side wall.

Streetlights panned across the front seat, not reaching the back, as she stopped at the main road. She pulled into the nearest lane and checked her rear-view mirror that all was clear. She accelerated through traffic lights, the white walk signal flashing into an empty intersection. The tires thudded over a joint in the road.

Box stores lined the street, set far back from the road, the laneways and parking lots vacant but for a single car. A traffic light turned red and she slowed, undecided on whether it was better to stop or blow through. The four-lane artery was empty behind her, wide open lanes and dotted yellow lines stretching in front.

Adams's voice was muffled from deep within the back seat.

"There's a street in three kilometres that will lead you through a new residential development. There are no cameras there yet and it connects to an old highway that leads out of town."

The restaurants and retail stores changed to a series of massive looming churches, startling in the flood of light that shone on their facades. Deserts of empty pavement surrounded them, the semblance of an oasis at its center either by accident or by design. When she turned into the development, the tiny blue arrow of the on-board navigation system indicated they were heading north. The half-built houses and newly minted curbs felt emptier than the wide-open streets. At the back of the development, at the end of a dead end, the new pavement turned to gravel before it changed to older, more worn asphalt. The vehicle's interior dropped into a deeper, more protective darkness.

The old road twisted through dense forest; abandoned, dilapidated houses shadows at the end of over-grown drives. At an intersection, they turned up the coast, and the road began its slow climb up the base of the mountain. Adams uncurled from the back seat and climbed into the front. It was a shock to have him beside her so far from their usual setting, and at the same time completely natural. She knew his shape, the precise strength in his movements. He rubbed at the back of his calf.

"Why did you let me go?" she said.

He stopped rubbing his calf and stared through the windshield. The trees grew closer to the road here, the upper branches forming a narrow tunnel the deeper they went. She slowed for a hairpin turn in the road, a layer of gravel skidding beneath the wheels.

Adams hadn't moved. When he finally answered his voice was stripped clean.

"After Freeman sent us that Gatherer for the base office, I ordered one. The biggest I could get."

She gripped the wheel and pushed harder on the accelerator, though there would be no escaping the dread seeping into the car and destroying the brief relief she had found.

"Who is it?" she asked.

He gave a ragged breath, and struggled for control he didn't get.

"Valerie—"

His voice caught.

"—and Camille."

Her stomach dropped. Adams's wife Valerie was warm and relaxed, insanely positive and not what she had expected for him. His daughter, Camille, was six.

"I'm sorry."

She was giving condolences as if they had died. But in truth, was there any other end to this?

There were no lights along the side of the road, the solid yellow line disappearing ahead of them into the darkness.

"I took it out as soon as Havernal got sick."

His words were short and strained, every syllable raw with guilt.

The opening of a tunnel appeared ahead of them, old stones set in a semi-circle around the arch, their headlights doing nothing to penetrate the darkness inside. And it suddenly felt like they had been wiped clean. Whoever they had pretended to be before had no place here, this tragedy and this darkness all that was left for them to do.

"Is someone looking after them?"

The lanes were narrower inside the tunnel, the stone wall close up against the side of the vehicle. Rows of stone bricks arched above them, built in another lifetime.

"She said that me being angry at home was only making things worse."

His voice was rough and she was stunned at this view of him. His invincibility stripped away by what the Gatherer had done.

Headlights appeared at the opposite end of the tunnel, hurtling towards them. The glare was so blinding that she latched her gaze onto the line of stones along the wall until it blazed past, her eyes stinging and her brow pinched as they were released on the other side of the tunnel.

A silver guard rail protected them from a suddenly steeper incline, a jagged, uneven cliff rising on the passenger side of the car. They curved around the cliff face, the glowing swath of the city below them, streets outlined with light, the Ferris wheel spinning incessantly close to the water. A city that shone with fever, the surface hiding the battle beneath.

"Stanton is still in command?"

Adams letting her go could have been covered up, put down as an error made in the heat of the moment. But seeking her out and being here now would be a blatant contradiction of his orders.

"Once Havernal took leave we started reporting directly to him. Anything that has to do with the Gatherer is under his command."

The open compound was distinctive amidst the density of the downtown, with paths lined with lights leading towards the inky blackness of the ocean.

"So what are you doing for him?"

"We were acting as a special guard unit for Alicia Freeman, mainly to gather information, until we were pulled away to—"

Bare rock extended in a steep cliff above the road, a few smaller stones scattered on the pavement.

"Find me," finished Maria.

They leaned forward at the same time looking up through the windshield to assess the threat of the falling rocks.

It would have been strange receiving the order to track down a soldier that had been part of your unit. Like hunting down a part of yourself.

"I expected you to show up sooner," said Maria.

The slope disappeared into darkness, nothing visible beyond the headlights.

"We didn't get orders to find you until you were seen in Rima."

"Are you following orders now?"

He hesitated, briefly enough to almost not be there.

The road curved around the mountain, the glittering outskirts of the city a band of light below them.

"No."

It was either a lie or part of him couldn't admit he had disobeyed orders.

"Then how did you know where I was?"

The city fell behind, the endless void of the ocean stretching beneath them. A lookout loomed out of the darkness in her headlights and she pulled over, driving down a short incline so that they were lower than the road and out of sight. She parked between two telescopes like any good tourist even though the blackness of the ocean blended with the starless sky.

Adams' gaze followed the headlight beams that pointed out over nothing before Maria turned them off and their world shrank to the blue and green glow of the dashboard.

"The movie theater was too public. If we were seen that would be the end of this."

"And what is this?"

He unclicked his seat belt at the same time he pulled on the door handle. Cold air flooded into the interior. When the door closed, a velvet silence descended, as well made as the car itself. His agitation was familiar to her. It had been the same when Havernal had asked her to seek out Storm and go against everything she had been trained to do. She and Havernal had been walking between buildings on the base and she had had a sense of being cut free, the lifeboat that had been so securely beneath her floating away.

That decision had been the first of many that would look renegade but had felt more right than countless orders she had followed before. It had led her to this lookout above the ocean, where the only orders she obeyed were her own.

She powered down the car and went to stand next to him between the two telescopes. She waited for her eyes to adjust, knowing there wasn't just blackness out there. There would be shades of darkness, the potential glimmer of a star or a lighter shadow on the ocean.

"There have been threats against the corporation. And Alicia," said Adams. "We're there to provide protection but it's more than that. The government doesn't want the Gatherer stopped. There's nothing to replace it. Valerie and Camille are using candles, wood for heat; the infrastructure has been abandoned."

She thought of the diesel barrels she had seen being transported by truck on the ferry when she had been looking for Storm. How valuable would that become once the Gatherer was abolished? She had thought the Diesel Train had been about fuel for their old engines but what they had really been doing was preparing for the future.

"I'll help you in any way I can but don't rub it in my face," said Adams.

She understood his sentiment, to keep this decision at arm's length. It would take some time to reconcile himself with it, if he ever did.

"I need to talk to Ari."

He turned to look at her. He would see little of her expression, the outline of his head and a cheekbone his only defining features.

"The guy from the original team?"

His confusion made her pause. Ari's name had triggered something for him.

"Do you know where he is?"

"Isn't it Freeman you want?"

His voice was sharp, his vulnerability gone now that he had a task to latch onto.

"Storm asked me to contact Ari. She said he was working for the corporation. That he was inside the compound."

He waited too long before he spoke.

"Freeman is inside the compound."

She looked back towards the city, seeking out the darker patch of the compound. It suddenly looked so much farther away.

"How is that possible?"

She hated the darkness, wanted to see his face.

"One of the protesters took her to his farm. I don't know why but it gave us an easy target. We got her out."

"You were there?"

Adams was an outline in the darkness, and she was attuned to him more through awareness and sound than anything sight could offer.

"How was she?"

"She was unconscious when we had her."

"But alive?"

She asked it as a question, but it wasn't. It was an order, a commandment that Storm be alive.

"Our orders were to deliver her to the compound. There's a building I don't have access to but that's where we took her."

"Don't they know it will kill her?"

The draw to go back to her was overwhelming.

"Stanton wants her there."

"For what?"

"I don't know."

She moved closer to the edge of the cliff, the waves crashing on the rocks below small traces of white.

"Or you won't tell me."

He spoke from close at her elbow, both of them standing at the edge.

"There's a new building on the compound, the size of a football field. None of our unit has access. Stanton has brought in a different unit. Guys he's used before. There are rumours but I haven't seen anything."

She could just see the outline of a pebble. She pushed it with her boot and let it drop over the precipice.

"What are the rumours?"

The pebble fell in silence, its landing lost in the waves.

"Some kind of test facility—"

She knew what it was before he said it, the image of the too-large Gatherers on the train looming large in her memory.

"And that's where Storm is?"

The mass of mountains overwhelmed the city's faint glow. Cold mist settled on her cheeks. There was even more reason to go back for her. Yet if she did manage to find her, how would she tell her she had failed?

"Can you get me to Ari?"

It was a necessary, critical decision and would destroy the last chance she had of going back for Storm. She could feel him processing the request.

He lifted his head, his gaze looking to the horizon as if he could see where his decision would take him.

"He was in Alicia's office the other day."

The revelation startled her and the access he had to information she needed.

"What did he want?"

"I don't know but whatever he wanted he didn't get."

"So he's there? Working for them?"

The crash of waves reached them from below.

"Alicia brought him on as soon as the problems started with the Gatherer. So that he could fix it. But his access is restricted and he has a personal bodyguard 24/7."

"Watching him the same way you were watching Alicia."

He didn't respond but didn't need to. So many VIPs didn't realize what they gave up by allowing security close to them. The wind wrapped around them buffering and pushing.

"I have some information that can help him. If I can get it to him it could stop the Gatherer." There was the faintest change in grayness where the ocean met the sky. Not a light but the separation was there. "Can you get me to him?"

He stepped to the telescope and bent his eye to look through the eyepiece. It was a pointless action, given that there was nothing to see. He slowly panned the lens across the horizon. Eventually he lifted his head, his hand still holding the telescope in place. It was strange to see him so still, the part of him that fed off his boundless energy somehow broken.

"Yeah. I can."

A beam of light suddenly struck the underbrush above and behind them, the headlights of a vehicle flashing on the cliff and into the light mist. The sound of an electric drive churning uphill followed after. It was too late to take cover and they stood motionless as the ball of light moved further up the mountainside, the whine of the drive gone before the light. They moved together, back to the vehicle, facing each other across the roof.

"You'll be court-martialled if we get caught," she said.

She was far beyond that but it would matter to him.

The interior light illuminated his frown as he opened the door. It was almost comforting to see his irritation at her telling him something he had already figured out. It meant they were still themselves and some things hadn't changed.

She powered up the vehicle and brought up the navigation system on the screen.

"Where to?"

TWELVE

ADAMS SAT ACROSS FROM Stanton as his superior talked on a tablet. He felt oddly detached from the realization that his military career was about to end in disgrace. A career he had wanted since he was twelve, every act, every decision geared towards becoming the best.

"It was a pleasure speaking to you."

Stanton's tone was warm and respectful and it was the first time Adams had seen anything remotely like a genuine smile.

Stanton ended the call and stayed facing out the window that provided an expansive view of the city. He looked at home in the corporate luxury, the ninth-floor office suiting his view of where he belonged.

"Thanks for coming in so early."

It had been well into the night by the time Adams had said goodbye to Maria, his sleep schedule so tortured and irregular another brief night wouldn't make a difference. He felt restless and wired, his agitation consuming every breath until Valerie and Camille were cured.

Stanton turned from the window and sat across from him, pulling the rolling chair in close to the sleek desk. He was too large for it, his knees almost touching the top.

Adams nodded but otherwise didn't respond. Stanton was acting like this wasn't a disciplinary meeting. That Adams and his unit hadn't messed up and let Maria go.

Stanton leaned forward.

Here it comes.

He felt weightless, numb, nothing penetrating beyond his fear for Valerie and Camille.

"How's your family?"

Adams didn't move, didn't blink.

"They're fine. Thank you, sir."

Stanton nodded and straightened a sheet of paper on the top of the desk.

"I understand they're sick."

Adams still couldn't move. He hadn't told anyone they were sick, hadn't expected this would be about them.

"Yes, they've been unwell."

Stanton abruptly pushed back and stood, looking out over the waking city. His bulk blocked almost half the window.

"Have you seen the new building that's gone up?"

His tone was conversational and Adams felt as if he were balanced on a steel girder high above the ground, no walls, no floor, a move in any direction fatal.

"Yes."

The building was behind the affiliate companies, so new the concrete was barely dry.

Stanton turned and smiled, and Adams instinctively pulled his feet underneath him, ready to rise.

"It's a treatment facility for the afflicted."

Adams couldn't stop from frowning, confusion, hope and wariness vying for dominance.

Stanton saw his reaction, had been expecting it. "The corporation is looking for a cure for the plague."

Adams had turned to stone. It took a long time for his mouth to move. "But they're denying it exists."

Stanton took a long breath in through his nose, his chest doubling in size. "They want to announce the cure when they acknowledge it."

He was breathless, afraid that a single breath would tear this possibility away. "Do they have a cure?"

His voice cracked, betraying him.

"They're close."

Adams searched for the place of calm inside himself, but couldn't find an anchor to hold onto.

Stanton strode casually around the desk, leaned against the edge. "I want to offer you a place at the facility for Valerie and Camille. They have all the best resources and they are getting results. They'll be among the first to receive the treatment."

The relief was overpowering, the lifebuoy solid and real in his hand. Adams swallowed and set his jaw. "I'd be grateful. Sir."

Stanton nodded, satisfied, his hands resting on the edge of the desk. "I'm happy to be able to help. You're an exceptional soldier."

Adams could feel the undercurrent beneath him, drawing away the foundation of his relief. It came with a great sadness followed by a resolve of what would have to be done.

"But we're going to need you to bring her in."

"Yes. Of course. I understand."

He didn't need to say who she was. He wanted Kowalski, and Freeman, though he already had her. They might have seen him let Kowalski go, or saw them after the theater – either way, they had him. If he wanted Valerie and Camille to live, he had to give them Kowalski.

"We need to know what she's after. And you know how she thinks."

She had been strong and feral on that cliff top. A centeredness to her he hadn't seen before. Everything she had been through had clarified and fortified her purpose to stop the Gatherer and prevent Stanton from having it. And maybe one day, she would understand.

THIRTEEN

THE MOUNT FOR THE spare tire dug into Maria's side. She tried to re-adjust but there was nowhere to move in the small space. The Elec Edition had room for two spare tires beneath the trunk, an area large enough for a small, tough soldier like Maria to squeeze into ... if she was six inches shorter. It was worse than being in a tank. They had only just started the drive and already she wanted to scream.

The thick smell of rubber caught in her throat as something mechanical engaged inside the vehicle and they slowed.

During an interminable stop, she strained to hear but the cover on her enclosure dulled sound. There was a pull and they were moving again.

Had this been a mistake?

Adams had been more stolid than usual when he had picked her up. He hadn't met her eyes when he had handed her the fatigues she had asked for. She had attributed it to his unease at disobeying orders but lying in this enclosed place, completely at his mercy, it felt like something more.

Another stop, this one longer and she pushed at the lid. It gave against the latch but didn't open. She thought the cover was thin enough to break through, if it came to that. But when would she know that she needed to?

The sound of the wheels was louder when they finally started moving again, and she guessed they were on the highway moving out of the city. Ari lived on a fenced property higher in the mountains.

The frame of the vehicle hummed, the vibrations spreading into the metal of her enclosure and her bones. She forced a few slow breaths and willed time to pass. The top of her head pressed into the side as they curved around a bend.

Finally, they decelerated, the hum lessened and they turned sharply. Tires crunched on gravel beneath her. A new agitated tension gripped her, shrinking her cell even further.

The low timbre of Adams' voice reached her, the responding voice resonating at a higher frequency. The raised pounding of her heart limited what she could hear.

Adams laughed.

Had a door opened?

The men continued talking and Maria ground her teeth. The guard was probably grateful for the distraction. Adams had said it could be one of their unit on duty and she pictured Hamel or Jones talking easily with Adams, oblivious of his extra cargo.

Would they have stopped him if they had known? Or let him through? She wanted to believe they would but there was no knowing the personal motivations of a soldier.

She heard a raised voice with the rhythm of "See you later" and they were rolling forward slowly, the vehicle tilting over the occasional rough spot. Adams was going overboard on giving the impression of having all the time in the world. She felt a rush of irritation, convinced he was doing it on purpose.

They stopped moving and she turned her head towards the sound of a door closing.

The air was hot and stuffy, the darkness and cramped quarters feeding into her sudden panic. Why hadn't he let her out?

Something mechanical, deep in the engine, ticked.

She pushed harder against the cover. The material flexed. She turned on her side, tried to force her shoulder into it. Nothing happened. She fought off a wall of panic and heard the trunk open.

Her relief was so strong she felt dizzy and then the lid was opening and Adams peered down at her.

"You okay?"

She ignored his offered hand and clambered out, taking deep gulps of cool, pine-scented night air.

They stood in a small clearing, surrounded by ancient pine trees, the cathedral ceiling of a large log cabin matching the trees' grandeur. A sleek modern couch and a massive stone fireplace were visible through the glass fronted living area.

"Is he here?"

A new kind of anxiety filled her veins, that she would take this risk and he wouldn't be here.

"The guard at the gate said he arrived two hours ago. He's probably asleep."

A well-equipped kitchen sat behind the open living area, the lights that flooded the cathedral ceiling spilling onto them and the gravel drive. A camera was mounted above the wide wood door, another at the peak of the cathedral.

"He has surveillance."

She turned away from it knowing it was already too late. Anyone at the end of that camera would have had all the time they needed to verify it was her.

"It's not installed yet. The perimeter fence and the cameras are all new."

Her gaze swung to his. It was calm, focused and held none of her alarm. The guys in the unit had always claimed that ice ran through his veins.

"How can you be sure?"

He sighed, his annoyance doing more than anything to calm her.

"I'll explain later."

The implication was that she would have to trust him. She didn't get a chance to decide if she did as Ari was suddenly standing in the living room, looking out.

"He's up."

Adams spun and she saw the recognition on Ari's face as Adams raised a hand in greeting.

She was suddenly uncertain, reluctant to follow Adams to the door. She stayed where she was, unable to take her eyes off Ari, he unable to take his off her.

He recognized her as surely as she did him, despite that he had cut his hair and wore only white linen pyjama bottoms tied at the waist. Would he greet her with anger or refuse to see her at all? She hadn't seen him since the shouting match at the lab after the release. She and Havernal had demanded that Storm stop the roll-out. Ari had watched all of it, smug in his certainty that they were too late.

They matched each other's pace towards the door, he inside and her out. They could have been reflections of one another in their suspicions and apprehension.

He became more real when he opened the door, his hair flat where he had been sleeping, a puffiness around his eyes and a dark, almost purple, bruising beneath them. A birthmark the size of a quarter marked his upper ribcage.

"Is Storm with you?"

He looked behind them, looking for her.

"No. Can we come in?"

The cabin smelled of wood smoke.

He considered her for a long moment, glanced briefly at Adams, before waving them in as if they were his guests. Perhaps it was an acknowledgement that asking his permission to enter had been a courtesy.

He disappeared into a hallway beside the kitchen and returned wearing a sweatshirt that read "University of British Columbia." His hair was straighter and his feet still bare.

"Have a seat."

He gestured to the two sofas that faced each other, both looking hard and uncomfortable. Adams stayed near the door, facing into the night. She had a moment of surprise when she realized he would let this be her show.

Ari knelt before the fireplace and crumpled a sheet of newspaper into a ball before placing it on the burnt remains of the fire.

"I thought you were together," Ari said.

He crumpled another ball and placed it next to the first. His hands were small and wide, the skin smooth.

"I had to leave her behind."

She kept her voice neutral, not betraying the guilt that decision still brought.

He paused mid-crumple, looked at her with eyes that missed nothing.

"Why?"

"Because it would have killed her."

It was only for a second but he seemed to deflate, his aloofness not as impermeable as he let on. He finished crumpling the paper and placed it carefully on the ashes.

"So she sent you instead."

He sat on his haunches, his elbows resting on his knees. The fluidity of his movements suggested martial arts or at least an awareness of his body beyond most civilians.

"Yes."

"And why would I listen to you?"

Ari had been the team member who resented her the most, openly hostile to the military and their attempts to interfere with the Gatherer. He pulled a handful of kindling from a box next to the fireplace, leaving several broken twigs on the stones.

"Because Storm sent me."

He laid the twigs carefully on top of the newspaper, balancing each on the next.

"And why would I listen to her?"

There was no mistaking his fury, despite the calm methodical exterior. He placed the last twig and turned to face her, his eyes completely black.

She started to speak and stopped, never having anticipated that he wouldn't want to hear Storm's message. She leaned forward, sitting on the edge of the seat.

"There are imperfections in the lattice," she said.

He gave a slight lift of his shoulders and opened his hands.

She felt the first warning of something not being right, of a pit opening up beneath her.

Adams had moved closer, and stood only a step behind her, his stance too aggressive until he seemed to remember himself and draw back. What was he doing? If he spooked Ari it would ruin everything.

"She wanted me to tell you," said Maria, "so that you could use it to stop the Gatherer."

Ari gave a dismissive shrug and a shake of his head.

"I know this already."

Her misgivings solidified as she grappled for something to keep her from falling into the pit.

"She asked me to tell you. She said you would know what to do."

He stood and moved behind the sofa, away from the fire he hadn't lit.

"She says a lot of things."

Maria stood, as if that action would bring him back to the fire.

"She said ..."

But what had she said? The imperfections in the lattice. There hadn't been anything else.

"I don't really care what she had to say."

She struggled to find words to respond. None of this was going as planned.

"She said you would help."

She couldn't let go of that promise. For if it fell away, she had a wide-open view all the way to complete disaster. She stepped forward and Ari moved into the shadow of the kitchen. He took a glass from an open shelf and filled it at the sink.

"It's been a long time since I've had to listen to anything that Storm said," said Ari. "Right about the time she took off."

Adams had stayed where he was. She could feel the energy coming off him as tense as if he were on patrol. A twig rolled off the ball of newspaper.

The empty glass clinked on the marble counter as Ari set it down.

"She was *sick*," said Maria.

Ari's fingertips rested lightly on the counter, but there was nothing relaxed about the pose, his stillness one of fury. "So was everyone else."

She thought of the twitch beneath Callan's eye in the documentary when they were all still together.

"She didn't know," she said.

Ari walked slowly back around the sofa, smooth and silent in his bare feet. Adams shifted his position.

Ari sat on the sofa facing them and stretched his arms along the back. He looked more middle-aged, the weight he carried too heavy for his young features.

"We had a conversation before she left," said Ari. "All of us. Everyone was experiencing some kind of symptoms. Callan was the worst, probably because he spent the most time in the test area. Daniel already had a rash on his side."

Maria could hear Storm's voice clearly when she had been lying in the enclosure at the cabin.

I didn't know.

"She knew they were all sick," said Ari. "And she left anyways. And put Alicia in charge."

He said Alicia's name with disdain.

"So she would keep delivering the Gatherers."

It was Adams who spoke, Maria distracted by Storm's lie. There was an uncomfortable logic to it, that Storm would know that Alicia would continue the distribution, get Storm's creation out into the world. Why else bring her mother in when they had only recently been estranged?

Maria sat down. Ari watched her with indifference, her realization insignificant compared to what he had endured.

Why would Storm lie about it? Was it cowardice, that she had fled when she should have stayed? Or that she had known that the team had symptoms, and released it anyways – at the same time as Maria had been trying to stop her.

Ari suddenly leaned forward. The collar of his sweatshirt was frayed, tiny threads brushing against his neck. "I am going to fix this. How it should have been done in the first place."

"You don't have access to the process," said Adams. "You're little more than a prisoner."

Ari looked at him with the same remote blankness.

"For now."

She was on her feet again without realizing she had stood, the hard stone of the hearth beneath her feet.

"Storm and Daniel were convinced it couldn't be fixed. That it had to be destroyed."

"Daniel's alive?" said Ari. There was real shock and confusion, she was certain of it. "Where is he?"

She faltered as she started to answer, and that was enough.

Ari's shoulders sagged, the haggardness that had been there earlier returning deeper than before.

"Of course not," said Ari. "No one gets free of this." He stared into the unlit fire, his focus far away until he shook himself, drawing back from whatever memory he had seen. "I'm not going to throw away the Gatherer because it needs an adjustment. It's like throwing away the airplane because it crashed a few times in early flights. It's admirable that they thought they could decree the Gatherer was unfixable but they're not here now."

"You're wrong."

He stood to face her. They were the same height, the black depths of his eyes at the same level as hers.

"I'm not."

She had moved into the ready stance without thinking, the urge to grab him and physically force him to do what she wanted overwhelming.

Ari smiled and she recognized that he was dismissing her, so secure in the power of his knowledge that she was no threat to him.

"If you won't do it for Storm, then do it for your team. They never would have wanted this to happen, especially Jana."

The color disappeared from his face, and the remoteness of his eyes was replaced by rage.

"Get out."

She had tapped into something that was barely below the surface, lethal and dangerous and uncontrolled.

"You can't walk away from this," she said.

"I'm the only one that didn't."

His body was tensing, focusing its energy. She adjusted her stance, fully ready. Adams stepped in beside her.

Ari pulled back, breathing in heavy, shaking breaths.

She could see the pain in him. His anger. The burden of shouldering this responsibility.

Adams stepped beside her, the way she had felt him move a thousand times before except it was in the wrong direction and he kept coming, not stopping when he should have. A flash of light reflected off the back wall.

She ducked away from him, the same way she would have done in training. He was ready for it, catching her shoulder as she tried to flee. She couldn't fight him, he was too fast, too strong. He pulled her shoulder and she strained against him. Why was he attacking her? The fire poker leaned against the chimney and she wrapped her hand around it and swung hard and fast behind her.

It connected with flesh, she heard a horrible grunt and it gave her the second she needed to break free.

She had a brief glimpse of Ari's confusion and shock and the gleam of headlights arriving from the drive. She was down the corridor where Ari had gone, past several closed doors, bursting out the side entrance to the sound of tires on gravel. She ran straight back, away from the vehicle, her feet silent on the bed of needles below the towering pines.

She heard voices, impossible to tell how many above her rapid breathing. Adams had been expecting them. Knew she would try to run.

THE GATHERER

She started to turn uphill, the harder route, and changed her mind. These men would know her and the choices she would make. She let her stride turn downhill, absorbing the slope in her knees, the trees flying by her as she focused on putting the greatest distance between her and the cabin.

FOURTEEN

STORM FLOATED IN A vast ocean, rising and falling with the rhythm of the waves, the sun bright and piercing above her. It felt as if she had been adrift for an endless period, her body less her own than another piece of flotsam caught in the interminable tides. She tried to move her arms and legs but the water held her tight.

She heard the sound of voices and she struggled to turn her head. Was it a boat?

She had a sudden flash of fear and she stopped struggling, remembering that people were more likely to be angry with her, that their help would only put her in more danger.

A wave crashed over her and she choked on salt water, a loud voice closer, as something supported her from underneath. Was it a dolphin? She was surprised that those stories of assistance would be real.

She could breathe again, the air strangely still, no warmth coming from the bright sun. The vastness of the ocean receded and the voices came closer. She had an awareness of hands under her shoulders, not dolphins, the sun the harsh cast from a light above her.

She grabbed for the edge of the tub, confusion and alarm stiffening her body, even as her hand fell through water.

"She's coming out of it."

It was a woman's voice above her.

Was it Maria?

She tried to twist and lower her foot to find a bottom. Her hands slapped at water.

"Hold still."

THE GATHERER

It was a harsher voice and she froze, terrified the hands would leave her to sink back into oblivion. She opened her eyes to the underside of a chin, and shoulders leaning in. A woman, fit by the strength of her shoulders and hands. A firm set to her mouth.

"She needs to come out," said a male voice.

"She's better where she is."

There was a chill on her shoulders as she was lifted, the warm water rolling off.

"She's terrified."

A pause as Storm tried to determine where she was but the sides of the tub were too high, opening to a grid of ceiling tiles.

"We'll lift her onto the towel."

She felt a horrible wrenching as she was dragged from the water and there was pain where hands held her. She felt the relief of solid floor beneath her, accompanied by the scraping of a towel on her skin.

She was lifted again and lowered onto a softer surface, the lights dimmer, her body suddenly protesting with a searing ache. At least two people moved around her. A firm, efficient prick on the back of her hand, and she turned her head to see Wesley inserting the IV. She was too weak to pull back, could do nothing but let her gaze follow the tube to her hand, a clear, unknown liquid dripping into her veins.

"What is it?"

Or that was what she wanted to say. Instead, her lips stuck together, her parched mouth resistant to words.

There was a searing in her arm as the liquid spread, like dry ice in her veins. She jerked her hand back, succeeded only in tugging against Wesley's grip.

"It's nutrients. To help with the depletion."

But there was something else, an underlying tension that rippled along her nerves as the drug progressed through her blood stream. She tried to reach for the needle's insertion point but he pushed her hand back down, holding her while whatever it was flushed through her system.

She searched for the other person in the room. A young woman watching with a blank hardness.

A wave of energy rolled through her, cells rallying to respond to the stimulus from whatever Wesley had given her. She was shaking, her sudden energy without a stable base to ground on.

They raised her to a sitting position and she searched the room for water, anything to quench her burning thirst. The tub she had been floating in was connected to a channel that flowed out of an opening in the wall, water shifting through it. There had to have been chemicals in with the salt, something to account for the soothing detachment. Did she even care? Her need for liquid of any kind was too great.

"Water."

Her voice was weak, like it had been a long time since she had used it.

Wesley nodded to the young woman, who turned and strode from the room. There was an agitation, almost itchiness on her skin.

The woman returned and held a glass of water to Storm's lips. Had time passed? Her hands were wide and strong like Maria's. Storm wrapped her hands over them, lifting the glass higher.

The woman stepped back and Storm tilted the glass to get every drop. When she finished, she gripped its round smoothness, holding it with two hands on her lap. The brightness of the room had receded, turning to a marvelous glow, whatever they had given her making the air vibrate like it was alive.

"How are you feeling?"

Wesley's voice had a rich timbre she hadn't noticed before, each tone resonating in her ears, the beauty of it a contrast to its lack of warmth. For he wasn't asking her how she was, he wanted to know whether whatever he had given her was working.

She splayed her hands on her thighs, letting the empty glass tip forward, the air cooling on the lingering dampness between her fingers. She could feel their strength, the muscles lithe and strong, the energy extending into her forearms, up her arms to her boney shoulders. It was a miracle to be strong again.

She took a deep, cleansing breath. How long had it been since she had felt this powerful? Ready to take on anyone or anything?

She picked up the glass again, felt the weight of its base and how easy it would be to shatter.

There was an amused exhale from the woman.

"Better, it looks like."

She had clear brown skin, black hair in a tight crop, and a crisp, pressed uniform. The sleeves were damp where she had supported Storm.

The surge of energy continued to grow, the blood pulsing along her veins, with the building of a deep energy at her core.

She pushed the blanket off her legs, and the glass shattered to the floor. She was stick thin, and a deadly white yet her legs were strong, her muscles begging to move. She swung her legs over the edge.

She walked over the broken glass, no choice but to move, not feeling the shards that must be in her feet. She pushed past the woman, needing to go somewhere, do something. The room was rectangular with the channel dividing the longer side and Wesley blocking the only door. Her heart raced and she was panting, sweat rolling down her sides. Bloody footsteps followed behind her as she circled the room, touching the walls, the floor uneven beneath her.

"It's too much."

The woman's voice battered her ears.

Wesley stood in front of her. "How do you feel?"

Raw words, without compassion or caring. She shoved him and he staggered back. At first surprised, then laughing.

"It's working."

The woman was too close at her side and Storm lurched away, unable to get enough air.

The unprotected door was in front of her. She lunged through it, into a long corridor of closed doors with light at the end. She needed to get outside, somewhere where this energy could seep out of her skin, expand outwards into the sky.

She was running now, her cut feet slapping on cold tiles in a larger corridor, the pain white hot. The sound of boots behind her did not stop her. She focused on the whiteness of her arms pumping in front of her. Pushing through a set of doors, she saw flashes of bedrooms through windows. Thin, stick people like her sitting up, lying down, haggard eyes peering out at her.

She ran faster, squinting in the blinding light before a sudden heaviness flooded into her legs, overtaking the agitation, dark and thick as oozing oil.

She stumbled, trying to reach the outside and release the energy and the heaviness. To be herself again. She caught herself on a door handle. The boots were close behind her. Waiting.

She sobbed in frustration as her knees hit the floor, the pain of her femurs jamming up into her hips. There was no attachment to it. An observation.

She let go of the door handle as she fell to the floor. She was gasping for breath, her body shaking as hands scooped her up and carried her back from the light.

FIFTEEN

MARIA PARTED THE LEAVES of the large fern, peering towards the dirt lane where she had hid the car before meeting Adams further up the road. Two RCMP officers stood beside it, the blue flash from their cruiser cutting across a nearby tree in the morning dusk. One of the officers spoke into a tablet, low enough she couldn't hear the words, and the other approached the car on the driver's side. At the door, he reached for the handle, an instinctive gesture on the odd chance the owner had left it unlocked.

When his hand made contact, the vehicle chirped back at him.

He lifted his head and she stiffened. She had the key fob in her pocket, the range of the vehicle's sensors wide enough to sense her presence. He surveyed the opposite side of the lane, turned to look in her direction. She crouched lower.

The second officer approached the vehicle on the other side, still talking into the tablet.

"Is the key in it?"

She leaned forward on her toes as the officer searched the car's interior. She moved carefully out of the ferns, taking shelter behind a large tree. The forest was lusher here with wider trunks and thicker cover.

A vehicle approached on the main, paved road, its whine and turbulence disturbing the forest. She strained to see through the trees but the foliage was too dense, the dusk still too thick. It could be Adams come to find her, or the men who had arrived at Ari's place. That betrayal rode cold on the back of her neck, pushing her forward.

The second officer scanned the woods as he spoke into the tablet.

Should she run? The other officer had begun searching the edge of the lane. They would know the vehicle was stolen by now but did they know it was her? Running would take her back towards Adams and the men, the burn from where Adams had grabbed her still hot and bright. She pressed closer into the tree, her breath rising in a white cloud. Frost shone on the nearby trunk. Any sane person would cut and run. Storm's lies and Adams's betrayal left the mission in shreds. Except, what if it hadn't been Storm who had been lying, but Ari, wanting to undermine her in the exact way he had?

The undergrowth thinned on her right where the ferns spread further apart and would allow her to move more quickly though with the possibility of being seen. Straight back, two offset trees made it impossible to pass and the paved road blocked her other side.

She peered around the tree. The men were focussed on the woods now.

"I'm gonna take a look."

The second officer's voice sounded closer now that he was under the trees, as if he stood on the other side of the trunk instead of thirty paces away.

The first officer suddenly lifted the tablet closer to his ear. She tilted her ear towards him, straining to hear, recognizing his sudden alertness.

"Get out of there!"

The urgency of the first officer's voice carried his words through the muffled dampness.

The officer who was several paces into the forest turned back, as the officer spoke into the tablet again. "On our way."

He was in motion, getting back into the cruiser as the second officer retreated out of the woods, hustling to the patrol car that was already turning around. It skidded as it sped out of the dirt lane, the siren wailing. Maria's back was to the tree, adrenaline priming muscles for a flight that was no longer necessary. A pine cone dropped to the ground beside her, her heart pounding as the forest settled back into the early dawn.

She could take the car and turn south, exchange it for another on the road, be gone from Rima and the Gatherer before anyone noticed.

She eased out from behind the tree, alert for sounds of returning vehicles, or anything at all beyond the sleepy rustling of the forest floor. She approached the vehicle cautiously, feeling exposed when she stepped onto the road where the men had just been. There was no trace of the search in the car, the dashboard springing to life at her touch. The slightest scent of cologne was the only evidence the men had been there at all.

The radio came on, a singer, a woman, holding a long-sustained note as Maria stopped where the dirt lane reached the wider paved road. Uphill would take her back into the mountain, downhill lead to the city.

The final chord faded out and the announcer's voice came on naming the singer and the song before switching his voice to the more urgent tones of a newscast.

"Early this morning, protesters breached the compound of the Gatherer Corporation following an explosion at the increasingly fortified area."

She held her foot on the brake, instinctively looking in the direction of the compound. She imagined she could see the exploded area and the chaos that would follow the attack.

And Storm in the middle of it.

Maria waited, listening to her gut on what Ari had said about Storm. It could be true. That she had known.

But it didn't matter now.

She turned the wheel, pointing the vehicle towards the city. When the wheels hit pavement, it jerked forward.

"Reports say that just before daybreak at the headquarters, during a shift change of the guards, an explosion tore a hole in the perimeter fence that has allowed the protesters to spread into the secure area and swarm the building.

"There's no word yet on who is leading the attack—"

She felt the satisfying pull of her gut as she accelerated, part of her mind cycling through images of an explosion, the compromised fence, and where Storm would be in all of it. She had a flash of the serene, manicured grounds of the compound, the serenity shattered the moment the bomb went off.

She checked constantly for the blocky outline of Adams' Elec Edition grill in the rearview mirror or approaching in the on-coming lane. But the road that wound out of the mountains was clear, the explosion at the compound having drawn the eye away from her.

"The security forces that normally guard the compound are blocking the protesters from entering the headquarters building. There are reports of several armored vehicles having left the base and heading towards Rima."

She drove faster, the forests a blur of green beside the black, winding strip of pavement. She needed to get to the compound before those reinforcements.

Houses became more frequent, bright bits of color between the trees. In the denser residential area, the trees were fewer and she scanned the sky for helicopters, anything that would tell her the level of the response.

"—We have reports the security forces and any staff on site have barricaded themselves inside the headquarters. Troops have arrived from the base, and have surrounded the protesters, who are now trapped between the barricaded entrance and the troops."

She felt a rush of sympathy for the troops and the security forces. An armed opponent was one thing, having to contain unpredictable, undisciplined protesters was a nightmare no military or police officer ever wished for.

She chose a route that ran parallel to the coast and came at the compound from the north. She parked the vehicle in the empty lot of a warehouse, one street over from the perimeter. She approached the side gate cautiously, using the long high hedge as cover, expecting vehicles or personnel at the narrow opening, relieved when her gamble had been right.

The side gate was abandoned, the gate left open, the light from the guard shack shining on an empty patch of pavement. She crept along the hedge, the place strangely quiet, a distant disturbance the only indication of the breach.

A quick dash through the open gate, and she passed the guard house, keeping close to the perimeter fence, alert for movement in the empty pathways and gardens. The underlying disturbance from the direction of the headquarters grew louder, shouts breaking above the hum. She steered away from it, winding deeper into the formal garden, passing the twisted paths of a dewy labyrinth as she moved towards the ocean.

SIXTEEN

STORM RUBBED AT THE two drops of blood where she had extracted the IV needle, leaving a red smudge across the back of her hand. She swung her legs over the side of the bed, pausing as she waited for the dizziness to subside. The hangover from whatever Wesley had given her showed itself in the piercing headache and a heavy nausea.

Her white shirt and shorts were new and clean, and bandages wrapped her feet. She willed her legs to hold her weight as she carefully stood, the pain in her feet cutting through the lingering fog. Her legs held, a latent strength in them she hadn't expected. She stood straighter. It could have been the residue from what Wesley had given her or the strange bath. Either way, she was grateful for the capability.

She crossed the bare floor of her concrete room. The door wasn't locked, her weakness and the stairs providing enough of a cage for her captors, and she leaned on the doorway for several seconds to gather her strength. She had counted thirty-two stairs when Wesley had carried her and they rose in a never-ending stack. There was no railing and she detected the faintest of burns from the lights.

She took one step at a time, her hands braced against the walls. At the third step she swayed in a rush of dizziness, her feet throbbing, the three steps feeling as high as a tower. She dropped to her knees, and crawled upwards, the concrete steps digging in her knees and scraping along her shins. She focused on counting, lifting her head only enough to see the next stair, looking neither to her destination or the fall back to where she had started.

Halfway up, she rested, her hip painful on the step, the wall rough from the tiny pockets and wrinkles in the concrete. Auras flickered at the edge of her vision. She had no choice but to move upwards, the descent equally hard.

The light grew stronger, spilling in from the corridor above, and she gathered strength from it, focusing on the light instead of the darkness below. Four steps from the top she paused, her thighs and shoulders shaking from the effort. There was a stagnant stillness from the corridor, no movement or life.

One. Two. Three. Four.

The tiles were smooth and hard beneath her palms, the coolness a relief on her stinging knees. She was at the end of the long empty corridor with the natural light of early morning at its opposite end. The opening of her stairwell was roughly patched, a metal bead marking the new edges of the opening and the gray of the patched drywall was unpainted. A cage newly made for her. Next to it sat the gleaming relief of her wheelchair where Wesley had parked it.

She rested against the wall, almost weeping at the sight of it. A noise came from the direction of the light. Was it a voice? She remembered again the wan faces she had seen through the glass windows.

It took an excruciating effort to stand, the wheelchair shifting under the sudden weight so that she staggered, digging deep into whatever reserve she'd been given to keep from crashing to the floor. She twisted clumsily into the cool leather seat, welcoming the support of the back and the release of pressure on her feet. She took a few moments to breath and several more to figure out how to move forward until she was rolling along the tiles, the empty offices passing by, the window to the outside growing larger.

At the double doors blocking the corridor, she hesitated. She didn't have the leverage to open them, and the field from the door opener could be contained within the wall or could be all around her.

Before she could think, or anticipate, she pressed the round button, wheeling back as the hum started, only the slightest heat on her sides as she scooted through.

The air was different on the other side, less stagnant, though there were no new sounds.

She slowed at the first room, straining to see in the window. It was a dim room, a figure lying curled on its side in bed. She continued on, passing a room that was dark. How many rooms had there been? She passed two more darkened rooms before she stopped again at a brighter room, with natural light. A woman sat on a bed with straight black hair to her waist and a magazine open in front of her. She was dressed in a blazer and jeans and could have been anyone on the street if it wasn't for the gray of her skin and the skeletal thinness.

A metal mesh was embedded in the glass, so the woman looked to be behind an intricate screen. Storm touched the cool metal of the door, wondering whether the protective mesh extended through every wall and window. When her fingers touched the metal, the woman looked up as if she had felt the contact.

She stood, steadying herself on the side table. There was no surprise in her gaze though it didn't leave Storm's as she walked carefully to the door. She had fine, delicate features, and round brown eyes, the starkness of her thinness adding a macabre element to her beauty.

The door swung inward, the woman leaning heavily on the handle for support.

Neither of them spoke, the woman's expression a cross between exhaustion and confusion.

"Hi. I'm—"

"I know who you are."

She spoke in a low, even voice, her light French Canadian accent adding a depth to it despite the unfriendliness of her tone.

Storm was surprised when she opened her arm, inviting her to enter. She wondered briefly if she should be afraid but the thought was laughable. Neither of them were strong enough to be a threat.

It was an awkward transition, the woman keeping hold of the door as Storm navigated the chair into the narrow space. The wheels rolled silently, and she entered the open part of the room, registering that it was larger than she had expected with two beds beside each other and a small form with near-black hair asleep in the second bed.

She stopped her chair, the woman supporting herself on the walls and the back of a chair as she followed.

She lowered herself stiffly onto the spot where she had been sitting. The pages of the magazine she had been reading showed bright cold images of snowy mountain scenes, the sky in the photos an impossible blue.

Storm's gaze was drawn back to the small figure facing away from them, the bareness of the room making her even smaller.

"Is she your daughter?"

It felt strange to whisper, too intimate for someone she had just met.

"Camille. You won't wake her. She sleeps most of the time." The woman didn't whisper. "I'm Valerie."

The line of an IV ran beneath the girl's covers. The IV next to Valerie wasn't attached.

"Did they not offer you treatment?" said Storm.

The woman looked up at the line looped over the stand, the full bag of clear liquid.

"I need to be awake."

It went without saying that it was for Camille, that her treatment was secondary to her daughter. The blazer, the jeans, all of it the pieces of normalcy she was trying to hold together.

"What is this place?" Storm asked.

"You don't know?"

Valerie frowned, her eyebrows thin sculpted lines. There was a peaked look to her eyes as she tried to concentrate. Storm remembered the frustration of not being able to break through the haze. Valerie closed the magazine.

"I—" Storm was embarrassed to be this ignorant, having been shuffled around on other people's whims. Her internal chastisement was equally as quick, for what did it matter if she was embarrassed? This was no longer about her. "They've been keeping me in a separate area. You're the first person I've talked to other than my…" What to call them? Captors? Handlers? Caregivers? "Other than Wesley."

Valerie's fingertips still rested on the cover of the magazine, her frown deepening as she examined Storm.

"What happened to your knees?"

Blood ran down her shins, staining her bandages a bright red. Again, she felt that surge of embarrassment that she had been reduced to crawling. She breathed deep, let the air reach the bottom of her lungs.

"I crawled up the stairs from my room. The concrete was rough."

Valerie's eyebrows rose briefly before returning to the frown.

"Didn't someone help you?"

Storm lifted her feet off the footrests and placed them on the floor, only the heels touching.

"There wasn't anyone around."

"I can wash them for you."

Valerie slid to the edge of the bed, readied herself to stand.

Storm held up a hand.

"They're fine the way they are."

She was frowning at Storms' knees, her mouth set in a grim line.

"Are you a prisoner?"

Valerie's eyes were bright, an edge to her voice that warned she was close to losing control. How hard would it be to care for a sick child when you could barely function? Storm had barely been able to care for herself.

"They are making me better."

She saw a softening of the woman's panic.

"Does it hurt?"

She had placed her hand in the middle of the bed, instinctively reaching for her daughter.

Storm thought of the urgency to run, the feeling that her veins would explode.

"Not so far."

"This is a treatment facility for the afflicted," said Valerie. "Camille and I only just arrived yesterday." She looked towards the small lump, her face bare with distress. "The trip was hard on her."

Valerie looked to be as badly off, never having made a real effort to get off the bed.

"Have people been getting better?" asked Storm.

It seemed impossible that she didn't know this.

"They offered us a spot so we took it. It was better than—"

She didn't say *nothing but that was the reality. There was no cure for this.*

"How many others are there?" Storm lifted her chin to indicate the corridor.

"I haven't seen anyone yet. We were supposed to get a tour this morning." Another concerned look at Camille, their introduction obviously postponed since neither of them had been capable. Valerie rubbed at her eyes. "I thought you didn't know this was a treatment facility?"

"I know that's what they're doing. I just have no idea where I am."

Through the square window, the view showed only gray and for a moment she thought the window was blocked until a ripple of dark ran through it. A shifting current in the fog.

Valerie had tilted her head, watching Storm with a clearer focus and a new distrust.

"We're at the compound." She gestured towards the side wall. "The headquarters is there, the manufacturing facility is there. Only a select few are permitted to come."

Storm rolled forward as if to get a better view out the window, but there was only the current in the fog. She had assumed it was a military base, with Stanton in charge, somewhere they could keep her out of sight. Yet this made a brutal sense. Why take her to a remote location, when they could embed her here? Close to the production line and the resources of the corporation.

"How did you get a spot?"

Camille whimpered in her sleep and Valerie moved to her side, leaning over her as she pushed the hair back from the girl's face. She murmured something in French. When Camille seemed to have settled Valerie tucked the covers close around her. As soon as she left the perimeter of the girl's bed, Valerie slumped, her movements slower and more forced.

She lay down on her bed, lowering gingerly against the pillows, her black hair fanned across the crisp whiteness. She closed her eyes and was so still Storm worried she had lost consciousness but after a few heartbeats her eyes opened.

"My husband works for the military. He's here protecting the compound. It's why we're here."

The wheelchair bumped into the side of the bed, Storm having tried again to get closer to the window. It showed the same stagnant gray and she was suddenly furious at her ignorance, needing to see so much more than that tiny square.

"How many troops are there?"

Valerie shook her head. Her eyes closed.

"I don't know."

Her face had relaxed, her body having overcome her will. With her pallor, the blazer and her hands folded on her chest, the resemblance to a corpse laid out in a coffin was unmistakeable. The finality of it frightened Storm, and she spun the chair, banging into the wall and the IV stand in her haste. Neither Valerie nor Camille moved.

She struggled to get the door open, making enough noise to alert the entire corridor, yet the row of doors remained closed.

The earlier brightness of the windows at the corridor's end had dimmed, tendrils of fog flowing in front of a darker swath behind. It obscured the grove of trees that should be there, the outlines of the buildings she knew by heart, void of any information at all.

She sat watching the waves of fog, her cut feet throbbing and aware that beyond the window she would know people, a whole organization that had grown up around her. Yet she didn't have the strength to cross the grass.

A shadow moved through the fog, the unmistakeable silhouette of Wesley walking towards the entrance. His shoulders were slumped, his head lowered.

Should she run? Or roll? She had no energy left for any kind of flight. The door opened and closed as he came through, his arrival echoing through the building.

He didn't react when he saw her, as if he had already known she was there.

"Going somewhere?"

He had tried for sarcasm, but it sounded more tired than anything else. She searched him again for a tremor or a more marked paleness.

"I needed some air."

He had his hands in his pockets and looked decidedly unmilitary despite the fatigues and combat boots.

"Same air up here as in your room."

He stood between her and the window, blocking anything that might be revealed in the fog.

"Does my mother know I'm here?"

He glanced at her bloodied knees and removed his hands from his pockets. He seemed to shake himself, a quick, rejuvenating jolt.

He spun her around to face back down the corridor. He was leaning over her, close enough she could hear him breath and smell the musty scent of his skin.

"Of course."

"I need to speak with her."

"What you should be worried about is getting better. We made some good progress yesterday and I think we should build on that today."

"I'm not getting better."

Part of her, yes, part of her was stronger but another part was damaged, like robbing one part of her to support the other.

They passed the row of darkened rooms and Valerie asleep on her bed. At the entrance to the stairwell, she caught a view of red chest hairs in the vee of his shirt as he bent to lock the wheels.

"Sure you are."

He threaded his hand beneath her knees and lifted her to his chest. She had no choice but to wrap her arms around his neck in an unwanted intimacy. It was humiliating to be so helpless, her body and Wesley betraying her.

"If you weren't better, you wouldn't have been able to climb these stairs. Or to figure out where you are."

He carried her down the steps and she held tighter, the concrete steps falling below them. He laid her on her bed, the fatigue she had been fighting against flooding in. He rummaged in a drawer beneath the bed before re-attaching the IV to the bruised back of her hand. She winced, feeling rawer and more exposed, and too tired to bear it.

Her eyes closed but she forced them open, resisting the warm flood into her veins. He had looked away from her, checking the level on the IV bag, and straightening a kink in the tube. It was the first time she had seen him when he thought he wasn't being watched.

He looked tired, a blue vein visible at his temple, the scab from a razor cut just below his ear. She tried to imagine him shaving. Was it in a barracks or did he have a home with people who cared about him?

The idea repulsed her, that there would be someone that could love him. She let her eyelids droop, taking what refuge she could in sleep, but they flew open before they were fully closed.

There had been a twitch below his eye. Had she imagined it?

He was unaware of her, fiddling with a clamp lower down on the stand. She dared not move, waiting for it to re-appear. Had he even been aware of it?

"The tests are killing you." Her words were below a whisper, the pull of the drug so strong, yet she knew he had heard as his focus returned to her.

She didn't even know why she had said it. Shouldn't she be happy the Gatherer was taking him?

He tightened the tape on the needle's insertion point and flicked at the clear tube.

"We have protections in place. We know what we're dealing with."
He was so sure of himself, convinced of his invincibility.

"They aren't good enough."

His face was narrow, the first signs of gray in the short hairs at his temple, everything about him precisely groomed so as not to interfere with his focus. She had seen the same drive in Maria, except hers had included those around her, while Wesley was slick and lean, not leaving any place for anything or anyone to catch onto. An eel slipping through the world.

"Not everyone is as susceptible as you."

There was his condescension again, like if she had only been stronger, the Gatherer wouldn't have gotten to her. Like there had been a choice.

The clear fluid streamed into her veins, his power over her extending into the blood that ran through her veins. She shook her head, trying to clear the creeping fog.

"Everyone in that room," she lifted her finger pointing upwards. "Is dying."

She let her eyes close, seeing the huge white Gatherer in the middle of the field, its gleam malicious and cunning. She recognized it as her real enemy. Not this man, or his army, or even the corporation. But this thing she had stumbled on. Bringing with it such power and destruction that it had changed the world. And her. And everyone who came in contact with it.

She wanted to stay awake, to explain it to him. But her eyes wouldn't open. She had fallen in too deep and couldn't find bottom.

SEVENTEEN

A BLACK ELEC EDITION SPED by, racing towards the gate, and Maria stepped into the shadows of the maintenance shed. A transporter sped by in the same direction with more soldiers inside and she shrank further back.

An occasional shout broke the stillness of the morning, the burnt smell of explosives sharp in the air. A gull floated above her, riding the ocean wind, and for a second she thought it was the one from the ferry where she had first discovered the diesel train. The gull tried then and now to show her an escape out over the ocean but the time for escape had long passed – if it had ever existed.

She listened for patrols that would be spreading out over the enclosed area. A search was the first thing they would do once the perimeter was secure.

In a moment of quiet, she darted from her protected place, crossing the paved service road and plunging into a thicker section of the garden, where the native rain forest had been allowed to grow dense, the walking path winding between tall grasses.

She heard the sound of a woman's voice, too close, and dove into the grasses.

"What was that?" The pitch of the woman's voice was high, fear vibrating through it.

Another female voice responded, calmer, though no less afraid. "I didn't hear anything. We're fine."

The calm woman was tall and thin, with straight, stringy hair, and heavy glasses too large for her face. The nervous one was

THE GATHERER

shorter and rounder, her eyes wide and frightened as she scanned the edges of the path. She was too scared to see Maria hiding only a few feet off the path, her fear focused behind her from wherever they had come.

"I told you we shouldn't have snuck out."

It was the rounder one, the edge of her voice so raw it was obvious she wasn't far from panic.

"How were we supposed to know they'd choose to attack this morning? When has anything ever happened at this time of day?" The scuff of their feet on the path drew away from her. "Besides, it's not us they're after."

Their footsteps stopped, the disturbance from whatever was happening at the headquarters an undercurrent washing through the grasses as sure as a morning breeze.

"Yes, they are. They don't care if we're only a programmer or if we're Alicia – to them we are all to blame."

The taller woman didn't respond and their footsteps resumed at a faster pace.

Maria ran in the opposite direction, alert now for other stragglers who had escaped the noose.

She heard the crackle of a radio, and pushed back into the grasses.

"... gate is secure."

She felt the closing in of the space around her, a pressure around her breastbone, tuned now to that solid perimeter.

There were no further sounds from the radio and after several minutes she continued on the path into a grove of fir trees. It was darker beneath the canopy that stretched high, creating its own sky. The disturbance of the protesters didn't penetrate through the cluster of trunks, the ground softer, still damp with the morning dew.

She paused, felt the vibrations growing beneath her feet and again scrambled off the path.

The pounding grew louder and a group of four military men, C7s held in front of them, moved fast towards the gate, or maybe the perimeter. They were strangers to her except for the uniform and training. She stayed still, blending with the undergrowth.

She breathed again once they passed out of sight, the echo of their boots remaining behind. A warning. Or an ownership.

She returned to the edge of the path, her hand resting against the deep grooves of a tree's bark, her fingers sticky where they touched. A few broken-off branches jutted from the trunk within reach, branches abandoned by the tree in favour of the larger, more ambitious ones pushing upwards to the sky.

She tested the strength of the lowest one. The truncated branch was thick where it connected to the trunk, its strength still intact. A disjointed path of broken branches led to the first significant limb. She heard the shout of an order from outside her protected glade, and the drone of an electric jet swooping low over the trees.

She climbed, using the branches for leverage and smeared her boots against the bark. She was confident in her ready strength, as she pulled and twisted, looking upwards to the next hold. Near the top she swung up and onto a branch, her feet dangling over the sides.

The smoke of the explosion drifted over the compound, its taste bitter and distinct. It touched the rooftops of the manufacturing facility and a larger black building. The shouting and incessant drumming reached her more easily here, and she climbed higher to see the source. The going was easier in the upper branches though she kept her ear tuned for the whir of the electric jets and the disturbance they would create in the air.

The top of the headquarters appeared in the distance behind the manufacturing plant, the windows glimmering in the rising sun. Protesters swarmed its base, a writhing mass of bodies, the crowd denser closer to the row of police officers that surrounded them. The officers were in full riot gear, stolid and formidable, the protesters like crazed marionettes bashing up against its impermeability.

Another group pushed against the barricade set up at the main entrance, military uniforms visible on the men who guarded it.

THE GATHERER

She heard a sudden burst of screaming and the protesters were fleeing, the white plumes of tear gas rolling through them. She knew the burn of the gas, the horrible flushing of eyes and nose that did nothing to relieve the searing pain. It wasn't necessary. The forces could easily contain the protesters but it wouldn't be just about containing the incident. This would be about sending a message.

The officers were pushed back by the surge of bodies, a break opening in the line so that a dozen or so broke free, racing for the grove of trees, the ocean, anywhere to get away from the gas.

There was a sick feeling in her gut as she heard the order called to bring them in. The officers took off after the protesters, like fully loaded tanks barreling down on a bicycle. Men, women, boys, girls, were tackled to the ground. Their cries of pain pierced up through the branches, clear and sharp to her spot in the trees. Arms were twisted hard, faces pressed into dirt, knees pushed painfully between shoulders.

Most of the teens were crying by the time they were being corralled towards the parking lot, the adults craning their necks to see where the younger ones were. All of them walked with bowed shoulders, cowering at any movement from their captors, having got more than they bargained for.

The protesters at the headquarters were being herded into a half-dozen transport vehicles that had been so quick to arrive they must have been waiting outside the gate – which meant the orders from the start would have been to take prisoners.

She pushed closer to the trunk.

It was unlikely anyone would look skyward, yet the awareness of what the orders likely were if they found her made the wind colder, her fall to the ground longer.

A group of four soldiers broke off from herding protesters and began a search of the compound. When they entered the grove, she pulled her feet in, the bark rough and cold against her cheek. When the pound of their boots had faded, her heart still mirrored their rhythm. She scanned the gray sky for a jet.

The headquarters, the manufacturing center and the massive new building were laid out below her, the heart of the compound and the Gatherer's strength. Her height above them didn't diminish their strength, if anything increasing their aura of impermeability. A single bird perched above a whole ocean of danger. The open hands of the Gatherer symbol on the headquarters caught the light of the rising sun. The wings of an angel were what they had once been called, now looking more and more like the wings of death.

Was Alicia there now? Trapped in her shiny tower the same way Maria was, with the looming bulk of the new building between them?

She faced the new building, the test facility as Adams had called it, and the place Storm was most likely to be. Was she captive in there? Or was she a willing participant, working alongside Stanton's team towards a common goal?

Maria lowered herself onto the branch, her back to the tree and settled in. The wail of a siren sounded in the distance, and somewhere below her, she heard the faint sobs of a person crying.

EIGHTEEN

ADAMS REMOVED HIS HOLSTER and belt and handed them to Hamel. He carried the C7 over his shoulder and felt his load lighten as he leaned it against the wall. Valerie didn't like Camille to see him with his weapons on and now that they were here, on site, he didn't want anything interfering with seeing his wife and daughter.

He was as nervous as if this were a first date, worried that the treatment facility wouldn't work out, that they would be angry he had brought them here. He ran his hands down his fatigues, wishing he had been able to change into his civvies.

"You ready?"

Wesley had surprised him when he'd arrived at his post with Hamel. Adams had been asking to see them but hadn't expected the visit to come in the middle of a shift.

"Yeah. You good here?"

Adams addressed the question to Hamel who had already taken up his post.

Hamel nodded and asked him to say hello to Valerie and Camille for him. A lifetime ago their families had held barbecues together. Before anyone was sick. Before the Gatherer existed.

Adams's post was at the far side of the compound, at the opposite corner to the treatment facility. He had assumed that Stanton had done it on purpose, to keep him as far away from his family as possible. They cut a diagonal across the compound, crossing behind the manufacturing building and in front of the test facility.

He nodded to the soldiers he knew and noted the flicker of distaste that crossed their faces when they saw him with Wesley. Rumors had started to leak out of the test facility … the experiments they were running, and the dead cows that were hauled out under the cover of dark.

"How are they doing?" Adams asked.

Wesley's stride was strong and he had power in his shoulders yet he still looked sickly, a rat that lives above ground but hasn't lost the darkness of the sewer.

"You'll be able to see for yourself."

Adams searched for a clue in Wesley's expression, worried about what he *wasn't saying, but his passive face revealed nothing.*

A soldier he didn't recognize guarded the entrance to the treatment facility. Wesley flashed some kind of identification and he let them pass. The building was strangely quiet, their boots echoing in the bare corridor. They passed doors with fragile people inside, most of them curled up, asleep.

Were they all connected to someone at the compound, their loved ones so desperate they had pulled every string to get them here?

At the sixth door, Wesley stopped.

"You'll only have a few minutes."

Adams pushed him aside, and was through the door, rushing towards the bed. Valerie's shocked, drawn face looked up at him. He was wrapping his arms around her, drawing her to him, when she stiffened.

His arms dropped.

"Did I hurt you?"

She smiled.

"I'm fine."

She was weaker than when he last saw her, her glorious black hair limp and dull. He looked to the bed beside her and the smallest of lumps under the covers.

"How is she?"

He rounded the bed, knelt on the floor so he could lean in close. Camille didn't stir, the stillness of her small, beautiful features like the veil of death. He brushed a lock of hair from her cheek.

"She doesn't wake up very often."

He heard the desperation and anguish in Valerie's voice, matching the pain inside his own chest. He had expected them to be better, for Camille to look up at him and smile, weak but on the road to recovery. He would have drawn them to him, held them close as he basked in the knowledge that they would be okay, having provided the solution to finally get them better. Instead, her stillness frightened him beyond anything he had ever known.

He lifted her small hand in his.

"Has she had a treatment? Have you?"

Valerie leaned against the pillows; the sheet smooth across her wasted hips. Her hips had once been voluptuous; smooth, round and perfect beneath his hands.

"They gave us something today and then tomorrow—"

She didn't finish, her eyes closed as she gathered her strength, holding onto the hope of what tomorrow would bring as much as him.

"Did it help?"

He could hear the pleading in his voice, for it to have made a difference.

Camille hadn't moved, impossible that her stark cheek bones and hollow cheeks could belong to his daughter. He had the overpowering need to take her in his arms. He stood and leaned over her, feeling the soft warmth of her breath on his cheek.

"Don't," said Valerie.

He didn't stop, pulling back the sheet so he could lift his little girl. Weeping sores covered her arms, and her thin nightgown and the sheet were wet with pus. He dropped the sheet, looking to Valerie, his horror reflected in her gaze except hers was deeper, harder, the injustice of it having had longer to take root.

He straightened the sheet over her shoulders and closed his eyes in a silent prayer that bringing them here had been the right thing to do. When he opened them, Valerie had her head leaned back, in a pose of such complete exhaustion that he saw everything she had suffered. How had he let this happen? He was the best in his unit, the best in his class. He kissed Camille's forehead, as if he could draw her suffering into him and be the one to carry it.

"Benoit."

There was a quiet strength in Valerie's voice he recognized, a command he had learned not to fight. She patted the bed beside her in a gesture that had once made his heart skip.

On his way to her, he caught sight of Wesley pacing outside the door. He wanted to slam the door in his face or better yet slam him into the wall. He kept control of himself, refused to engage his anger. It was not what his family needed from him right now.

He leaned carefully against the pillows next to Valerie, her hand in his as fragile as Camille's.

"You'll both get better. You'll see. This is the best place for treatment."

His words sounded hollow, rife with fear instead of certainty. She squeezed his hand in reassurance and he saw what Valerie surely had already known. A camera was mounted in the corner, its dark lens marking every move he and his wife and daughter made. His body responded, his muscles poised and his ears alert. He was on display here, every move as critical as if he were on patrol.

She placed both her hands around his and leaned into his shoulder. He ached at feeling her so close beside him, his longing to hold her so deep it broke him wide open. She lifted her chin, so her mouth was beside his ear.

"People don't get better here."

He shook his head. Squeezed her hand, even as he looked to Wesley, who he couldn't see through the door.

"Why would you say that? They have the best resources here, government funding. This is where Storm Freeman is being treated."

Her eyes were a deep brown, the depths of which were the only place he had ever felt home.

"She came to see us."

"Here?" He spoke in a low whisper.

She nodded a single time.

"Are you sure it was her?"

She didn't answer right away. She had always had that pause before responding, a moment to gather her thoughts. He wanted to move in front of her, shield her from the camera, from all of it. She held his gaze, a finality in it that frightened him to his core.

"She was in a wheelchair, with blood on her knees. She said she had crawled up the stairs because no one was around to help. I don't think she came here by choice. They are holding her."

"But I've seen her. She's better."

He felt her shift away from him, saw her irritation in her eyes. "Were you here? Did you see what I saw?"

The sharpness in her voice returned him to his senses. Familiar and heartbreaking, that he had used this time to make her angry, to not listen.

"I'm sorry."

Her gaze briefly flicked to the camera. She lifted her hand to cup his cheek, though her touch was fleeting, the gesture too much for her to sustain.

"She didn't know where she was. She was asking me for information."

The room darkened, the natural light from the window shifting with the clouds, and all his alarm bells were telling him to get the hell out of there.

"That doesn't make sense. The news is that the treatment is working."

She sagged, the weariness in her frightening him. He laid his arm carefully around her shoulders, and she whispered in his ear.

"It's not."

He forced himself to sink deeper into the bed, to not respond to the slamming of his heart. Wesley's shadow filled the doorway before he stepped in. Had he heard? Were they being monitored that closely?

His eyes locked on Adams.

"You're needed at your post."

He wasn't. There were a hundred other soldiers that could do that job.

"We need a minute."

Adams's tone was harsh, filled with the anger, and not how he should be speaking to Wesley. He expected him to deny it, but instead he nodded, letting his gaze move from Adams to Valerie.

"I'll wait outside."

Neither of them moved as he retreated, their only communication the tight squeeze of their hands. The black camera peered down at them, a relentless eye in the corner of the room.

He buried his nose in the top of Valerie's hair, breathing in the faint scent of her shampoo, feeling the touch of her forehead on his chin.

It had been a mistake bringing them here. Selfish of him to drag them away from their home. He would take them back, tell Stanton they didn't want the treatment.

He forced himself to stand, keeping his back to the door. He wouldn't be able to hide his pain, not with Valerie, and he didn't want Wesley to see it. He leaned down to kiss her and she briefly held his face in her hands, the touch so light, her lips on his like a whisper.

"Take us home."

He nodded, a cold hard urgency making it impossible to speak. He placed his hands on either side of her face, and she held onto his wrists, preventing him from letting her go.

"I will."

He turned and rested his hand on the top of Camille's head, unable to stop his hand from shaking. He looked to Valerie a final time, leaning into the bed as if he were still beside her.

He met Wesley at the door and when it shut behind him it felt as if he had been punched.

"If anything happens to them, I will find you."

It came out as a threat and he didn't care. Adams was faster and stronger, and bristled with the desire to physically force Wesley to tell him the truth but the slightest shift of Wesley's gaze through the

THE GATHERER

window to where Valerie sat vulnerable and sick in bed, slammed shut the idea of laying a single finger on this treacherous man. He stepped around him, intentionally brushing his shoulder. It was juvenile and ridiculous, but he needed this man to know there would be consequences if anything happened to the center of his world.

NINETEEN

Storm gripped the arms of the wheelchair as it bounced over the threshold, the last yellow streaks of the setting sun visible through the banks of clouds on the horizon. The paved path rolled smoothly beneath the wheels and Wesley pushed her quickly, a lightness to his gait that was new.

She lifted her nose to the breeze off the ocean, taking in long deep breaths, the air cool and fresh in her lungs. The glowing points of light on the path extended ahead of them, the series of lights growing stronger as the day dimmed.

"Were Valerie and her daughter moved?"

Their room had been dark when they passed, with an air of abandonment rather than sleep.

A soldier stood at the intersection of the paths. They slowed long enough for Wesley to show his ID.

They turned onto a newer path, with crushed gravel over dirt, their pace slowing.

"It's not like I have anyone to tell," said Storm.

The manufacturing building was a blaring beacon of light, a spaceship ready to take flight. The new structure beside it was painted black with only a single light above a steel door.

"They have been relocated."

And likely because of her.

She saw a movement in the corner of her eye where another soldier stood further out in a grassy section, standing guard. Another soldier stood along the edge of the new building.

"Has something happened?"

The tires crunched on the gravel, the evening breeze blowing softly.

Storm twisted in the chair, catching sight of *another soldier near a grove of trees* and several more near the lighted parking lot.

"What's going on?"

This wasn't about protecting the compound, this was an occupation. The employees that would normally have wandered the compound were nowhere to be found.

Their pace didn't falter, the looming blankness of the new building growing larger. She put her feet to the ground and tried to stand. The chair jammed into the back of her heels. She lurched forward, managing to catch herself before she fell.

She turned in a circle, counting over a dozen soldiers within view. She faced Wesley and the chair.

"Where do you think you're going to go?"

He spoke with derision and it aggravated her that he was right, her frustration providing the smallest surge of energy.

"You have to tell me something. None of this makes sense."

She stepped off the path, in the direction of the parking lot.

"Neither does what you're doing."

She didn't care. Why get better if she couldn't use it to regain some of her lost freedom and actually do something about everything that had gone wrong?

The white hands of the Gatherer logo shone at the top of the headquarters, beneath the clear dark sky. The top story was brightly lit, in a glow that seemed to originate from the center of the building, clear and bright compared to the damp darkness around her, and the unsettling watchfulness of the guards.

"I want to see my mother."

"You'll see her tomorrow."

He spoke with impatience, and moved the chair forward so it was closer to her feet.

A shadow passed in front of the headquarters window.

She shook her head, chastising herself for being as ridiculous as if she were still a small child.

"I don't believe you."

Her energy had waned and yet she lingered, not wanting to return to the confines of the chair. Since she had felt the tiny kernel of energy inside her, she had been returning to it, checking that it was still there, so afraid that it would disappear. The walk across the grass would kill it, render her back where she had started. She returned to the chair.

Two soldiers guarded the door to the dark building, neither of them acknowledging her as they passed through. The vestibule was a stark white room with several small portals in the wall. She had to stand for the eye scan and what she guessed was face recognition, the steel door only opening when she and Wesley had been cleared. It was a sharp contrast to the original, open transparency of the compound, when the whole world had been invited to see what they were doing.

They entered a wide, brightly lit corridor of gleaming tiles and blank walls. There was a familiar smell of new equipment, the chemical scent of fresh wiring, and a restlessness that spoke of energy and movement. She had a sudden memory of the lab when they had all been hard at work.

The corridor stretched ahead of them, doors on one side spaced far apart. Halfway down he stopped the wheelchair and locked it in place, his movements precise and efficient. He draped an x-ray blanket over her and, panicked, she tried to squirm out from beneath its weight.

"It's just a precaution." He handed her the balaclava. "It's not a test."

She crumpled the smooth stiffness of the material into a ball, whatever it was made of not enough to protect her from anything. "Please don't do this."

She sounded weak and pleading, but she couldn't take another test. That deep guttural pull terrified her more than anything she had felt in the city.

He pushed her forward. She tried to stand but he held her down with a hand on her shoulder.

THE GATHERER

They had entered a long room and for a moment she thought they had entered a green house, the smell of earth and growth filling the high ceiling. Rows of plants spiralled out from a central point, the inevitable Gatherer in the middle. A bank of terminals ran along one wall, several conduits laid along the floor between the terminals and the Gatherer.

The air was strangely inert with a deadness to it despite the plants. She felt suddenly isolated and bereft though nothing had changed.

She braced for some kind of field, yet the dull lifelessness in the air continued, seeming to grow thicker as they approached the sea of plants. They were all spider plants, varying from bright green at the edges to brown then white as the rings approached the center. The pattern was circular, its uniformity surprising, even the plants in the outer rings showing signs of damage though they were over thirty yards from the device.

"You're mapping out the damage," Storm said.

Wesley stood beside her, gazing out like a farmer over his field.

"We had no other way to gauge it, since we don't truly know where the Gatherer gets its energy from." He emphasized the "we" in such a way as to imply that there was someone who did know, and she was it. "But we had to start somewhere. To get an idea of what is really happening."

"You're looking for a cure."

The relief of it was astounding, that someone with resources and money was actually looking at this seriously. Despite the despondency and grimness of the place, she felt a tiny flash of hope.

Wesley stood among the plants, the long leaves brushing against his shins. If he felt the vacuum surrounding the plants, he didn't show it, his shoulders lifted, a victorious smile on his lips.

"We're measuring the speed the plants move nutrients through their leaves. To see if the Gatherer alters that functionality."

He strode back to her, his lips pressed together as if he were trying to suppress a grin yet only succeeding in creating a distorted smile.

"But there is something better," he said.

He pushed her down an aisle left through the plants. The closer they got to the Gatherer the more despondent she felt, her moment of hope crushed beneath an overwhelming layer of sadness.

Wesley whistled quietly as they passed close to the mammoth device, even as her sense of hopelessness grew so intense it felt as if she would choke. like a dark swirling pit around her feet. As they drew away, the constriction on her throat eased, and while an underlying sadness remained, it no longer consumed her. She looked behind her, to see what had caused such a violent emotional response. There was only the ring of dead plants, bits of green reappearing as they drew further away.

"Do you not feel that?" she asked.

Wesley didn't respond as they approached the opposite wall, the smell of earth and manure intensifying.

Wesley backed her through another door, the stench of a barnyard thick enough that she gagged. When he spun her around, she pushed back in the chair but there was no getting away from the rows and rows of cages and the skittering sound of thousands of rats moving inside their tiny cells. The rat in the cage closest to her had a sleek brown coat, its narrow face lifted up to her. She wanted to pull her feet up, away from this sea of death.

People moved in between the cages, making notes and recording observations. Underneath it all lay the undercurrent of despair, as if the world itself was about to end. The woman closest to Storm looked up briefly, the only one who seemed to have noticed them, middle-aged, a marked blankness in her eyes beyond the usual scientific detachment. She looked as if she were utterly alone, her movements slow as if she had lost the will to live.

They wheeled forward, Wesley explaining the details of the observations. Storm barely heard, unable to take her eyes off the rodents in their cages, their alertness and energy growing less the closer they drew to the Gatherer. Patches of missing fur appeared on the rats until in the inner circle they lay on their sides, some panting, others not moving at all.

She couldn't get a breath, the sense of futility so strong she was certain death would come at any moment. It was like the impending doom she felt before a seizure but this came from the outside, something creating a vast hole of devastation and misery.

Wesley stopped the chair.

"—you can see the rats here are more affected, many of them unable to eat or lift their heads. Some have even shown suicidal tendencies, whatever the Gatherer—"

The rows stretched in a long arc, a series of rings around the Gatherer. The same long arc as the corridor where she had found Valerie and Camille and the corridor that had led to the weapons test.

She looked behind her, the latched entrances to the cages were evenly spaced along the row. They used the same layout for the plants, animals and humans, and were running tests on all of them.

She thought she would throw up or scream into the high opaque ceiling.

"Get me out of here."

"There are other things I wanted to show you." He sounded disappointed, her reaction unexpected.

"I can't stay here."

"There are no fields here, nothing to harm you."

He only thought she cared about the fields, the devastation that surrounded them not even registering in his mind. So what of the human patients that he had promised to treat?

The Gatherer had multiple conduits running out of it and was attached to a frequency generator and a power supply. It was a bastardization of the simplicity of its original design. There was a grimness to the crystals, almost a darkness, whatever light and beauty long since stripped away.

"Please."

She saw an image of Daniel lying still and wasted after death, the grief she had been carrying morphing into a despair that was unending. Her head was in her hands, the skittering of the rats inside her head.

The chair rolled forward, slowly at first but gained speed, her emotions lightening as they moved. By the time they reached the outer wall, she was able to take clear, measured breaths.

He pulled her into another room, this one smaller, a more traditional clinical lab with microscopes and rows of test equipment. Trace fields rippled across her skin and they passed quickly, the scientists barely having time to lift their heads before the door closed behind them.

She smelled food and coffee. Chairs were scattered around a moulded plastic table, and a counter stood with a sink and cupboards on one wall. Wesley parked her a safe distance from the refrigerator.

He had his hands on his hips, like a parent standing over a misbehaving child, his disappointment and disapproval evident though he tried to keep a neutral face.

"What was that about?"

The room was stuffy and the smell of old food caught in her throat. At least that pit of hopelessness had gone. She looked over her shoulder at the closed door, unable to shake the feeling that it would follow her.

"There is something wrong in there."

That was an understatement. The rats had been bad enough, but the blackness around the Gatherer had been a physical manifestation of nothingness, complete annihilation.

"Of course. We're mapping the damage of the Gatherer." The inflection in his voice made it clear the blame for that was hers. "You can't expect it to be pretty."

She hadn't expected it to be pretty and it astounded her that anyone felt she still needed to be reminded.

"Have you had problems with the staff?"

A frown.

"The demands have been significant, given our time constraints."

A chair scraped on the floor in the next room. Wesley lowered his voice as he sat down and leaned forward. "Not everyone is cut out for this kind of work, but we have the right people now. We're making progress."

Storm's pulse had calmed, the quietness of her mind startling after the violence of the despair.

"Progress towards what?"

There was a scar over his right eye, pink and shiny, a flaw in his pale skin.

He rubbed his fingers across it as he considered his answer. "Understanding how the Gatherer affects people."

"It disrupts all electrical systems," said Storm. "I thought that was obvious."

"Yes. We see that. But to what extent? Do larger Gatherers affect people faster? Does a smaller capacity mean less damage? How is the damage occurring?"

She had tried to answer these questions when she had been in the Yukon. But she hadn't had the background or the resources to set up tests.

"You're a biologist," she said.

"Of a sort. I specialize in how animals, including humans, and plants respond to outside threats."

'Threats' was a vague word, and she was sure he had used it intentionally.

"I got permission to show you this," he said. "Because I wanted you to understand what we're doing. No one else has come close to this level of investigation. We're starting to develop models of how it works, starting to be able to predict outcomes."

"So why do you need me?"

A coffee cup had been left on the counter next to the sink, a stained trail on its side where the liquid had spilled.

"The models are unpredictable. We thought as a creator and one of the afflicted you would be able to provide unique insights."

"You'd have to show me everything. Otherwise I won't be able to correlate my own experience."

She had the sudden awareness of Maria, as if she were in the room listening.

I have to be here, she explained in her mind. They've made a weapon. They're running tests. Being on the outside isn't going to help us. She was aware of using the word "us," still thinking of her and Maria as a team.

Wesley nodded; his eyes narrowed as he watched her.

A calendar had been tacked to the wall with a cartoon sketch of two perplexed scientists looking down at a table above a caption she couldn't read.

There must be something they can't fix if they were bringing her in. These labs and experiments were not something they wanted the world to see – though the real danger wasn't in what there was to see, but to feel. How could you measure that? The complete annihilation of hope and life, so that all that was left was despair?

"Of course," said Wesley. "You can have access to whatever you need."

She felt a deep fear that didn't come from that pit. What had happened to allow her to see all this?

"You'll have to bring what I need to my room. I can't be in the lab. Or the test areas."

"Of course."

"And I want to meet with my mother."

He paused before he nodded, his expression too veiled for her to read what had passed there.

So it wasn't going as well as Stanton had professed. Something had happened and they believed she was the one to fix it.

She turned her head. Aware of the two Frankenstein Gatherers. Beasts that had been tortured and warped into something unrecognizable. She felt a sudden sympathy for them. And an understanding. This wasn't about Wesley or his researchers, it was about her and the Gatherer. The way it had been in the beginning.

There was a relief in that simplicity, and she felt the kernel of energy that had returned to her over the past days solidify.

"I need you to tell me what you've done."

TWENTY

THE HEADLIGHT BEAMS HIGHLIGHTED the chain link fence, gleaming on the three rows of barbed wire and the electrical wires that twisted through them. The night air was cool and damp and the white clouds of the soldiers' breaths floated up from the thirty armed men waiting at the gate. Six personnel carriers lined up behind them, ready for the afflicted that would be loaded in. Not like cattle, Adams kept telling himself. Like people, sick people who needed help.

His pulse was high, his nerves agitated. He did not have the cool focus he usually achieved before a maneuver. He reminded himself these people were civilians, most of them sick or incapacitated, but his worry for Valerie and Camille kept surging bright and hot, refusing to let him settle.

Patel unlocked the chain holding the gate shut, the fence put up in panicked haste when the plague had first arrived. The chain clattered to the ground and Adams flinched before checking the roofs of the closest building and the shadows between them.

He rolled his shoulders, trying to ease his jitters. These people would be unarmed; this was an exercise in relocation and bringing help to people in need. Yet why were they arriving at night and why were the plans of relocation not shared with those that were to be most affected?

He took up his position at the back of the line. The Colonel had asked him to go along and be his set of eyes. It also conveniently acted as a reminder of how lucky he was to have Valerie and Camille being treated in the compound.

They moved quickly, their footsteps echoing against the dark facades on the warehouses, their path growing darker as they drew further away from the gate. Some of the men had their night vision goggles lowered but Adams kept his off, preferring to let his eyes adjust to the moonlit night. It would be bad enough when they burst into the main warehouse where the afflicted had taken refuge, they didn't need to look like faceless robots when they did.

There was the dim glow of windows in a warehouse up ahead, the flicker of candlelight. A fire burned outside the door, in a pit set up in the middle of what had once been a street. Half the group of soldiers fell away, vanishing into an alleyway, in the direction of the dwellings along the river. Adams wanted to pull back, approach slower, so the people would understand they were there to help, but the leader of the mission had been chosen for his ability to get things done, not his empathy.

Two people sat at the fire and one of them bolted through a sudden sliver of light where the warehouse door opened. The second positioned himself between them and the door, as if he had any chance of stopping them. The man was thin, long hair pushed back from a receding hair line, with a gauntness to him that marked him as afflicted.

"What do you want?"

The unit took up positions around the struggling fire, some moving down the alleys on either side to block other exits. This could have been done so much differently.

"Sergeant Patel of the Canadian Special Forces. We're here to transport the inhabitants to another location."

Adams was positioned closest to the door, a thin strip of light showing where it had been left open.

"No one told us about this."

The glow of the fire illuminated one side of the man's face.

"It's a new support program for the afflicted. You'll be taken to a facility outside the city where you will receive appropriate care."

THE GATHERER

A woman with long gray hair stepped out of the warehouse, followed by a young man with a thick beard, a woman with a closely shaved head, and a young girl with tangled blond hair and tattered fairy wings that caught the light of the fire. He tore his gaze away, focused on the others that continued to pour out, all thin, weak, none of them armed. Many were in pajamas and he wanted to tell them to go back to bed, have a warm drink, anything except stand on this barren pavement on this cold night.

A tall, dark haired man pushed past one of the afflicted. He walked without frailty, his sharp eyes taking in the soldiers and the crowd as he came to stand beside the gray-haired woman. The young girl moved to the other side of the older woman and held her hand.

"I'm Marty and this is Romero," the gray-haired woman said, indicating the man beside her. "Can we help you?"

Her face was worn, lined with a tiredness that spoke of exhaustion rather than illness. She had a natural calmness to her that made him think she was a caregiver of some kind.

"We have instructions to transport everyone to a safe location outside of the city."

"Has there been an attack?"

"There will be proper facilities. Treatment."

"What kind of treatment?" said Marty.

"You'll be briefed on the details once you've arrived. The location has been made ready for you."

Patel wouldn't have been told the details of the treatment. It might not even be true.

"We weren't informed of this."

It was Romero who spoke, the type Adams recognized as a self-appointed leader, though it was Marty who held the authority.

"It's safer to move you at night," said Patel.

It didn't need to be said that it was for the protection of the rest of the population. For those who still believed that the plague could be transferred between people. Even some of the men in the unit were nervous, keeping a greater distance than necessary, despite their briefing.

"We have everything we need here."

It was Romero again. Adams watched Marty, the riveting intelligence beneath the compassion, and the young girl who chose her hand to hold.

"There are some that are too weak to travel," said Marty.

"We have space for everyone. Different needs can be accommodated. This area is no longer safe for you."

"It's never been safe."

It was an angry response from the woman with cropped hair, who had emerged from behind Marty, her arms folded across her chest.

"What kind of transportation?" said Romero.

"There are personnel carriers parked at the entrance to the dark zone. We can take everyone."

A few of the afflicted made for the warehouse door, crowding at the door in their rush to get in. The older woman's face held a profound disappointment, interlaced with her endless weariness.

"We can't go with you," she said.

"This isn't a choice."

"Those transport trucks generate electric fields," said Romero. "There will be fields throughout the city. These people are too fragile to be exposed to that."

"We've mapped out a route with the lowest possible exposure."

The young girl was scrutinizing each of the men in the unit, methodically moving her gaze from one to the next. When she reached his, her eyes widened, he the first one to return her gaze.

He nodded but the gesture confused her, and she looked away. It felt as if she were searching for someone, the same way he looked for Camille whenever he saw a young girl.

"We don't need your help."

Romero still didn't get it, blustering like a fool that doesn't understand the world has changed. Marty laid a hand on his sleeve.

"This isn't about help."

Romero looked down at her with irritation. This wasn't the first time he believed her to be wrong or weak.

"You have an hour to pack up your belongings. We can help transport the weaker ones to the trucks," said Patel

"We need more time."

Marty had made the request, she at least understanding this wasn't a choice, negotiation of the implementation her only option.

Romero stepped in front of her and Adams hoped he would be the one to restrain him.

"Are you proud of yourselves? Preying on the sick and the weak? They are getting better here. Can you say that about where you're taking them?"

The men behind Patel leaned forward. They knew what was coming even if this idiot was the last one to figure it out.

"You should use this time to help them get ready," said Patel. "The building is surrounded so please don't try to escape."

"Are we in the dark ages? Banishing the sick and infirm like lepers? Where is your sense of decency?"

Romero was wasting his breath and everyone knew it but him. This decision had been made hours ago, if not days, and his grandstanding changed nothing.

His swept-back hair fell forward with the force of his indignation, his movements the loose, ineffectiveness of the untrained.

Marty and the girl had moved back. The girl's face was blank, her eyes brooding, holding an anger too intense for her age.

Is this what would happen to Camille? Her illness stripping away innocence along with health? He felt sick, his irritation at the man swelling beyond any rational reaction. He gripped the rifle harder. He could feel the other men doing the same, all of them willing to be the one to take this guy down. Patel spoke, even and unyielding.

"These people need to be where there are proper facilities. And medical staff to help them."

"We are helping them," said Romero. He crossed his arms.

Patel's signal was subtle, invisible to anyone except the team. A soldier opposite Adams, positioned slightly behind the idiot, stepped forward, and leveled his rifle at Romero's kidney. The few remaining afflicted scattered, most retreating into the warehouse, a handful remaining, including the little girl.

The idiot made the mistake of trying to fight back. Adams had to admire his confidence in himself. They weren't authorized to use their rifles in this mission, perhaps the guy had guessed that, but the soldier had him on his knees without even trying.

"Take him to the trucks," said Patel.

"I need to get—"

A soldier twisted the guy's arms as Patel stepped around him.

He spoke directly to the older woman, giving her the details of what they were expected to do. She nodded, though her attention seemed to be focused elsewhere, perhaps calculating the damage this would do.

They hauled Romero to his feet, letting him walk on his own, the rifle held behind him more as a reminder than a threat.

"Megan!"

Romero turned around, still surprisingly cocky in the face of the rifle. The girl lifted her chin, her gaze still cool though perhaps it was more numbness than anger.

"Bring the network."

There was a softening of the blankness, so that for a moment she looked like the child she was. She nodded and let go of Marty's hand. The woman briefly squeezed Megan's shoulder even as she discussed logistics with Patel.

Megan floated as she walked, her tattered wings making her lighter on the ground.

"Go with her." Patel barked the order at Adams.

He stepped in behind her. Her glance was more curious than afraid when she looked back at him, and a space of calmness opened up inside him.

THE GATHERER

They stepped into the warehouse and he scanned for potential threats. The few people in the near vicinity shied away from him, his heavy gear and rifle harsh in the bare meagerness. A rope of LED lights circled the upper perimeter of the warehouse, casting a weak shadow over the area below where dozens of candle flames and lanterns were in motion.

He paused, he had expected a few dozen but the bobbing lights stretched far back into the warehouse, hundreds of bodies torn from their sleep. He stopped Megan with a hand on her shoulders.

"Wait here."

She nodded, turning to face back towards the door, like she knew what he was going to do. He stuck his head outside.

"We need more vehicles."

He got an acknowledgement from Patel who was already instructing someone to call for more as Adams turned back inside.

"Okay," Adams said when he returned to Megan.

An aisle ran down the middle of the warehouse, single beds and bunk beds spread out in a senseless chaotic pattern around it. Megan skipped in front of him, the lightness of it strange in the panicked shuffling around him. At the side wall, a soldier stood next to an exit, with another on the opposite side.

Colorful comforters were bunched on some of the beds, photos hung off bunks, and books lay next to almost every cot. A woman in pajamas, swaying slightly, struggled to remove a photo taped to a bunk.

He breathed in, shocked at the sight of so many of the afflicted in one place. It wasn't his job to question orders. He carried them out. They had brought personnel carriers to transport the infirm. How could this be the right way to do this?

Megan had gotten ahead of him and he had to hurry to catch up to the flash of pink taffeta bobbing up ahead. A man sat on a bunk, bare boney knees poking up to his chest, the candle beside him spluttering as he watched Adams pass. The skin rose on Adams' neck, like being watched by someone who is on the verge of dying, their claws reaching out to pull him with them.

Halfway down the aisle, Megan stopped. When he caught up to her, the full expanse of the warehouse overpowered him. Rows and rows of beds, all spiraling outward, the ceiling peaking above them at the mid-point of the arch. An aisle crossed perpendicular to the main aisle, where he and Megan stood, the center of the X.

He turned slowly, with a feeling that he was missing something that he needed to pay attention to. Yet he could see no aggression in the people as they gathered their things, no one acting like they were trying to hide something.

"Can you help me with this?"

Her voice was light and melodic, the angel wings well suited, a natural manifestation of this strange child. She crouched over a device embedded in the floor. A battery and wires and for the barest of instants his heart leapt, thinking it was a bomb. But the wiring resolved into something simpler. A central power source for some kind of network. How was that possible?

The afflicted had to be away from all currents, the fields they created a special kind of torture.

Megan detached wires connected to a small pulse generator, set to a level to be almost not there at all.

"What is this?"

Dirty curls hung around her face and she had copper wires woven into her wings.

"Doesn't it hurt these people?"

Her curls bounced as she shook her head. She pointed to a tiny round dish lodged inside the structure. It was made up of minute crystals, the whole contraption smaller than his palm.

"Is that—"

It made no sense.

"I got the idea from Storm when she was here."

"She was here?"

Megan lifted the device carefully, cradling it against her ribs. She held it protectively, seemed to pause as she closed her eyes and lifted her chin. The circles were dark beneath her eyes, her curls lax, the knobby knees below her tutu sharp points. She opened her eyes to see him watching and it felt as if she saw him and everything he had done.

She knelt down and covered the hole in the network of tiny wires with a piece of plywood.

"Does it help these people?" he said.

She smiled suddenly, wide and bright, a remnant of the child she must have once been. She waved her arm like a TV host to take in the whole warehouse.

"Can't you tell?"

Some of the residents struggled to move, others helped the weaker ones put on clothes. It didn't look like any of them had been cured or were getting better. Yet how much worse would they be if this tiny experiment wasn't here?

"Is it made of the same materials?"

It looked like an exact replica of a Gatherer, delicate and strangely beautiful.

He shook himself. It was a bow of crystals held in the grubby hands of a child. Not a cure. He was grasping at straws.

"Is there anything else?" he said.

She held the small dish tighter against her ribs as if she had sensed his dismissal. Didn't matter. He wasn't here to make her feel better.

"Do you have other things you need to get?"

She was frowning now, reacting to his change of tone as if he had disappointed her.

"Just this."

She walked back the way they had come, wings bobbing, a tattered piece of material dragging behind her. The heels of her runners were cracked at the back, and her jeans had a dirty patch on the seat.

He wanted to scoop her up and carry her away from this place of false hopes, back to where Valerie could look after her. Except his thought stopped mid-way, for Valerie could barely look after herself. More likely it would be this young girl looking after Valerie and wasn't that what she was already doing? Looking after others?

He took a final look into the hole the tiny device had left, the heart torn out of the network.

He moved to the back of the warehouse, slowly herding the sick and infirm towards the main door. There were hundreds of them. A crowd of struggling sick people being rounded up from the place that had to have become home. Their lack of protest made it worse – the injustice of the plague was only opening them up for more suffering. A blanket slipped off the shoulders of a woman and fell to the floor. He bent to pick it up.

She accepted it without a word, the touch of her cool fingers like the briefest touch of a butterfly. Like the fairies Camille swore lived in the tree beside her room.

Bile rose in his throat. He swallowed against it, willing the cool detachment of the mission to flow over him. Except anxiety and fear didn't let it settle. He was sweating, his palms slick on the rifle.

They had reached the halfway point and the other two soldiers flanked him on either side, a net to catch all the passengers. Patel had insisted on calling them passengers, or patients. Yet these were prisoners, in every sense of the word.

He scanned the crowd for the top of Megan's fairy wings, but she had been enveloped by the crowd. Was that tiny dish the key to fixing all this? Or the dream of a sick little girl?

The warehouse behind him was a network of empty cots and bunks, sheets hanging off hastily left beds, splashes of color from clothes left behind, and a single candle burning in the back corner.

"I'm going to check that out," said Adams.

The solder on his right nodded and moved over to fill his position.

THE GATHERER

His footsteps echoed in the emptying warehouse, its size separating him from the low murmur of the corralled passengers, like disappearing into the back of the supply depot when it had been cleared out. Except it had been humans that had filled this space, making the absence of them deeper.

He threaded his way between empty bunks, stepping over a pair of forgotten slippers, his shoulder brushing a plastic bag hanging on a post. Pillows still showed the indents of people's heads, the blankets likely warm if he were to touch them.

He lost sight of the candle as he wound his way further back, the dim flicker re-appearing when he changed to a different aisle. He had thought the bunks were in rows. Instead they curved in long arcs towards where Megan had removed the tiny Gatherer.

At first, he thought the candle had been forgotten in the rush to leave but as he drew closer the outline of a pair of feet and legs appeared beneath a woven blanket of bright blues and blacks, the torso and a turned head appearing as he drew closer. A mane of long gray hair spread out on the man's pillow, his eyes closed, his white gloved hands folded on his chest.

Adams knelt down beside him, the concrete rough and hard beneath his knees, and pressed his fingers to the man's neck.

The man's eyes opened, and he turned his head. Adams dropped his hand. His eyes were shadowed in the semi-darkness, but Adams had the impression of an intensity that belied the corpse-like position of his body.

"No one left behind," said the old man, his voice deep and raspy. He hadn't moved other than his head, but Adams had tensed, responding to something he couldn't see.

"Everyone is being shipped out," said Adams.

The man held his corpse-like pose, only his head turned to look at him.

"I'm staying here."

"You can't."

A folding chair had been set up beside the bunk, as if for mourners keeping vigil.

"There is no one anymore that can tell me what I can and can't do." The man returned his gaze to the underside of the bunk, closing his eyes as he spoke. "So, what are you? A Sergeant? Corporal?"

Adams looked closer at the man.

"Sergeant."

"Since when do they send special forces to collect the sick and the weak? Expecting a fight?"

He needed to get this guy to stand. Walk out on his own.

"The dark zones aren't safe anymore. These people need better care."

The man chuckled, though it was half-hearted. Other than the blanket he had no possessions. Nothing to connect him to this world.

"And you people are here to give it to us?"

Irritation bristled up Adams' back. He was wishing he had sent one of the other guys to investigate.

"I'm just following orders."

As soon as he said it, he knew it was the wrong thing to say, the man's burning eyes turning on him. Like something from a different world in this dark corner.

"Does that absolve us from responsibility? I've always wondered."

His tone was mocking, his body still deathly still. If he hadn't felt the man's pulse, he might wonder if he was real, or something his conscience had cooked up.

"You've served?'

His cackle sent chills down Adams' spine.

"I've been serving since the day I was born. And it's never done me any good."

"Then you know I have to get you out of here."

"There's nowhere you can take us that the plague won't find us."

The man's stillness had grown heavier, a weight around Adams' neck.

"You need to get up."

There was a long inhale from the man, his chest rising before the long slow exhale, like he was breathing in the world and keeping part of it inside of him.

"The others will be leaving soon," said Adams.

"They don't need me anymore."

The silence was thick and deep as if the other passengers had never been there and it made Adams restless, wanting to be back with the group. A thin wire, taped to the floor, ran below one bunk to the next. The outer tendrils of Megan's web.

"I can't leave you here."

The man lifted a hand, the first sign of movement, a weak wave of the glove dismissing him.

"Not my problem."

There was a noise from the front of the warehouse, the rattling screech of a metal door rolling open.

They would be loading the passengers into the shielded backs of the trucks, blankets and drinks provided for their comfort. Completely inadequate for what these people needed. Again, he swallowed against his nausea, his distaste refusing to settle.

He shifted his rifle so that it hung across his back. He would have to carry him. He pulled back the blanket and immediately dropped it. A violent, oozing red rash covered the man's legs and chest, his arms above the gloves swollen and red with hives. He wore clean boxers but the sheets around him were stained yellow from pus.

He recoiled, his heart hammering inside his chest. The man watched with hard, flat eyes, his gloved hands folded over his chest.

Megan's web wasn't doing anything. He had been a fool to believe it. This attack on the man's body went far beyond anything a feel-good holistic web could touch. Is this what waited for Valerie and Camille?

In a sudden, clear purpose the remote detachment of the mission locked into place. He needed to get out of here. Cure or not, he needed to be with them. Moving slowly but purposely, he wrapped the man in the blanket, with as little pressure as possible. The man watched him, with eyes that seemed to understand every thought, every doubt, every hesitation that had ever gripped him.

He was about to lift when the man spoke.

"It won't help anything."

Adams took shelter within the detachment, focussed on the task at hand.

There was a hiss of the man's inhaled breath as he lifted, the smell of infection and decay overwhelming. The blanket was a soft, tight weave under his fingertips.

The man was lighter than he should be, with the shoulders and hips of what had once been a larger man.

"Please."

It was a gasp, agony, the man's eyes wide and terror-ridden, unable to find a place without pain. Adams' coolness hardened, a shell of layered ice. It wasn't him carrying this fragile man, not his hands that were causing this pain.

His footsteps reverberated through the empty bunks. It took longer to reach the main aisle and he was aware of every moment he caused pain. Time attenuated, the trip back taking hours instead of minutes. The aisle stretched forever; the few patients still left at its end, far away. He held his arms still and kept his torso rigid as he walked. The man's ragged breath kept time with each step.

Megan waited at the central intersection, no longer carrying the tiny Gatherer. She watched his approach with that distant blankness. She gave no acknowledgement when he passed but for the tracking of her eyes, her light footsteps falling in behind him.

The remaining passengers, a few dozen, parted when he arrived. Marty was helping load people in, and she paused when she saw who he carried.

"He shouldn't be moved," she said.

Adams climbed the steps into the truck, and she stepped out of the way.

"Put him on the empty mattress."

She had adjusted quickly, knowing what she thought didn't really matter, each of them taking shelter within their respective roles. He laid the man down gently, his rifle shifting on his back. The man's eyes were closed, his breathing shallow, his head turned away from Adams as if he could turn away from the pain he had caused.

A young woman with delicate, bird-like hands placed a pillow under his head as Adams carefully unwrapped him. The man didn't open his eyes, seemed to have retreated into whatever comfort he could find. Adams wanted to say something, yet words didn't come.

The passengers already loaded waited for him to leave, and he understood why.

He turned, bracing for an attack, except it wasn't physical.

Marty waited for him at the bottom of the steps, the final passengers behind her. She let him pass without acknowledging him, but her dismissal was without judgement and he was grateful for it.

TWENTY-ONE

Storm asked Wesley to stop the wheelchair at the junction of the two paths. Her mother sat at a picnic table, in the middle of the empty outdoor area in the far corner of the compound. She faced away from Storm, towards the ocean, the mid-morning sun highlighting the red in her auburn hair.

"I can walk from here."

Wesley hesitated, either from an expectation that he was to be at this meeting, or an uncertainty whether she could make it that far.

"I'll make my own way back," she said.

He still looked unsure, but they had passed a dozen soldiers on the way from the treatment facility. She would be well protected and contained.

"Don't push yourself too hard."

She placed her feet on the ground, the chair shifting as the brake locked in place. Her legs were unsteady but stronger than they had been in weeks. She lifted her chest and drew in a long full breath, her lungs opening up.

"I'll leave the chair here in case you need it."

Wesley still faced towards her mother; half-balanced on his toes as if he would come with her. A mist of water sprayed up from the ocean and cooled her cheeks.

"I'll be fine."

She straightened the cuffs on the jacket he had provided for her and made her way along the gravel path, the agitation in her veins for once not the result of a field. Her mother was still facing away, the dark blue of her suit the sole point of color against the faded perfection of the gardens.

At the scuff of Storm's foot, her mother turned, her sculpted bob unmoving, the sunglasses framing her face so large Storm couldn't see her expression. Her mother moved out from behind the table and Storm had the impression her mother had gotten smaller, her shoulders narrower under her suit. Storm stopped before she reached her, aware their reunion was being watched by Wesley and the half-dozen soldiers visible from where she stood.

Her mother pressed her lips in a smile and half-raised her arms in an invitation for a hug. Except she and her mother didn't hug. Hadn't since Storm was young. Her mother stepped forward, covering half the distance between them and Storm met her halfway. Her arms were thin around her mother's shoulders. Her mother's arms lay around her waist and Storm knew she would feel the wasted flesh on Storm's ribs.

Her mother squeezed tighter than Storm expected, and she instinctively squeezed back. The breeze played around them and Storm was surprised they still clung to each other.

When they moved apart, neither of them knew what to do next. After a moment's hesitation, Storm took the seat with her back to the ocean, the breeze pushing into the back of her head. She pulled at her collar to keep the wind from finding its way into her coat.

Her mother sat across from her and squinted as she laid her sunglasses on the table.

Over her shoulder, Wesley stood next to the wheelchair. He was all rigid lines and hardness, waiting at the edge of the manicured lawn.

"I'm so glad you're safe," said her mother. There were deeper lines around her mother's mouth and a looseness to her skin along her jaw. "After that horrible video ..."

Her voice caught in an emotion Storm couldn't read.

"I'm better now."

Storm had kept her tone measured as if there wasn't so much more that she needed to say. Her mother's gaze swept over Storm, taking in the too-large suit and the skeletal paleness of her hands. "You're so thin."

Storm lifted her hands and spread her fingers, the tendons high ridges beneath translucent skin. She could barely remember when they had looked any different.

"Daniel's dead."

She hadn't known she would say it but had suddenly needed to tell someone who would understand, her grief thick and black.

Her mother's expression barely flickered, other than a slight pressure in her lips. "I'm sorry."

"Did you know?"

Her mother shook her head, hardly a movement at all.

"You said you would look after them." She hadn't meant it to sound like an accusation but how had he been left to suffer in that substation, little more than a rat in a sewer? "They were sick. Just like I was."

Her mother shook her head in exasperation. "I offered help. They didn't want it." She flicked her wrist in dismissal. "And besides, Ari isn't sick." Her tone was cool, almost angry.

"Is he here?"

Storm had leaned forward, her ribs pushing against the edge of the table. In the distance, the manufacturing facility gleamed in the morning sun. She could imagine Ari in there, coding and testing in search of a solution. She wanted to be with him, testing her theory, even arguing with him about it.

"I brought him in once we knew something was wrong. I thought he would be able to fix it."

"What is he trying to do?"

Her mother shrugged and exhaled in frustration. "It's a firmware upgrade, to limit the frequency of operation, last I heard."

"Is he succeeding?"

"He claims it will stop the plague."

"I need to see him."

THE GATHERER

Someone had carved a rough outline of the Gatherer symbol in the wood of the picnic table. Its simplicity was surrounded by other carvings of a gull in flight, the towering fir trees, and a worker on a riding lawnmower. Her mother laid her hand flat over the carved Gatherer symbol before she responded.

"Things here aren't the same as when you left."

Over a dozen guards watched the open spaces between buildings, the mass of the test facility looming over all of it.

Her mother lifted her chin and closed her eyes, tilting her face to catch the sun. There was an exhaustion in that brief pause, her mother's gaze lingering on the ocean when she opened her eyes.

"You won't have the control you once did," said her mother. "You won't be able to go near the process."

"What are you talking about?"

The coldness of the wind pushed beneath the table, wrapping around her ankles.

Her mother placed her second hand over the carved gull. Several dark age spots mixed with the freckles on the back of her hand. Half covered by her wrist was a different carving of the upward hands of the Gatherer symbol tipped over and the carved ball of the earth rolling off.

"After you destroyed that Gatherer in Three Rocks, there was an attack on the compound. Protesters barricaded us in the headquarters and the military arrived to get us out."

Storm had seen the video clip after the attack where her mother had confirmed the corporation would continue production of the Gatherer and that they were doing great things for the world.

"But the military was here long before that," her mother continued. "As soon as you first left, they were waiting. It was all hush-hush, no one in uniform. It wasn't until your stunt in Three Rocks that the guards became visible, and they put sentinels at the gate."

Storm could see a half dozen guards from where she sat.

"So they're controlling the access?"

She followed her mother's gaze to the movements of a female soldier as she paced the shoreline. She was short and compact, her no-nonsense stride reminding Storm of Maria.

"It's more than that."

The flatness of her mother's voice gave away so much more than any outburst of emotion. Storm finally understood, the refusal to confirm the plague, the testing of the cows and rats.

"The decisions haven't been yours?"

Her mother shook her head, as she looked over Storm's shoulder to the ocean, her hands still positioned over the carvings on the table.

"Mom?"

Her mother looked slowly back to Storm, the focus returning, as she shook her head again.

"I'm little more than a talking head, hiding their tests and acts of war behind the good will of the corporation."

"There must have been something you could do."

Her mother laughed, quiet and cynical.

"Storm. Listen to me. It's not like it was another corporation. The military is an arm of the government, it's national security. The Gatherer is something too important for them to lose."

Storm should have recognized it sooner. Ari had. Warning them, the first time Maria and Havernal had shown up at the lab, that there would be powerful forces that would want to get their hands on the Gatherer. It was why they had released it so quickly and soon.

"I had the choice of stepping down or staying as spokesperson."

It took a moment for Storm to understand, that her mother had made the choice to stay. Her mother's eyes were beyond weary, the blue faded. "I still don't know if it was the right thing to do."

Her admission unsettled Storm, for her mother had never harboured doubts on anything, even when she had been wrong.

"Why didn't you tell me?"

Her mother drew her hands into her lap, the depths of her

THE GATHERER

exasperation allowing her expression to soften. "I didn't want them to know where you were."

Storm thought of the Suburban and electric jet that had broken the peacefulness of her clearing in the Yukon, and how the corporation, the local police, and, she now understood, the military had all wanted to claim her as their own.

"They found me anyways."

"But at least you had time to heal."

Her mother held her gaze, the determination there still uncowed, despite the strain and the humility.

Storm leaned forward, the fatigue she continually fought suddenly close and present.

"I haven't healed. Whatever they are giving me helps for the moment, but it isn't a long-term fix. I'm still susceptible to fields. My body aches, and I can feel the bursts from that transmitter."

A transmitter had been installed on top of the headquarters and she could feel the prickling across her skin. She lifted her arm as if she could show her mother the agitation of the signal. Except there was nothing to see but her thinness and transparent skin.

Her mother reached up and grabbed her arm, bringing it back down to the table. Her fingers were cold, the grip too tight. In the distance, Wesley paced behind her chair and checked his tablet.

Her mother followed her gaze, her disgust clear on her face. When she looked back to Storm it looked as if her eye had twitched.

"Did your eye just twitch?"

Her mother shook her head as she released Storm's hand. There were deep pouches under her eyes, and she looked shrunken. It would be easy to mistake the plague for fatigue.

"No. No. I'm fine."

"You've been so close to the processes the whole time. You need to be careful."

Her mother's look was long, and Storm squirmed under her gaze.

"Not everyone gets sick."

Her mother's matter-of-fact tone soothed her, and she sat back, easing herself back from imagining the worst wherever she looked.

"They will once the aberrations they're testing are released," said Storm.

Still at the junction of the path, Wesley appeared to release the brake on the chair.

Storm leaned forward, her frustration at Wesley's incessant hovering making the word harsher than it needed to be. "*Mom.*"

She saw her mother brace herself, rally whatever energy still remained to respond to Storm's request. It made her heart break. She wished she could tell her mother to leave, that she didn't have to hold on anymore. Except they weren't there yet.

Wesley started pushing the chair towards them.

"Can you send Ari to see me?"

Her mother immediately shook her head. "I don't know where he is. He hasn't been in the compound for weeks."

She felt the hope drain away, replaced by frustration that every time she tried to hold onto a solution it slipped away. Wesley had almost reached them, the certainty in his expression coming into focus. He parked the wheelchair parallel to the end of the table, the gravel crunching beneath his boots.

"I thought I'd bring this over, to save your strength."

"Can we have another minute?"

He smiled, not moving. "You need to save your strength."

"I can handle a few minutes of sitting on a bench," said Storm.

He blinked, the small bristles of his hair barely moving in the wind. The guard held his place at the crossroads of the two paths.

Her mother touched her hand. "I'll come and see you. Once you're stronger."

Storm nodded, not sure if her mother was playing to Wesley or if she hadn't understood that Storm wasn't getting better. She rose, her legs unsteady, disheartened by the extent of her fatigue after even this short meeting. She took the proffered chair, not knowing if she would ever be free of it or him.

TWENTY-TWO

STORM SAT AT THE small desk in the Faraday cage they had set up for her in the control room. The screen where she had watched the test of the Gatherer was dark, and a small number of technicians worked at their stations.

The cage was in the shape of a cylinder, the walls made up of a fine mesh that created a path directing any charges or fields into the ground, leaving a neutral space at its center. A narrow opening acted as the door, running from the base of the cylinder to a point just below the ceiling. It was better constructed and more sophisticated than the one she had made in the Yukon, the seamless mesh walls gleaming where they reflected light.

She could have moved in and out of the structure but so far, she had stayed inside its protection, the fields from the terminals and lights all the deterrents she needed to stay in one place.

She caught the technicians watching her when she looked up from the reports Wesley had provided. Their expressions were curious, if wary. She didn't mistake them for potential allies but that didn't mean they couldn't work together. Each of them with a different goal.

One of the staff was the blank-faced woman she had seen on her first visit, checking the rats in the cages closest to the Gatherer. She didn't smile, her black hair pulled back into a clip and didn't wear a uniform. The set of her mouth was less grim than it had been that first day, yet she moved tentatively, almost skittish, as she checked her screen and the report open beside her.

Abruptly she stood and approached Storm's cage, moving past it towards the coffee machine.

"Excuse me?" Storm called, the woman startling at Storm's voice. "I had a question about the data."

The woman hovered outside the narrow opening, coming to the edge of the enclosure but no further. She was in her thirties, with dark eyes, the hair in her clip thick and coarse. She looked tired. Harassed, almost.

Her name tag read Lillian and Storm smiled.

"Hi Lillian, it's nice to meet you."

Lillian seemed frozen on the spot, one hand shoved in her pocket, the other gripping the coffee mug. The legs of her jeans showed below the coat, their hem ending right above a pair of scuffed light blue crocs. Several decals had been attached to the holes in the shoes, too faded to be identifiable.

"Did you want to come in?" said Storm. "It doesn't hurt."

Storm lifted her chin to indicate the mesh walls but her attempt at humor didn't register. She pointed to a graph in the report with an exponential upward curve.

"It shows here that the capacity of the gathering process is exponential as the size of the crystal structure increases."

Lillian still hovered beyond the entrance, a frown creasing her forehead, her gaze not quite focused. "Major Wesley can answer any questions you have."

The mesh cast a broken shadow across Lillian's face, exposing the darkness beneath, whatever was haunting her having come home to rest.

"Is he here?"

Storm looked towards the row of terminals and Lillian's gaze followed hers, but they weren't fooling each other. They both knew he wasn't.

"He's off-site this morning."

It surprised her that Wesley would leave her unattended on her first day at the lab.

THE GATHERER

"Would you mind? I'm trying to understand the changes that were made to the Gatherer to increase its capacity. I would have liked to run a model myself but—"

"You'll have to wait until he comes back."

She turned and walked away, providing Storm with a view of the back of her white lab coat.

Storm pursed her lips. Why go to the trouble of setting up the Faraday cage in the control room if he wasn't going to allow her to interact? He could have just brought the documents she needed to her room.

Three other technicians besides Lillian, occupied the room, all male, two middle-aged and one, with a ponytail, young enough to be in his twenties. They all stared intently at their screens and she would have loved to know what they were working on. She could see flashes of the occasional graph or a window open while a process ran, but they could have been working on something completely unrelated to the Gatherer and she would never know. Except nothing happened here that wasn't about the Gatherer. The entire, massive building was dedicated to the Gatherer and its secrets.

She refocused on the data, determined to find the pathway that would allow her to stop it permanently. The material that Wesley had provided formed a pile of paper over an inch high, much of it focused on the early data on how the Gatherer operated and it was taking her significant time to sift through to find where it failed.

"Can I get you a coffee?"

Storm lifted her head to Lillian standing in the opening.

"That would be great."

She didn't drink coffee since her nerves couldn't handle the stimulation. Lillian's movements were slow and precise at the coffee machine. How much of that was temperament and how much was a result of being immersed in this lab? The other techs didn't appear to be affected, yet they didn't move around as much as Lillian and that might be how they coped.

Lillian stepped into the enclosure, the rise of steam off the cup accompanied by the bitter smell. Her gaze lifted to the high walls of the enclosure, turning in a circle to see the whole circumference.

She moved a stack of papers aside and placed the coffee next to Storm, the liquid black and clear. She hadn't even asked how Storm liked it.

"Thank you."

Lillian nodded before waving her hand in the general shape of the cylinder. "Do you notice a difference?"

"I do."

She didn't mention that it didn't stop the traces of despair from licking at her thoughts, like a waft of smoke from a smoldering fire.

"Do you?" asked Storm.

Lillian glanced at her before she looked away. "No. I'm not one of the – afflicted."

She had paused before using the word, and when she did it had come out dismissive and afraid. She moved away from the desk, towards the opening.

"I had a question," said Storm. "Since you're here."

Lillian hesitated, looked over her shoulder towards the other technicians.

Storm flipped to a different page than the one she had been looking at earlier. "It shows here that the specimens' health declines more rapidly as time progresses. Does this happen to all the subjects?"

Lillian came back to the desk slowly and looked down at the graph. Storm didn't think she was actually seeing what was there, her gaze shifting sideways as if distracted by whatever had brought her in.

Storm flipped further through the printout, the pages flicking quietly, before she stopped at another graph that showed the response of the rats.

"It's more pronounced in the rats." Her revulsion swelled whenever she remembered their small, ravaged bodies. "Is this something that is being pursued?"

Lillian rested her finger below the graph. It took her a few moments to respond. "I noticed it first in the plants. Since that's my area."

Storm thought of the single test Daniel had run on a rabbit. She'd never heard what, if anything, he had learned.

"We didn't do this kind of testing," said Storm.

Lillian nodded as if Storm had confirmed something.

"It wasn't necessary until they built the larger capacities," said Lillian.

Storm looked up at her, but Lillian kept her gaze on the page. Was she talking about the plague? Or was it the despair? She was sure Lillian felt it but was she even aware?

Lillian flipped through the pages, the faintest smell of citrus coming off her clothes. She stopped at an entire page of data, showing the amplitude of the rats' electrical activity in the different rings of the test area.

"It's getting bigger."

Lillian didn't indicate the graph but Storm understood.

"You're talking about the despair."

Lillian moved the coffee mug to the side and pulled the pages closer. Anyone watching would assume they were discussing the data. She flipped to another page showing the mortality rate of the plants.

"I hadn't named it yet," said Lillian. But she was nodding, accepting Storm's analysis.

"Is it being investigated? Is Wesley aware?"

She wore a shiny gold stud in her ear, the back mismatched silver.

"I've told them about it, but I don't think they understood what it is. Or they aren't listening."

"But you feel it?"

Lillian nodded, for the first time letting her gaze drift to Storm's.

"And so do you."

Storm nodded. She didn't know how Lillian had known, but she had recognized Storm's reaction. Both of them able to see it in the other.

"What do you mean, it's getting bigger?" said Storm.

Lillian looked past the mesh to the other technicians and the mosaic of green and brown inside the test area.

"I could show you. If you can manage it."

The despair was an emotional pain, not physical. But perhaps that was Lillian's point. Did the rats die faster because they had lost the will to live? Yet the plants didn't feel, so why would they exhibit the same pattern?

"I can."

"I'll need to get permission."

Lillian stepped away, then turned back.

"Pay attention as we get closer to the middle. Last week it was at row ten. This week it's at row twelve."

She wanted to ask if Lillian had mapped it out, how she knew, but she was already through the opening. She spoke with the young man with the ponytail, who looked at Storm repeatedly as he shook his head. Eventually, though not happily, he picked up the phone and made a call. Lillian returned to the cage and when he pushed his shoulders through the opening, sweat glistened on his upper lip. His face was wide and flat, his eyes too far apart.

"They are replacing the Gatherers today so there won't be much to see but we can take you on the same route you saw earlier."

"Thank you."

She stood, taking the arm Lillian offered as support, even as she marveled at the ease of moving, like a lock had been released from her muscles. The wheelchair was parked outside the cage, and she was aware of the faint fields from the terminals as she sank into it.

She was getting better, the burn of her nerves a step down from her earlier reaction. The young man pushed the chair, taking a direct route to the door. She held up a hand to stop him.

"We need to go around, away from the terminals."

He stopped and swung in a sharp turn, his maneuvering rougher than Wesley.

"I'm Kevin."

THE GATHERER

The introduction was abrupt, almost rude, but she didn't pay attention. She had known countless young men like him at school, unable to comprehend even the simplest social graces.

"It's nice to meet you, Kevin."

Lillian held the door and Storm was assaulted by the dense moistness of the air and the heartbreaking rings of plants in different stages of death. A long, shriveled leaf lay in the aisle in the outer ring, the faintest of crunches audible as they rolled over it. She kept her awareness tuned, waiting for the change that would prove Lillian's assertion that the despair was spreading and existing independent of the Gatherer operation.

There were no people in the testing space, the circle green at the outer edges before it turned brown then white at the inner rings. The whir of a forklift at the center was the only noise in the hushed silence. There were more fallen leaves as they drew closer to the center and the clear space where the forklift had lifted the Gatherer and was carrying it towards a bay door at the far end. A leaf caught in the wheel swished quietly as it was pulled along the concrete.

Lillian walked close beside her and Storm had a sudden memory of walking beside Maria, the low brush of the marsh stretched out around them. There had been mist in the trees and she felt the exhaustion again and the certainty they would never find their way out. She hadn't known if she could trust Maria, at that point not recognizing her razor-sharp intensity as grief for Havernal, her commander. And had their flight made a difference? Maria gone off to find Ari with an idea that was a long way off of a solution, the Gatherer's power having expanded and grown so that it was a different device than the one Storm had created, more loyal to its new masters than it was to her. She doubted she would be able to do anything about it, the world and the destruction of it too big, too corrupted for her to—

She counted the rows from the middle. Eleven. And her thoughts had turned dark when they had entered the sphere of number twelve.

She looked up at Lillian, her drawn face as desolate as Storm's thoughts.

Lillian nodded in acknowledgement.

The leaves on the plants were white, their shriveled ends like dead fingers hanging over the edge of the planters. The only green leaves were behind them, faded and struggling, in the outer rings.

She shook her head, struggling to rise above the hopelessness, to step outside herself and recognize it for what it was.

Lillian's shoulders had slumped, and Kevin's pace had slowed, his feet dragging with each step. It felt as if she were choking, the weight of the despair so strong it was crushing every thought. They reached the center where the Gatherer had been, the conduits that had connected to the bottom like huge leeches sucking the life out of it and everything around it. She wanted to bury her head in her hands, protect herself from what felt like an attack. And then they were moving away from the center and the world lightened. She took a deep breath, running a hand over her face, surprised to find it wet from tears. Lillian was bent over as if she could barely stand.

When they reached the outer edge, Lillian stood taller, but still stooped, not fully recovered from the burden. Even Kevin was subdued, the self-importance gone from his voice.

"Is that what you wanted to see?" he asked.

"Yes. Thanks." Storm's voice was raw, rife with the experienced grief. "How long have these tests been going on?"

Kevin hesitated and looked to Lillian.

"Six months," said Lillian.

"And how many Gatherers have you had to replace?"

Lillian and Kevin were in a stand-off, either not permitted or unsure on what they could share.

"You wanted to see the rats as well, didn't you?" Kevin pushed her towards the next door.

Lillian didn't immediately follow, and Storm could see her struggle. No one would willingly immerse themselves back in that hopelessness.

Kevin was already moving through the next door, pushing into the stench of animals, manure and misery.

The sensation was stronger here, the thickness of the despair arriving hard and fast at the twelfth ring. Many of the animals had curled into tiny balls of fur in the corner of their cages. She fought the urge to sob, the desolation in those cowering balls a reflection of her own despondence.

How could she have left Daniel behind? The rest of the team was dead before she had had a chance to say good-bye. Every rash and twitch of the afflicted in that warehouse was hers. All of it leading directly back to her guilt.

The rats in the inner circle weren't curled into balls, but stretched out in death, tiny paws curled in mid-anguish. She was hunching low in her chair, her shoulders barely above her knees. The urge to cover her head with her hands and give-in was overpowering.

She gripped the arm rests and forced herself to sit up and face the memories as a by-product of this despair. They were vibrant and beyond real, so terrible that you could barely look away.

Lillian had her hand on Storm's shoulder, not to comfort, but to keep herself erect and moving forward. Was she able to step away from the despair, or was she in its thrall?

This Gatherer looked more ragged, one of the panels removed to reveal the inner workings. The concave dish and its crystal structure were a hundred times the size of her original design, and with a darkness to it like a blown fuse.

Something at the back of her mind was trying to tell her something, connecting that darkness to something she already knew but the thought wouldn't form.

Kevin stopped the chair and walked angrily to the panel lying on the ground. He slammed it back into place, hit it with the heel of his palm to lodge it back in. His face was flushed, his jaw so tight it jutted out of his chin. She cowered away as if he would strike her. Her fear derailed the desolation long enough for a thought to break through: Anger wasn't far from despair, if you were still fighting.

By the time they reached the outer circle, she could barely hold her head up. Her thoughts had cleared, the hopelessness reduced to a sadness, yet she was battered and worn, that trip delivering enough emotional sorrow for a lifetime.

They pushed through another set of doors, bursting into the cool, smoothness of a corridor she recognized. The one Wesley had followed to take her to her room. They traveled the slow curve of the metal wall back towards the control room, their pace faster, as if Kevin was trying to outrun what he had felt in the test area. Lillian lagged behind them, out of Storm's sight.

What could possibly create that kind of response? It was connected to the Gatherer, but that wasn't the question. It was how the process, designed to draw off energy and condense it into a usable form, was somehow drawing off something deeper and more essential. She felt a prickling along her skin, and not from any field. It was an awareness, dark and threatening, of whatever the corrupted Gatherers had unleashed.

They entered the control room in silence, Kevin positioning her outside the cage. Lillian was beckoned over by one of the other technicians, the two of them re-entering the room of plants. What would it take to go in and out of that devastation all day?

"I'd like to go back to my room."

Kevin looked more haggard than when he first pushed his shoulders into the enclosure, as if he hadn't slept in days.

"We don't—" He sighed with pure weariness. "I'll see what I can do."

It was a soldier who came for her. One of the armed guards that stood at the entry points between areas. There was a neutrality to his expression that was as frightening as Lillian's.

She had hoped to exchange a glance with Lillian before she left, something to show her support and let her know she had felt the pool of despair. She saw her in the midst of the wilted plants, before the edge of the window cut off her view.

TWENTY-THREE

MARIA CROUCHED BEHIND A tree trunk, out of sight of the lights that marked the path through the night-time grove. The patrols were less frequent than she had expected, most of the soldiers' efforts focused on securing the perimeter now that the protesters had been removed.

She moved away from the path, towards the south side of the campus, where she could see the contrasting silhouettes of the manufacturing center and the test facility Adams had told her about. Her stomach was hollow with hunger, her mouth parched with thirst. She picked a blade of grass and chewed on the end.

She moved parallel to the path, walking half-blind between the spots of light from the lamps. The consistent strike of waves against the shore sounded on one side, but her attention remained on the quiet coming from the front gate and the entire complex.

There would be several guards at the gate, if not more, but it was the lone patrollers she had seen from her perch above the trees that worried her. Their footsteps and shadows would be as hard to notice as her own.

The two guards she had noted earlier stood at the main door of the test facility. The side facing her was unprotected with not a door or even ventilation grate breaking its surface. It was the length of at least a football field, the height more than a warehouse. The entire structure was painted matte black so that if the manufacturing center hadn't been behind it, it wouldn't have been more than a starless shadow against the night sky.

The door to the building opened and the guards stepped aside to let two women pass. Both wore fatigues and carried pistols at their waists. They spoke briefly to the guards, their stances relaxed, as if they knew them. The women moved away, their farewells a brief, muffled disturbance before the compound settled back into quiet. Was Storm in there?

Maria moved along the edge of the grove, the trees curving back towards the compound's side entrance, drawing her away from the building. There was a sound in the trees behind her and she dropped into a crouch. The noise had come from the ground, an impact made by something heavier than a squirrel.

She kept her breathing shallow as she listened to the absence of rustling in the grove. She heard another footstep, aware of the strange stillness in the trees. There was a movement on her right and she saw a silhouette moving between tree trunks with a rifle held in front.

She crouched lower, ducking her head to hide the glow of her skin. She couldn't make out much more than his outline. He stopped, looking out towards the ocean, the horizon black. He couldn't have seen her or he wouldn't have left himself so exposed.

There was the sudden smell of cigarette smoke, its burn dry in the grove's dampness. The tip rose, glowed brighter, and lowered, showing the faint features of a young man. Smoking on patrol was wrong on so many levels, which meant they must have brought whoever they had close at hand for security. She heard voices coming from the entrance again, the grove providing cover for both her and the soldier.

Eventually, he ground the butt into the dirt and moved away. Part of her wanted to give the kid shit for being so stupid. Most of her was grateful for it.

She gave him a several minute head start and then followed, keeping to the edge. The maintenance shed had been back towards the side entrance and the one place she might get water and food without being seen. She stopped when she had gone as far as she could in the shelter of the trees. The lawnmowers and maintenance trucks were parked in a neat row on the other side of an open area that was as wide as a double lane highway. It would be impossible not to be seen when she crossed it.

An outside faucet stuck out along one wall of the shed, taunting her from across the open area.

Towards the ocean, a soldier faced away from her, his stance revealing he held a rifle, just like the others. No other soldiers were in sight, the darkness at the edge of the compound deeper and closer on her skin. She moved back a few steps and felt along the cool dampness of the forest floor through leaves, twigs and painfully sharp thorns until she found what she needed. A branch about the width of a rifle, her grip around its girth close, if not exact. It was too long, and she bent it slowly, pushing the break into the earth to muffle the crack of wood.

The weight of the stick was close to what she needed, the length not far off, the rest of it completely hopeless except when viewed from a distance. It would have to do. The night was growing old and she wasn't going back up that tree without food and water.

She chose her exit point carefully, slipping into the stance and mindset of being on patrol before she left the trees. She imagined she was stepping into the streets of Kabul. Her pace was slow and careful, eyes continually alert for threats.

The grass gave beneath her feet, her back prickling with cold and the certainty she wasn't fooling anyone. She gripped the rifle harder, pretending it wasn't rough tree bark she was holding but the familiar weight of a C7.

She forced herself to put one foot in front of the next. Walk like she was meant to be there. A searcher, not the target.

The soldier near the ocean looked towards her and she adjusted her body position to block the branch, still moving forward like she was meant to be there. A cold sweat broke out on her sides as he turned away. Another soldier stood on the roadway that came from the side entrance. If he was the soldier from the grove, she couldn't recognize him at this distance, and that gave her a degree of comfort. Well – if not comfort, at least it postponed a desperate attempt at escape.

She had crossed halfway across the open space, the safety of the grove twenty paces behind her, the shelter in the maintenance shed not guaranteed. Same pace, same alertness. Just another patrol in a long night. She could imagine the ridicule if her team saw her. They might even be watching her, recognizing her from across the green. The stick was so much worse than the ancient hunting rifle she had carried when they first caught her.

She was close enough to the building she could see the wet spot beneath the faucet where it dripped onto the pavement. It took all her effort not to attach her mouth to the spigot and let it gush down her throat.

The soldier towards the ocean lifted a walkie-talkie off his hip and spoke into it. Should she run?

She changed her trajectory ever so carefully towards the side of the building away from him. He replaced the walkie-talkie and stayed facing the ocean. She listened for a sudden change in the quiet of the compound, vehicles starting up or soldiers on the move.

She was in front of the main entrance, moving away from the seduction of the faucet. She moved methodically towards the other side. It was darker around the corner, and she felt the slightest easing of tension as she passed into the shadow. She took a moment to breathe. And listen. The night's rhythm unbroken.

For a moment, she wished there was someone to tell that she had fooled them with a stick. Amanda would appreciate it, but it was Storm she wanted to tell.

She passed a closed window on her way to the back of the shed where the sound of the ocean was louder, the white caps of the waves marking the shoreline. It was empty of sentries, the moon casting a long straight beam along the top of the water, seeming to end at the two doors. One was a large, rolling door and the other a locked utility door. She tossed her stick behind an overgrown shrub.

THE GATHERER

She pulled at the utility door, its solid resistance destroying any chance she had of forcing it open. The larger door was secured to the ground by a padlock through a metal ring . She pulled at it in frustration, already turning back to the window.

As she turned, the lock twisted and she felt the clasp release, the curve of metal swinging free in her hand. She looked around, suspecting it was a trap. But there was only that same beam of light on the water and the empty stretch of grass. She said a brief prayer to the God of lazy maintenance staff.

She slid it out of the ring and laid it carefully on the ground. With controlled force, she inched the door upwards. The vibrations of each move rippled through the sheet metal. She expected at any moment someone would step around the corner, or there would be a sudden blow to the back of her head.

When the gap was large enough, she slid underneath, the concrete cold on her back, the interior dark and still. She waited several moments for her eyes to adjust, and then eased the door closed. The air smelled of mowed grass and earth with an underlying scent of food. Her stomach growled. A row of windows around the upper edge allowed the dim light that outlined the bulk of some kind of machinery taking up most of the floor.

Two squares of glass along the back wall refracted her distorted shadow back at her. She approached carefully, skirting around the bulk of the machine – a lawnmower, by the smell.

Beyond the first door, the shapes of four chairs emerged from the shadows, arranged around a square table. There was a small kitchenette against the wall and the hum of the fridge from the corner. She closed the door and made for the sink, taking huge gulps directly from the tap. The initial pain of swallowing was followed by pure, cool heaven.

She wiped her chin as she moved to the refrigerator, the stark white interior mainly empty but for an old pizza box, a half-eaten cake, and a container of coleslaw with a few dregs remaining.

She grabbed two slices of pizza and swallowed big chunks as she stood in the shadow cast by the moonlight through the window. The view showed the route along the hedge she had just taken, not the wider view of the compound and the guards – which she would have preferred. A glint of light reflected off the ocean beyond the hedge, near where the perimeter fence extended out into the ocean, preventing anyone from gaining access without a boat or a strong breaststroke.

She grabbed another slice and the coleslaw and carried them into the open area, walking quietly to better hear any noise from outside. She had expected the second room to be a storeroom and was surprised when the door opened onto an office with a large monitor sitting on the desk, conscious of the hard square at her breastbone, from the small SD card Amanda had given her.

There was little floor space between boxes and discarded equipment, forcing Maria to navigate a narrow path to the desk. Shelves lined the walls, displaying dusty, old manuals and discarded machine parts. The smell of dirt and engine oil filled the room.

The desk chair had been worn in by someone larger than her and she felt reduced in size by its ill-fitting contours. She tapped the keyboard and the screen brightened immediately, showing a spectacular aerial view of the compound with a login window at its center. She checked over her shoulder, confirming the glow of the screen was hidden from any windows, before she flipped up the strap of her bra and drew out the card, the small square warm from her body heat.

She powered down the computer, the screen flashing to dark, and let it sit for several seconds before she slid the card into the SD port. The silence in the shed was complete, her every move echoing around her. She gently pressed the power button, the whir and clicks of the start-up process pushing into the quiet.

She held her breath as the LED above the port flashed, watching it flicker as a screen of code appeared and immediately went blank. Had she just sent an alarm to someone at headquarters announcing she was here? Or was whatever program Amanda had put on that tiny piece of hardware even now streaming through the compound's network, giving her a foothold in the entire system? The monitor flashed again before opening onto a screen that looked remarkably like the one she had seen at Amanda's.

She placed her fingertips on the keyboard and carefully typed.

Welcome to paradise.

She waited for what felt like several minutes, the LED continuing to flash, but it was likely less than thirty seconds.

Took you long enough.

Maria smirked as she started to type her reply: *Where is she?*

Halfway into the second word, the window disappeared, and the screen went blank, before it began to flicker, blurting bits of code. She pictured Amanda at her wall of screens, her fingers a blur on the keyboard as she wormed her way past firewalls and verifications.

If there even were any.

The first rule of protecting energy assets, before the Gatherer, had always been a physical barrier to keep attackers out. But if your attacker was inside your perimeter already past the fortifications, would you expect to find them there?

The screen flickered and flashed, protesting whatever Amanda was forcing it to do. Maria had a weird sympathy for it, having once been at the receiving end of that control.

Taking her coleslaw with her, she shoveled spoonfuls into her mouth as she checked the side window. The sky was solid black, with no hint of the day that was to come, and no soldiers in view.

It felt as if she was wildly waving a lighted flare above her head, yet the compound barely breathed, the area as still as if the plague had never happened.

She replaced the empty container in the fridge and wiped the spoon on her pants before returning it to the drawer.

She was moving faster now, aware that the time when she should have left had already come and gone. The office felt different with the screen alive, as if all the features of the room had been drawn into that shimmering rectangle.

The image finally stilled and formed into a diagram that showed an overview of the compound. A red beacon flashed dully in one corner within the perimeter of a building she had only seen the corner of from her perch. She felt the air go out of her, at seeing Storm's location, the red beacon sending jolts of urgency along her nerves. It was better than seeing a lighthouse in a storm or the searchlight of a helicopter coming to take you home.

She refocused on the diagram, making sure she wasn't missing any details, though there was little information beyond the flashing dot. It showed Storm in a smaller, more accessible building which would make her easier to find, and easier for them to guard. The monitor went dark for an instant before the original login screen with the aerial photo returned.

She slid the SD card from its port and returned the chair to its original position, knowing that while the screen showed its normal login, Amanda was burrowing into the corporation's network, following connections as she uncovered whatever they had left exposed. She wished she could follow her, learn what she did, but she would have to wait and pray for a time when Amanda would be able to tell her what she had found.

TWENTY-FOUR

Storm lay on her back surrounded in darkness. She had no way to gauge the time of day buried in the earth, but the memory of the rats was still so strong it felt like it had been minutes instead of hours since she had left them behind. The only thing that reached her down the long stairs and through the open door was an undisturbed stillness.

The night had once been her domain, her best work done in the remotest hours of the day. She hadn't felt that clarity since being sick and she thrilled at being awake now, even if it was dampened by her awareness of its fragility.

She rolled onto her side and sat up, testing the strength of her legs as she stood. With her hands in front of her, she walked carefully through the darkness, feeling along the wall until she found the crack of the door and the cold metal of the door handle. She climbed carefully, moving upward into a lighter grade of darkness, her heart pulsing and her breathing labored when she reached the top. She had paused several times, refusing to resort to her hands and knees and had managed the entire set without crawling. She smiled into the empty corridor, wishing there was someone she could tell this astounding news. Wesley would quiz her, pester her for details, but he wouldn't care how good it felt to be able to climb these stairs alone, the trajectory of her health no longer straight down.

Moonlight from the window at the far end of the corridor gleamed on the tiles, shining a light on the brighter end of the building compared to the deep darkness where she stood. She by-passed the square shape of her wheelchair, running her fingers along the cool smoothness of the wall to guide her.

The clunk and release of the double doors echoed down the hall and out into the entire building. The hardness of the echo chilled her, the disturbance encountering nothing that would interrupt its path, she the only inhabitant in a building meant for so many more.

She stopped at the third door where she had first seen Valerie and Camille and eased it open, the room slowly coming into focus as her eyes adjusted to the deeper darkness. Moonlight glinted on the steel rail of the empty bed, the mattress stripped and bare, and a beam cut across the top of the empty table as if there had never been anyone there at all.

The emptiness frightened her and she pulled back, closing the door behind her. She moved faster through the building, feeling the need to put distance between herself and the finality of it. In the foyer, the light from outside was bright enough to define the handrail below the window. The grass and trees in the grove were brighter still, a stage lighted for the soldiers that were equally defined. Two stood in the parking lot towards the front gate. One at the pathway that led into the grove. Another was outside the door at the bottom of the ramp, a guard meant for her. She would have liked to continue onto the grass, wander the grounds as she had once done, but it wouldn't be tonight.

She gave the elevator at the base of the stairs a wide berth though she detected no field. The stairs leading up were rough under her feet, and she used the railing for balance and support. When she reached the landing, another window faced the ocean, trees to the left, the maintenance shed a dim outline in the distance.

She climbed further, slowing to catch her breath as she reached the second floor. The stairs ended at another open area with ceiling-high windows looking towards the front gate. She moved soundlessly across the cold tiles, stepping into the brightness that streamed in the window. The brightness was more than moonlight, coming from floodlights that blazed on the front gate. It took her several moments to understand what she was seeing, though the floodlights showed everything in stark detail. Over a dozen guards stood inside the gate, more ran out on either side along the perimeter fence, at least two dozen within view. It was what was beyond the gate that made her step closer, the railing at her hips stopping her from going further.

The roadway had room for two vehicles to pass going in and out of the compound, and a pull-out lane for several more if required. All of the pavement, all of the space, was filled with people, sitting, standing, holding signs, all facing towards her. An open lane had been left through the crowd, with enough room to allow a single vehicle to pass. A man, in fatigues, stood at the mid-point, facing the guards. The fatigues suggested military, or at least combat, except he was far different from the soldiers on this side of the barrier. The pointed fingers and angry words she couldn't hear marked him as the chosen voice of the protesters, or perhaps himself.

There were hundreds of them, maybe a thousand, spread out along the fence. There could have even been more, the view blocked by the lush gardens and the trees. She felt weightless and out of breath, fixated on the anger of that single man, and the ripples of it that echoed through the crowd.

She should be out there, standing in front of them and explaining, or at least promising to make it right. But could she even do that? Or would it just be more lies?

The tests on the plants and rats were to gauge the limits of the Gatherer, how much damage it could do and how it did that damage. They had called this a treatment facility but she was beginning to understand she was the only patient still being treated. And that treatment often felt more like an experiment.

The single protester approached the gate, the soldiers shifting positions as he drew nearer. She turned to descend the stairs and demand she be allowed to talk to him, to all of them, but they would never allow her that. She watched him face off against a force he could never beat.

The hopelessness of it deflated her, robbed her of that brief period of energy, yet it was different than what she had felt in the lab with the rats and plants. This sadness came from inside of her, a response to the conflict and fear she had delivered into these people's lives.

The desolation in the lab had been an external force that sucked everyone and everything in the vicinity into its depths. And it was growing. She saw again the burnt-out crystals of the Gatherer that had been carted away. Burnt-out shells of what they had once been. She returned to the original process of the Gatherer, trying to see what could be happening that could create the despair. It was the permanence of it she didn't understand. During the process, she could at least conceptualize that something in the way it gathered energy would have an emotional component; except why would it still be there when it stopped? Even after the Gatherer had destroyed itself by reaching too far and too high?

The protester paced in front of the gate, taunting the guards. They didn't move, their positions set and held regardless of what the protesters said or did.

Was that how it was for the despair? Once it was locked in, it couldn't be dislodged? Yet it didn't make sense. What could it possibly be locked into? This was energy, there wouldn't be anything to hold onto.

She stiffened at the sound of voices below her from outside. They were arguing, one of them low and measured, the other higher and more frantic. She stayed locked in place, the view of the gate retreating and replaced by an awareness of the confined emptiness of the building, nowhere to go where she wouldn't be found.

She heard the door open and soft quick footsteps hurry down the first floor hall. Not the boots of a soldier, but someone smaller, lighter, headed for her room.

The guards at the gate hadn't moved, and the soldiers along the paths stood absolutely still. Whoever had arrived was known to them, had clearance to be here.

THE GATHERER

After the clang of the double doors, the silence returned. They would find her eventually and she strangely had no fear. Her time of hiding was over.

She moved away from the window and down the stairs, stopping at the first landing, knowing the one who sought her would return when they found her room empty. It could be Wesley, though the stride hadn't matched his, or her mother's. For a moment, she thought it could be Valerie but she wouldn't be here without her daughter and likely couldn't walk at that speed.

Even though she was expecting it, the slam of the doors of the person returning startled her, and she felt the unexpected distress of her heartbeat, her body still not equipped for sudden stressors or attacks.

The foyer was bright with moonlight, the footsteps disturbing the tranquility as they approached. He charged into the brightly lit area, small and lithe and frenetic, his head down as he made for the exit.

She stepped into view, opening her mouth to call to him, when he looked up. He stopped, his expression a mixture of relief and apprehension.

"Ari."

"Storm."

"You came."

He nodded, as speechless as she was, because there was so much to say. Muscles bulged beneath his shirt where they hadn't been before, a broad chest straining against his well-fitted shirt. He had cut his hair and his skin glowed, a ridge of light highlighting a full healthy cheekbone.

"It's good to see you." She didn't add "so healthy," though that was all she could think as she stared, her mind filled with the image of Daniel's emaciated body. "Did my mother send you?" Her mother had known where he was. Or had found him.

"It won't be long before someone sees that I am here," he said.

She followed his gaze to the blackened dome that hid a video camera. She had a flash of irritation at her own stupidity. It was how

Wesley had known to come find her when she had been with Valerie and Camille.

"Can they hear us?" she asked.

"In the rooms. But not here."

She beckoned him to follow her up the stairs, needing distance from the guard, if not the cameras.

They stopped at the second landing, looking out over the stand-off at the gate, and the continual shifting and changing of the crowd. His short hair made him seem smaller, more conservative than the thick black mane he had once had.

"I'm surprised you came back."

He tried to say it casually, but there was an accusation there.

"Because you thought I was dead, or because you thought I didn't care?"

He exhaled sharply. Her abruptness had caught him off guard, yet what did he expect? They had never been anything but blunt with each other.

"Both."

There were protesters visible through the trees on the far right, the crowd larger than she had thought.

"I would have come back sooner if I had known," she said.

She didn't indicate the crowd but it filled their view, impossible to ignore.

"You knew before you left."

Her grip tightened on the rail. "Is that why you came here? To accuse me?"

She wondered what he had been through, that would make him so intent on laying blame.

"No."

He seemed to collect himself, had at least the sense to look chagrined.

"We were all sick, but we thought it was stress. None of our symptoms were the same," she said.

"We ignored what we didn't want to see."

A series of soldiers lined the perimeter as far as she could see, immobile amidst trees and bushes that swayed in the wind.

"Maybe."

"If you hadn't all taken off," said Ari, "we would have seen it sooner and might have been able to stop it."

"Even if we had stayed, after the fire we weren't together. We wouldn't have seen it."

"I would have."

His certainty was unyielding, using it as a shield to obscure what had really happened. She resented that he would accuse her of this, when they had all been part of it, made the decisions together.

"We can't change it now," she said.

She felt strangely disconnected in the stillness of the building, while the wind battered the crowd and the soldiers with equal fury.

"Then why did you come back?"

The entire compound seemed to be swaying, their place on the landing the only point of stillness.

"To stop it."

"Better late than never."

She stepped away from him, moving back towards the stairs leading down.

He moved quickly, stood in front of her, the health evident in every movement becoming an irritation.

"Storm. Wait."

His face was different now, not trying to hide the pain or the loss.

"We all wanted it to turn out differently." She said it gently, understanding his pain better than anyone else.

He gestured back towards the window.

She paused before conceding, taking the moment to control her own pain and anger. She moved back to the window, unsure whether she should, felt the vertigo of the shifting landscape. Ari stood beside her.

"Kowalski came to see me," he said.

She turned to him quickly, his words sending a jolt of excitement through her.

"When? Is she safe?"

He was watching her carefully.

"Didn't you detest that woman?"

Maria had been obnoxious when she had first come to the lab with Havernal. Storm had called her vulgar and uncouth, but what she really had felt was fear.

"Nobody is the same person they were anymore," said Storm.

His nod surprised her.

"She came to the house but I don't know where she went. There were people looking for her."

"Did they find her?"

Her hands were sweating on the railing and she eased off the grip.

He shrugged, her fate not his concern.

"Did she deliver my message about the imperfections?"

One of the protesters waved a sign that read, 'We know better.'

"We're way beyond that now," he said.

"I know."

It was naïve that she had thought her design element would have remained secret. And she wondered how much more of her knowledge was out of date, irrelevant in this new world.

"I was sorry to hear about Daniel."

He spoke with a heaviness, a recognition perhaps that they were the only two left standing. The memories of Daniel, Callan and Jana crowded around them.

"How did you know?"

The protesters could have announced his death or the corporation could truly know everything. Inside this building, inside the compound she knew nothing at all.

"Kowalski told me."

"He built a lab in a decommissioned sub-station. Was trying to find a solution even though—"

THE GATHERER

She stumbled on the words. He had known it was killing him and kept going.

"That sounds like Daniel," said Ari.

For an instant they paused, lost in the memories of their friends.

"There has to be a way to stop it."

The tension returned to his body, a tightening of his hands on the rail, the slight turning away from her. The sensation was so familiar she had a memory of him from the lab, his back turned to the rest of them, immersed in his programming.

"The military controls the entire compound," he said. "We have to work with them, or they will shut us out of everything. If we are outside of this," he waved his hand to indicate the perimeter and the soldiers, "we won't be able to do anything."

"Even if it means helping them build a weapon?"

He turned back to her, his shadow mimicking the shift on the floor behind him.

"You've seen it?"

"Yes."

He exhaled, seemed suddenly lighter, his gaze lifting up to the bright sphere of the moon. "I'd only heard rumours."

It seemed impossible that he could be here and not know the carnage of rats and cows that was being created within their line of sight.

"It kills instantly," she said. "Within a radius of about fifty yards."

He still had his gaze on the sky, above the stand-off at the gate. "We always knew there was untapped potential. We just never dreamed how much."

There was so much they hadn't seen, including how much their chance invention would ruin their lives. Though not Ari, who seemed healthier than he ever had.

"Do you know why you didn't get sick?"

Tiles in shades of gray formed a mosaic on the wall, a stepped design that lead nowhere.

"The only thing I could come up with is the fish."

She half laughed, checked to see if he was joking.

"What does that even mean?"

"The aquarium in the lab. I sat beside it all the time, it was between me and the test area. It's the only thing I could think of that was different than the rest of you."

She had stopped laughing, trying to see where his idea fit.

"They use ocean water as part of the cure."

He looked up at her, his eyes brighter, his mind struggling to find the same connections she was. "The effects are only temporary. It helps with the symptoms but it's not a cure."

They were silent, trying to make the pieces fit but it was elusive, coming from a place they still didn't understand.

"Is that what you're working on? A cure?" she asked.

The lone protester had returned, walking resolutely towards the gate. At least a dozen soldiers waited for him, and she could feel the desire on both sides for it to escalate, an opening for them to act.

"I've been working on limiting the operation of the Gatherer into a single channel. It's not a cure for what has already been done but it will stop any further damage from the ones that are out there."

"They aren't trying to limit it to a single channel," she said. "They're trying to expand it. You must know that."

He looked to the camera, perhaps wondering who was watching.

"After its release, I'll be moving over to apply the same principle to the larger Gatherers that you saw."

"And you're going to do it?"

His face was shadowed with a weariness she hadn't noticed under the health.

"I chose to stay here—"

She ignored the recrimination and perhaps he sensed that, for he seemed to lift himself and focus out beyond the window.

"—and do what I could. Which meant coming here and working with whoever held the greatest influence. At first it was your mother, but the military arrived shortly after, and since then I have been answering to them. They have incredible resources and whatever I ask for, I get. This firmware update we're sending out won't fix everything, but it will at least stop causing harm. And once I've done that, they'll allow me to move to the test area and start collaborating on the larger units. Applying what I've learned with the smaller units to the larger ones."

He had turned towards where the large black building would be, out of sight behind the wall.

"It's not a larger unit. It's a weapon," she said.

"That's one of its applications. But there are others, that could change the way we live. Bring us access to energy and processes that have been out of reach."

"And ways to kill."

He pressed his lips together, not able to hide his irritation.

"You and Daniel always believed that you could find a perfect energy source that would save the world. It doesn't exist. Every source has flaws and it's a matter of finding a balance between the benefits and the damage."

"That's not how the Gatherer was meant to be."

The protester had stopped several strides from the gate, his arms crossed.

"But that's what it is," he said. "Just like any other energy source, there are consequences to its use."

"The consequences are too high."

"Are they?" His voice had risen, echoing in the stairwell. "Worse than nuclear bombs, nuclear waste? You need to accept all of what we created. The good and the bad."

"I won't."

"Then you will be relegated to the sidelines. The new Gatherers and everything they achieve will be done without you. Is that what you want?"

His words felt like repeated blows to her body. Had he always been this kind of scientist? Clinically weighing the benefits against the damage and in some disconnected lab deciding the suffering would be worth it?

"Have you been to the dark zones?"

He shook his head, more in irritation than as a response.

"I'm not saying people aren't suffering, but we are fixing that. The Gatherer can still do all the things we imagined."

"So you haven't been." She looked up at the camera, didn't care who was watching or even if they listened.

"I saw Jana, when she was dying." His anger arrived quickly, in a sudden fierceness to his boy-like features. "If we'd seen this sooner I could have saved her."

His voice echoed back at her, neither of them attempting to lower their voices.

"It's too late to save the Gatherer," she said.

She thought of the despair that was spreading, the permanence of it, as she caught a movement in the corner of her eye. Wesley was speaking with one of the guards standing at the edge of the parking lot. In no hurry. Which meant he wasn't worried about what Ari would tell her. The information he had was useless to her.

"Wesley is coming."

She nodded towards him.

Ari watched his casual progress across the moonlit grass.

"He's a monster. Be careful."

The silence around them solidified, as if strengthening itself against the coming intrusion. She thought of the strange intimacy of Wesley's care for her, the possessiveness of the control.

Ari turned to her and spoke quickly, his anger gone.

"We could work together again. Make the Gatherer into what it should be."

"I don't want to fix it."

It was a familiar place for them, arguing over a decision, both of them intransigent. Other times they had found a middle point. This time she wasn't so sure.

They heard Wesley speaking with the guard below.

"It's not about what you believe. If you don't work with them they have no use for you."

Wesley's footsteps were climbing the ramp from the entrance.

Was he telling her that if he hadn't chosen to do what they wanted, he would have been killed?

"When are you sending out the firmware update?"

"Within a week. Two at the outside."

Wesley had started up the stairs and she stepped away from the window, her shadow vanishing as she moved out of the light.

"Let me know if it works."

"It will."

Wesley came to the first landing, uncharacteristically dishevelled in casual pants and a t-shirt. The darkness of the ocean spread out behind him.

"Mr. Chaudhary. Ms. Freeman." His formality was mocking, and she felt the confines of the facility tighten, her options growing smaller. "It's good to see the two of you reunited."

A guard stood behind him, the only visible feature dark hair and broad shoulders.

"But, Mr. Chaudhary, you aren't authorized to be here."

"Ms. Freeman asked me to come."

"Did she? And who facilitated that for you?"

His gaze had turned to Storm and she had a sudden fear for her mother, somewhere in the compound, as much a prisoner as she was. She wondered how much they could see of her, their faces blurred by shadows. The world she now lived in devoid of light.

Storm was aware of how unprepared she and Ari were for this kind of confrontation. They might be brilliant but in this situation that wasn't going to help.

"Could you escort Mr. Chaudhary back to the headquarters?" said Wesley.

The soldier stepped back, creating an opening for Ari. Ari hesitated before he stepped towards them, pausing briefly at the top of the steps.

"It was good to see you."

"You too."

As the footsteps of the two men retreated down the ramp, Wesley climbed to the landing where she stood.

"You made it up the stairs." He was standing too close, and she could hear him breathe. "You're getting better."

She retreated to the window. There was a brightness to the eastern sky, a change of shade, but it could have been the spill-off of the streetlights rather than the hope of a new day.

"But how long will it last?" she said.

He had moved forward, standing half in and out of the light.

"As long as I want it to."

The parking lot shone like a beacon against the lightening sky, its light a stubborn brightness against the broader lightening world. She laid her fingers against the cool glass as several guards moved past the gate and surrounded the single protester. In the time it took for her to understand what was going on, he was being escorted to a waiting vehicle, his hands in handcuffs, his shoulders slumped.

Wesley moved behind her.

"Shall we?"

TWENTY-FIVE

STORM FLOATED ON THE surface, the water shifting gently beneath her and the taste of salt on her lips. The water was the same temperature as her skin and she moved her hands occasionally to remind herself where she stopped and it began. A pad supported her head to keep the electrodes attached to her forehead out of the water. The leads from the electrodes ran across the floor to a separate shielded room where Wesley peered at a monitor, tapping keys and changing settings as he monitored her response.

She wondered if he could see her brain activity as she returned again to what Ari had said about the aquarium. The water could have provided some kind of barrier to the damage the Gatherer had done or stabilized the area around it after the tests had been run. She tried to remember the kinds of fish that had swam inside, whether the water had been saltwater or fresh.

There was a sudden change of light and Wesley came into view above her. He peeled the electrodes from her forehead and coiled the wire around his hand. Would water be able to block the damage of the larger Gatherers, if it actually had on the smaller ones?

She let herself slip fully into the water, only her face above the surface, absorbing every ounce of health she could from the salted bath. Was it repairing the burned synapses as she floated here, returning her body to its former health? She was almost afraid to pay attention to the subtle changes: her sleep that was deeper, the smallest of distances from feeling she was about to fall apart, and the ability to think beyond getting through the day or whether she would withstand the next exposure to a field. She skulled her hands below the surface and let them float upwards until the knuckles broke through the water's edge.

Wesley was at the side of the tub again, waving to indicate she needed to get out. She floated a second longer in a moment of pointless defiance.

A small kick propelled her to the ladder, her body protesting as she stood into the cooler air. Water ran off her body onto the ladder, the edge of the tub, and the floor. The soaked briefs and tank top clung to her thighs and breasts, so little left of her that wasn't exposed.

Wesley handed her a crisp, white towel, the threads rough on her skin where it wrapped her shoulders. He moved with the same matter-of-factness as before, as if she wasn't mostly naked in front of him. Waves still rebounded against the walls of the tub, crashing over each other at the center. She ran the towel down her legs, trying to conceal how good this nugget of strength felt.

"Did you add the salt?" said Storm.

He had turned away from her to grab her robe, trading it with her for the towel. There was a hesitation there and a reluctance to share. He watched her put on the robe, and tie up the waist, showing no embarrassment at this strange intimacy and yet he stumbled at sharing anything to do with the treatment. She stepped away from the small pool of water that had formed at her feet.

"It's ocean water, filtered for particulate."

She turned back to the tub, stunned at how therapeutic it had felt and at the new evidence of the power of the water. She checked the side of the tub for intake tubes, looked to the control room to see if that was the source.

"How often do you replenish it?"

Did her being in the water deplete its electrical balance? An exchange of energy at some level that would require the water to be replaced or rebalanced in the wider body of water?

He tossed her towel into a laundry hamper on his way to the door.

She circled to the top of the tub, her hand running along the edge.

"Does it need to be fresh?"

"You should get back to your room."

She rounded to the other side of the tub and he came beside her. An open channel ran from the tub to a cut out in the wall. Water ran through it, murky with the particulate that hadn't yet been filtered out. She squatted down and dipped her fingers into the surface, rubbing it between her fingers. It was wet, and cool, like all the water she had ever touched.

"How does it work?"

He had stayed at the top of the tub, as if part of him wanted to hold her back, while the other took a step forward.

"What made you think of it?" she said.

It was brilliant in its own simple way. Submersing the afflicted in the electrical neutrality of the water to try to force the system back into balance.

"We first noticed it in one of our patients. They were standing in the ocean three to four times a day because they swore it made them feel better. We experimented with different minerals and additives, but the ocean water worked best. Even saltwater we created wasn't as good."

The words spilled out of him, crowding together.

"Is it permanent?" she said.

He stood at the edge of the channel, his hands deep in his pockets as if to control his urge to touch the water as she was.

"We don't know. The patient who was soaking in it reverted once they were exposed to a field."

It had been the same with the web Romero had created at the warehouse. A temporary balm to ease symptoms. But not a cure. Something about the Gatherer altered the electrical balance of a person so definitively that it was permanently changed. So she would be temporarily better here, but not out in the world.

The channel ended at the wall and a door that would be opened when the channel needed to be refilled.

"How often do you change the water?"

"Everytime."

She nodded as she stood, distracted by the exchange of energy between water and patient.

She chose to let him push her in the wheelchair.

"How does it correlate to the other patients?"

They were out in the hall, rolling down the empty corridor towards the stairs to her room. They had seen no one on the way to the bath, and the corridors were still as empty, dark uninhabited rooms marking their path.

"We haven't tried to rehabilitate them."

She turned to look up at him, thinking of the suffering Camille and Valerie had endured, and the small gains she felt every day.

"Why not?"

The dark window of the rooms that had once held patients rolled by.

"We're verifying that it works before we administer it to the weaker patients."

"They're only going to get weaker if you don't treat them. No one was weaker than I was when I arrived."

She tried to stop the wheels of the chair and succeeded only in burning her hand from the rub of the tires. Valerie and her daughter had travelled thousands of miles in the hope of relief.

"It's not ready yet," said Wesley.

"You used it on me."

She had twisted in her chair again, holding on to one armrest so she could see his response. His chin was clean-shaven, a rash on his neck from his razor.

"They need to be treated," said Storm. "To at least have the hope that they can get better."

He spun the chair around and backed her through the door. She held onto the door if only to get his attention. He pulled her hand free with no effort at all. The door scraped against her legs as it closed.

"The patients aren't your concern."

The air was staler in the back half of the corridor, she and Wesley the only living beings that ever disturbed it. She tried to stand, annoyed at his relentless push forward, and succeeded only in jamming the chair into the back of her ankles.

"You asked for my help and this is what it looks like. I need to know all of it."

They approached the opening to her stairwell, a rectangle devoid of light.

"We didn't bring you here to save the world. You're here to find out why the large Gatherers are failing," said Wesley.

He bent over and set the brake on the chair, his shoulder brushing hers. He moved to lift her and she stopped him.

"I can walk."

He held her in the chair with a hand on her shoulder.

"You need to save your strength."

She hated that he was right, this staircase was not where she should spend her energy.

She let him thread his hands beneath her knees and shoulders, and lift her in a quick, easy movement. She hated his hands on her and she held her head away from his chest, not wanting to hear the vibrations of his voice.

They were at the top of the steps, the steep openness of it yawning below them. He held her above it, the same way he held her above the ravages of the Gatherer. All he had to do was let go and she would crash back into it, too injured and sick to climb out.

"The larger Gatherers are failing because you're pushing them past their capacity," she said.

He started down the first step, the rough gray of the staircase ceiling sloping downwards, pockets and abrasions showing on its surface where it hadn't been properly smoothed.

"And what about the despair?" she said. His grip tightened around her legs. At least he wouldn't be able to deny it now, she had felt his reaction, knew he understood. "It's not something that can be ignored."

"It only showed up once the Gatherers started failing at the higher levels," he said.

"So you ignore it and hope it goes away once I figure out why it's failing?"

They were halfway down the stairs, his grip and torso unwavering.

"It had to be there before. It's growing, which implies there is a foundation for it to grow out of," she said.

He shook his head, an abrupt, irritated movement.

"It's not a living creature. It doesn't grow. Something about the failure disturbs the balance of energy in the area. So when we rectify that interruption, it will no longer happen."

They reached the bottom of the stairs and Wesley held her tighter as he maneuvered her through the door. When he put her down, he held out his hand to steady her, the support withdrawn as soon as she stood on her own.

She crossed to the bed, taking a moment to appreciate how good it felt to be without pain, her mind clear and focussed on something he had said.

Disturbing the balance of energy.

As if one side had been weighted too heavily, or something had been taken away. Like an absence. If it was an absence of energy, then the Gatherer was depleting its source and it wasn't replenishing.

She stopped, looked up at Wesley in astonishment.

She almost asked him to take her to the lab, to test her theory except she didn't need to. The same way she had always been able to follow the process of the Gatherer in her head, she had known what that despair represented by feel. The depletion she and Lillian had experienced – and Kevin – was so deep and fundamental, it could only come from an absence, an essential balance that had been altered.

"What is it?"

She shook her head, his interruption threatening to take her off track. She understood now. The despair was not a phenomenon of its own but a symptom, an indication of the complete depletion of the life energy in that location. And once created, it could expand without the Gatherer, like a black hole that drew life into it.

Wesley stepped closer.

She shook her head again, ran her hands over her face, trying to brush away the wonder at this realization.

Giving us access to a level of energy the world has never had.

Hadn't Ari said the same thing? Looking to the power, and not the consequences.

"Tell me what you figured out."

She could see his panic, that she understood something that he hadn't. Something he had missed.

She lifted her shoulders, let them settle back, luxuriating in their lightness and strength.

"I'll tell you when those patients receive their treatment."

He stood absolutely still, and in the quiet she heard his elevated breathing, as fast as if he still carried her. The color in his face grew, flushing red with his anger. He stepped close enough that she could smell his sweat.

"I don't have to negotiate with you. You will do what we ask you. And solve the problem we give you. Nothing else."

His fury frightened her, his strength a sudden, volatile thing. She stepped back, her heart beating wildly, her hope and insight tarred black by the awareness of his ability to cause her harm.

"Sit down." He rolled the IV stand from the corner, the stand tilting with the force of his grip. "If you want to save the world, you're going to need your health."

He was sarcastic and dismissive, already knowing what she would choose.

Slowly, with every part of her screaming not to, she sat on the side of the bed and swung her legs up.

He was already injecting a syringe into the IV bag, his fury in every abrupt, efficient movement. He gripped her hand, too tight, and she flinched, expecting him to jam the IV needle into her vein. She hardly felt it.

He dropped her hand on the bed, flicked the tube, and checked the bag. He didn't look at her and didn't speak until he reached the door on his way out.

"I'll be back in an hour to take it out."

She listened to the short chop of his footsteps on the stairs, and the sudden absence of them when he reached the top.

TWENTY-SIX

Amanda carried her coffee cup from the kitchen, craving the jolt of caffeine after a long night exploring within the computer systems of the compound. She rubbed the back of her neck, trying to ease the muscles that had locked into place around three o'clock. She placed the coffee on her desk in front of the wall of screens and tapped on the keyboard as she sat.

It had been over twenty-four hours since she had shown Maria Storm's location and it was as if Maria had simply vanished. Amanda had managed to access the compound's camera network but it hadn't helped in figuring out where Maria had gone.

She forced her thoughts away from the anxiety that had grown as the hours passed, ignoring the part of her that was convinced Maria had been caught.

The feeds slowly came online. One showed the main green area, another showed Storm's room, and—

"Shit."

A soldier had just emerged at the top of the stairs that led from Storm's room. He was walking fast and looking annoyed as he took out a phone. He spoke a few words, impossible to read his lips, before he nodded his head in affirmation and ended the call.

She checked Storm's room. She was on her bed, an IV connected to her hand, giving every sign of being asleep except that her eyes were open.

The soldier exited to the outside, and Amanda flipped to a different view. He walked purposefully across the open lawn, cutting right towards the large black warehouse. The day was cloudy, giving her good clear images, but it left the compound gray and grim, the black building looming over all of it.

A second person came into view and she pulled her chair closer as she zoomed in. From his height and energetic walk, it had to be Ari, the only other member of Storm's original team still alive. She had witnessed him visiting her in the middle of the night, saw their argument even if she hadn't heard the words, and now here he was in a suit jacket, shaking the soldier's hand and looking like he was going to a job interview.

Had Maria reached him? Ari nodded frequently, his energy a contrast to the stillness of the soldier. He looked like he was excited to be there, but was it an act? Or was he even now, relaying Maria's message? Or is that what he and Storm had argued about?

She punched at the keyboard, annoyed with watching conversations that she couldn't hear. She was about to look for different, closer angle, when she saw what the two men were waiting for.

A huge man was strolling along the path from the direction of the headquarters, dressed in some kind of uniform. Ari and the soldier practically bowed when the larger man arrived.

She glanced at Storm, thin and still far from health, isolated in a room that was little more than a cell while these men met above ground in the light and air. Where the hell was Maria?

The three men moved towards the door at the base of the black warehouse, Ari in the middle. He was speaking rapidly, gesturing with his hands, the group looking small and insignificant in the shadow of the building.

She stared at the door after it closed, the guards outside as motionless as Storm in her bed. There was no point in trying to follow them inside. She had tried multiple times to access the systems inside that black tomb, but it was like it didn't exist at all.

She moved through several camera views, catching again the angles that showed its exterior. Her eyes burned from the hours she had spent searching for Maria's shadow moving against a building or disappearing into the trees. She couldn't have just vanished.

She returned to the feed on the entrance, but the men hadn't reappeared.

She stood, pacing in front of her desk, her fortified house for the first time feeling more like a cage than protection.

She sat back down, the scenes before her unchanged.

What the hell was Maria waiting for?

TWENTY-SEVEN

"THE MESSAGE WILL HAVE more validity coming from you."

Storm couldn't move, the impact of what Stanton was saying leaving her as immobile as if he had run an electric current along her nerves.

"We have a cure and the corporation will be distributing it shortly."

"Do you?" said Storm.

Beside her, her mother's only visible reaction was the push of her fingers into the table so that the skin showed white around the shiny red hardness of her painted nails. They faced the fierce intensity of Stanton and the smaller, more restless energy of Wesley across the conference table.

"We're very close."

It was Stanton who responded, but it was Wesley she looked to. His gaze briefly met hers before it slid away. They had refused to give the patients the treatments and yet suddenly they had a cure.

"You're asking me to lie for you."

Color rose into Stanton's cheeks. He was leaning forward, his shoulders halfway across the table.

"I'm asking you to give us some time. Get the protesters to calm down. We don't need any more people getting hurt."

No matter what she did, more people would get hurt. The only question was whether it was through the violence of the protests or the Gatherer itself.

"Isn't it enough to announce she is back at the corporation? That alone should calm people down," her mother said. She had come to the meeting in her role as CEO, her hair coiffed, her voice cool and laser tight.

There was the slightest flare of Stanton's nostrils as he exhaled, a bull barely kept in check. Her mother smoothed the top of the conference table. It still had the shiny untouched surface of lacquered wood.

"I'm happy to do that," said Storm. "To officially announce I'm back at the helm."

She sat back in the padded chair. The off-gas of the new upholstery made her mildly nauseous as she straightened the lapels of the suit jacket Wesley had dropped off that morning. It was too large for her and felt as if she were wearing someone else's clothes.

"You'll do whatever I tell you."

She hadn't expected him to accept the compromise, he and Wesley singing the same tune. She laid her hands on her thighs, a fear of impossible depth wrestling with her desire to tell him to go to hell.

"And if I don't?"

Her mother's hand shifted towards her, as if that would stop her.

Wesley had his eyes lowered. The slightest upturn of his lips made it hard to breathe.

"Do I need to spell this out for you?" said Stanton.

Stanton filled all the available space in the conference room, which was just large enough for the table and six chairs. It had a new smell and bare walls, a room planned for something and never used. A single window looked over a grove of trees, the room several stories above the ground. The natural light of the cloudy day coated the room and their faces in a flat grayness.

"If you don't mind," said Storm.

Stanton draped his arm across the back of Wesley's chair. Storm knew what he would say. The lever they held over her head was the only thing that mattered. But there would be a finality in hearing him say it and she wanted all of them to understand what he meant to do.

"Wesley has done excellent work developing a protocol to return you to health. Your growing strength and your belief you have a choice here are both signs of that. But the situation is simple. No press conference. No treatment."

"And once it's done, would I be allowed to leave?"

Stanton gave a huff of disbelief, half laughter. Wesley had sat up, alarmed. Stanton raised a hand to appease him.

"One step at a time. It isn't safe for you out there. With the fields, and the number of people looking to take out their revenge. You're safer here."

"I'll take my chances."

Stanton had leaned forward again, his elbows on the table. There was no patience left in his gaze, if there ever had been.

"You don't seem to understand. I am not offering you a choice. After the press conference you will remain in our care."

He lowered his chin ever so slightly towards Wesley. "Care" implied whatever horrid experiment Wesley chose for her. She had been so ill on that video, there would be no questions if she died.

"And if she agrees?" her mother asked, in a tone indicating they were discussing the terms of a manufacturing contract rather than Storm's health.

She was trying to show Storm the benefits, the only way she knew to keep her daughter alive.

"She continues her treatment—" Stanton opened his hands to show his benevolence, "—continues her work with Major Wesley on the Gatherers we're developing." His hands folded again. "And doesn't destroy everything she has worked for."

He was certain of her response. A spider with two flies caught in its web. For who wouldn't choose life? She wanted to live, to feel her body grow stronger and permanently shed the pain and weakness that traveled with her.

She stood and moved to the window. The fir trees reached to the sky, the canopy its own dense, protected world. The clouds almost seemed to touch the trees as if there were no separation between boughs and sky. Her leg muscles were strong, and she had the energy to lift her chest. Panic fluttered there, at the thought of letting the strength slip away and the pain that would replace it. Yet she couldn't stand up to a microphone and say this. Recorded forever so that it could be replayed at will – her capitulation, her weakness, and above all her selfishness, the final proof that she was not the savior that the world – or she herself – had believed her to be.

"And after she has helped you, and she's healthy, she'll be free to go?"

It was her mother again. Telling her this was the choice she should take.

Storm turned at the sound of Wesley's voice, speaking quietly into Stanton's ear. Stanton nodded before they both looked up at her. The table had stretched, so they suddenly felt far away.

"She'll be able to choose at that point whether she wants to leave or continue her work."

It was a lie. A promise they never planned to keep and both she and Stanton knew it. His fatigues were vivid against the blank walls, his shoulders impossibly wide. She hated his brawn and his power, wanted more than anything to strip it away from him.

She returned slowly to the table, her hands shaking as she pulled back the chair. She rested her elbows on the table and forced herself to breathe, letting the anger run smooth and deep. The words caught in her throat. He was right. There was no choice. Agree to say a few words or return to the pain of the plague, unable to think or do anything beyond survive. If she could even do that. The words would betray everyone who had ever believed in her. Daniel, her team, Megan, the thousands of fans who had reached out to her, and Maria.

Wesley had lifted his head, as if he sensed his victory. She tasted self-loathing and defeat and her complete failure to fix what she had done.

"What do you want me to say?"

Stanton's frown smoothed, and his chest rose and fell in a deep breath. Her mother's head dropped for an instant, the only outwards sign of her relief. Wesley smiled. Stanton drew a folded sheet from inside his pocket, straightening the creases before sliding it across the table.

"It's not long. A few words about how sorry you are for any suffering you've caused, and then moving quickly to the good news of your return to the corporation and the release of the cure."

A few words. A single typed page that would take only a few minutes to deliver.

You can endure anything for ten minutes.

It had been Daniel's counsel when she had been a guest on a late-night talk show.

If you want it badly enough.

Except she didn't want this.

"There will be a teleprompter. That is just to help you rehearse."

She could barely read the words, let alone repeat them for practice.

"What about the fields?"

A teleprompter meant cables, cameras and lights.

It was Wesley who answered. Her caretaker.

"The press conference will be held outside on the main green. All electrical equipment will be shielded. We'll also do a session in the water beforehand so your system will be stable."

She imaged she could feel the handcuffs clicking around her wrists, locking her to that treatment, her health. Her self-loathing flowed and raged around her so it already felt as if she were going under. The strength had gone out of her legs when she stood and she was unsteady, as if pushed by the torrent. The same way the river had tried to drag her downstream before Maria had come back to save her. Except Maria wasn't here to save her this time. Or to help her make an impossible choice.

Her mother smiled with pressed lips and gave her the slightest nod. She moved to hug her but Storm turned away. Stanton extended his hand as if they were sealing a business deal and she didn't shake it. It was bad enough she held this vile piece of paper in her hand.

Wesley held the door for her.

"I'll check in on you in the morning."

Stanton's words weren't so much of an assurance as a warning. A reminder of who was orchestrating this performance. Her mother moved to follow.

"If you have a moment, Alicia?"

It chilled her to hear him use her mother's first name. She turned too late to see her mother's reaction; the door already closed.

TWENTY-EIGHT

MARIA'S BODY HURT AND no matter how she shifted on the branch she couldn't ease the ache that had settled in after a second night in the tree. She had struggled to stay awake in dangerous places before but none as precarious as this swaying treetop. Despite her vigilance, she had dozed, jolting awake each time with all-too-real dreams of falling.

She moved carefully to a branch slightly above where she had slept, testing each step before she weighted it, her cramped muscles protesting at the movement. The new branch faced east and she looked down at the growing activity in the open green space between the large black warehouse and the building where Amanda said they were keeping Storm.

A few dozen chairs had been set up in neat rows. One crew was busy constructing a platform that looked like it would be some kind of stage, another was setting up lights and speakers to broadcast whatever was being announced. Soldiers stood on guard around the edges, the colorless gray morning leaving only their solemnity and purpose.

She sat carefully on the branch, letting her legs dangle on either side. Sap stuck her fingers together and crusty smudges covered most of her clothes.

The barricades in front of the headquarters were gone, the transport vehicles no longer parked in the lot. Soldiers lined the paths and buildings and had surrounded the area where the chairs and stage had been set up. The largest concentration was at the gate, faced off against a crowd of protesters that blocked off the road but for a narrow column.

THE GATHERER

She was too far away to recognize any of the soldiers, but she knew their training, the orders they would have received. She ached for that simplicity now. Orders issued that you were to obey, and it was not your job to worry about the why or the consequences.

Inside the compound, there was no clear route through the soldiers. They would be close enough to recognize she wasn't carrying the right weapon, and, if they knew what to look for, who she was. The rocky shore of the ocean showed the straight attention of several soldiers. Half of them looking in towards the compound, the other half out towards the ocean.

"How are you going to get out of this one?"

She said the words under her breath, hoping for a solution that wouldn't mean she would be trapped in this tree until she fell out from exhaustion or dehydration.

The screech of metal carried on the wind and she turned towards the gate where the protesters had grudgingly parted to allow an electric coach bus to inch between the wrought iron posts. The guards closed in behind it as soon as it was through.

It moved slowly, with some of the soldiers lining the bus on either side as it moved inward. It was a charter bus, its digital sign scrolling RESERVED into the dim morning. It stopped on the road at the point closest to the stage, and Maria had to catch herself from leaning too far forward as she waited for the door to open.

Two soldiers came out first, and after a pause, while the new soldiers and the ones on the ground arranged themselves in a line, a heavy-set older woman lumbered down the steps. They searched her bag, patted down her body, and scanned her eyes before she was allowed to be escorted towards the chairs. The young man with long hair that followed her off the bus received the same treatment as did the older, clean cut man behind him. Each of them was escorted to the chairs and over the course of what felt like hours, the seats filled up. Most of the attendees had tablets, some carried cameras with long lenses, a few came in pairs, with an announcer in a suit leading and a more disheveled cameraperson behind.

The wind had grown stronger and some of the attendees turned their backs to it, the ones with long hair continually tucking it behind their ears. Maria held tighter around the branch, the tree shifting beneath her.

Static blared across the compound as a mic was tested. A podium with the white symbol of the Gatherer had been positioned at the front of the stage. Maria gripped the branch and leaned forward, to hell with the swaying tree. A copper shield was being set up around the mic and the distance carefully measured between the speakers and a particular chair on the stage.

Either Storm or someone with the plague was going to appear on that stage.

She stiffened at the sight of a tall, cocky soldier striding across the green, followed by several others in uniform. Stanton. His gait and aggression were unmistakeable. She half expected him to lift his head and look up to her place in the trees, no amount of camouflage enough to hide from him.

Her fingers dug into the sticky bark as he bypassed the black warehouse and went directly to the building where Storm was being held. She had the illogical need to run in ahead of him. Stand between him and Storm.

Stanton and his followers entered the building. The empty bus had withdrawn to the parking lot and the people in the chairs waited or talked in small groups, surrounded by a ring of soldiers. The wind had grown and the day darkened, so that some of them pulled on jackets, the heavy clouds rolling in across the ocean drawing the light into itself. There was a dampness under her clothes as if the coming rain had already arrived.

Three guards erected a canopy above a table full of sound equipment, the only bit of cover on the entire green. The heavily guarded black warehouse and Storm's equally guarded building would refuse to give shelter to the crowd if the rain began, the bus in the distant parking lot the only option. Her options were even more limited.

THE GATHERER

Stay in the tree and hope to remain unseen or return to the ground and take her chances at avoiding the regular patrols and the countless soldiers looking for something to alleviate their boredom.

Two of the soldiers from the canopy threaded a cable beneath the stage and she realized she had drawn the wrong conclusions. The measurements had been for something else, the field from that cable enough to cause anyone with the plague serious harm. She watched as they covered it with black mats beyond the stage and connected it to a bank of outlets that was powered by a feed from the manufacturing facility.

She looked for what was missing: In the midst of the manicured pathways, the multiple buildings, and electric gate, there wasn't a single Gatherer. She looked harder, beyond the edges of the buildings, deeper into the clusters of bushes. No sleek line of a Gatherer broke the continuity. Hadn't there been a Gatherer that the entire compound had been built around?

She tried to remember where it had been, when she and Havernal had made that futile trip to see Alicia. It had been where the colossal black building now stood, having consumed that shining white Gatherer and everything around it. Did that blackness power the entire compound now?

There was a sudden alertness as the crowd looked towards Storm's building. The soldiers stood straighter, weapons lifted higher, bodies ready. Stanton and his followers had emerged from the building, surrounding two new people as they moved towards the stage.

There was the distinctive red of Storm's hair and the darker auburn of Alicia beside her. The tree stopped swaying, the ocean stopped rolling, and the clouds froze in place. The only movement was Storm's confident stride, her shoulders lifted in a blue tailored suit.

Her gut twisted. Shame and anger rushed in to form a calamity of betrayal. Had Ari been right? Storm was strong, healthy, and looked more like her real self than Maria had ever seen. Storm leaned down to say something to Alicia and wavered slightly as she stood straight again. So not a hundred percent, but better, unrecognizable from the woman Maria had left behind.

Her relief astonished her. A tension unwinding inside of her so she took her first full breath in weeks. Yet it was tainted, the suspicion that Storm had used her, tearing open the shame she had tried to get over after Storm had released the Gatherer under her nose. She had fooled her again.

Her fury came quickly behind it, tightening her muscles and enlivening her nerves. She almost hollered at the small group, exposing her anger for all to see.

Her culpability stopped her. For these soldiers weren't her friends, she wasn't part of that team. They would incarcerate her. Charge her with the attack on the Gatherer in Three Rocks, Coulter's death, the explosion at the headquarters, the penetration of the protesters into the compound, and whatever else they could pin on her. She would be the scapegoat they needed.

Storm stepped up onto the stage first, directly above the cable the soldiers had installed. She pulled at her sleeves as she waited for her mother to follow. If there was a field, Storm wasn't feeling it. There was no way she could hide that kind of pain.

Stanton directed Storm to the chair second from the end with Alicia beside her. Storm hadn't even looked at the mats that covered the cable on its run to the manufacturing facility. Was she so strong that she didn't need to be aware? Had they really worked a miracle on her?

Maria needed to get out of the tree and be doing something other than watching from a distance, ignorant as everyone in that crowd. She wanted to hurl the thousand accusations crowding her head at Storm and to get as far away from Stanton as she could. But above all she wanted to stand in front of that microphone and tell the crowd not to trust them. Not to be fooled the same way she had.

Her anger was so fierce and pure it felt as if she could fly down to the makeshift stage.

THE GATHERER

Alicia clasped Storm's hand. It was an unusual gesture and hard to tell from the distance, but it looked as if Storm pulled her hand away. But could she read anything into that? Storm and Alicia's relationship was uneven. Two strong, stubborn females convinced that they knew best.

Stanton spoke with the young soldier who had tested the mic. The young man nodded several times before he retreated to the sound table. The canopy snapped in the growing wind.

The players in the scene were strangely still, a moment in a play before the action begins. Storm dipped her head to listen to something Alicia was saying. She smiled, nodded, playing the dignitary ... or was it a grimace? Maria couldn't tell at this distance. The suit hung off Storm's thin shoulders and she had her arms pressed against her sides. Her head was lifted, scanning the crowd, a regal tilt to it that befitted the creator of the Gatherer.

If Maria was closer she would be able to tell how much better she was. Up close, there would be cracks, a tremor, or a hesitation that would show the effort. She cursed the tree and her ridiculous situation, even as she recognized its protection. Without it she would have been caught, locked away in a cell and not a witness to whatever this was.

There was a screech and all eyes turned towards the gate. Three black SUVs idled outside the gate, waiting for the slow slide of the iron bars. They were the newest version of the Elec Edition, far more powerful than this slow cavalcade would ever need. These high-performance vehicles, like the soldiers that filled the compound, were for show. She felt a deep sense of loss that Storm had been drawn into this circus of image and illusion, and that if she stayed too long she might never pull her free.

Guards flanked the vehicles once they cleared the gate. Four on each side of all three vehicles. A standard procedure. Guard each like it held the important target.

Stanton stood and adjusted his uniform, a dress uniform he only used for the most important occasions. Alicia rose, followed by Storm who looked unsteady.

The vehicles left the paved road and traveled over the grass to the stage. The crowd had risen, their tablets lifted, and the cameras pointed, whoever was inside the vehicles having achieved the entrance they wanted.

She could almost see the tentacles reaching out from that cavalcade, twisting around Storm and her mother, inextricably connecting them to Stanton and whoever was in the vehicle. Though she already knew.

She had the urge again to let go, let herself swoop down and knock everyone off the stage, grab the mic and expose their lies. Except there was something in the way Storm was watching the vehicles approach, the lift of her chin of endurance rather than pride. The men from the RCMP protection emerged from the vehicles first. Three from the front car and three from the back. They were unnecessary with the number of soldiers around the set up, but they would want to be seen doing their job. Their presence was as much as part of the show as anything else.

One officer got out of the middle car, followed immediately by the professionally tousled sandy-blonde hair of the Prime Minister. He smiled and waved even before he was standing. The sight of his stolid confidence, and the wide smile with which he greeted Stanton increased her agitation. Stanton grasped the Prime Minister's hand and laughed loud enough at his joke that Maria heard it from her tree branch.

The Prime Minister stepped to meet Storm and Maria gripped the branch harder.

Storm dipped her head to greet him, nodding as he held her hand in his for what felt like too long. Was there some kind of exchange? Or message? Something he was telling her even as the world watched? Storm abruptly moved to the side, letting her mother move in to be introduced. Had it been intentional? To break whatever hold he had tried to exert over her.

Storm moved back from the two, giving them space, but her progress was blocked by Stanton's bulk. He steadied her with a hand on the small of Storm's back. Storm jerked away as if she had been burned and the ribbon of doubt grew thicker. Had it been a reaction to physical pain? Or was it a reaction to Stanton publicly trying to exert his control?

Storm and Alicia sat first, followed by Stanton and the Prime Minister. The journalists settled into their seats. Again, the players were strangely still, as if the first act had ended and they waited for a signal for the second to begin. Was the distortion her own? Or was there a forced rhythm to this performance?

It was over a minute before Stanton rose. He held onto the lectern as if seeking to exert his will over the sleek, contoured podium. She had been awed by that embodiment of power when she first met him, finding a comfort in being guided by the certainty in his vision. That had changed the moment she left Ottawa to find Storm, her respect for him destroyed the moment he denied the plague's existence.

"Thank you all for coming. Once you hear today's announcement, you'll understand why it was so important that we get this message out. You're an integral part of that and we couldn't do it without you. All of you were selected for a reason — whether because you represent a newspaper, are a phenomenon on YouTube, or are considered an influencer. We wanted to trust this message with the best there is—"

Maria shifted on the branch, wondering if the pandering was as obvious to its targets as it sounded to her. She couldn't see their faces and could only gauge their reaction by the set of their shoulders, the rhythm – or not – of their fingers on their tablets.

"This is a reminder that there is to be no live transmitting of this event. When you hear the announcement you'll understand the precautions we've taken and the necessity of removing and holding anyone who chooses to disobey this requirement."

Storm showed no expression, the stillest one of all, her face turned slightly towards the ocean, intentionally exposing herself to its cool dampness of the breeze.

"—But this announcement isn't mine to make. As you can see, there are more important people here than me."

He gestured towards the Prime Minister and Storm.

"That honor resides with the Right Honourable James Callow. Please welcome our Prime Minister."

There was the purposeful stride of the Prime Minister as he again shook Stanton's hand and took his place at the mic. His hands rested on the podium, his shoulders relaxed, his touch lighter, though equally as deadly.

Surfer boy is what they had called him in her unit. For his beach boy looks, but mainly for his ability to surf above scandal as if none of it had anything to do with him. He smiled widely out at the crowd, the force of the smile ruining its ability to create trust.

"This is the second time I have been on a stage with Storm Freeman. And each time it is a privilege and an honor to share the stage with her."

Storm's head was still turned to the ocean as if she hadn't heard. Was she suffering? Her attention already drifting?

"When I first heard of the Gatherer, I was astounded and awed by its possibilities. I knew even then it could deliver an energy freedom that would usher in a whole new relationship with the power that feeds our society. And I wasn't surprised. I wasn't surprised that it came from Canada.

"It allowed us to take our values and principles and deliver them out into the world. Canada was ready to be a world leader and the Gatherer was proof that our time had come."

Alicia looked briefly to where Storm was looking and turned back, whatever Storm was focussed on not something others could see.

"—The Gatherer has delivered abundance to the world, and our home."

He hadn't mentioned the plague, or the riots. Did they really think they could still ignore it? When protesters lined the gate less than a hundred metres away? No matter how carefully selected these journalists had been, they wouldn't buy a whitewash. One of the journalists had lowered his tablet and leaned in to say something to the heavy-set woman that first got off the bus. She was shaking her head.

"We all know this. We have lived the abundance of the Gatherer. Seen it spread across the world. What you don't know is the good news that Ms. Freeman is here to deliver. Normally, I like to keep these kind of announcements for myself—" A few people in the crowd laughed half-heartedly. "—but this one I will leave for Canada's superstar, Storm Freeman."

The sound of her name seemed to jolt Storm from her reverie. The crowd was cheering, louder than for the Prime Minister, who waited expectantly at the podium.

As Storm stood, her mother squeezed her hand in a show of support. Or was it? Storm had pulled her hand away again. It could have been because she was moving towards the podium or it could have been a refusal.

The crowd had stood, along with everyone on the stage, clapping in a way that felt different, as if their expectations for her were higher.

Her presence at the podium went beyond the Prime Minister's. Her thinness and her paleness only added to the sense that she was different than everyone else. She held a single sheet of paper in her hand, that she laid carefully on the lectern. She took her time adjusting the mic higher than it had been for the Prime Minister.

"Hello."

She smiled, and there she was again, owning the crowd, and drawing all the light in the clearing towards her. The crowd could feel it, leaning forward, Storm as much as a force of nature as the Gatherer.

"It's good to see you."

There was more applause, punctuated by hoots and whistles, the mood of the crowd friendlier. Maria had the strange sensation of happiness blended with terror.

"So much has happened since we last spoke."

People had calmed, picking up on Storm's solemnity. It was a side of her they had rarely seen before. Maria squeezed her legs around the branch, feeling suddenly so much less secure.

"I wanted to start with an apology. For any harm that I have caused through the Gatherer. If I had known that it would hurt anyone I would never have sent it out into the world."

It angered her that it had to be Storm that mentioned the plague; the Prime Minister and Stanton too cowardly to claim the truth of it.

"It is a revolutionary device, and it has brought our world great things. Changed the fate of our country."

There was a smattering of applause as she turned to acknowledge the Prime Minister. He beamed back at her. Stanton sat straight in his chair, as if perched on a horse announcing, *Look at me. I did this.*

Maria wanted to strike him down, cast him from the pedestal he didn't deserve.

Storm had paused too long. She was looking out over the crowd as if noting every face. At some she paused longer, and one of them she greeted by name. When she finished, she looked to the manufacturing facility, the headquarters, and the dark shadow of the new building.

"Cat got your tongue, Freeman?"

It was a call from the audience, somewhere in the back.

The Prime Minister sat with one leg crossed over the other, but his relaxed calmness had changed to an act, his shoulders as rigid as Stanton's.

Storm's gaze had moved back to the ocean, a view she would have known by heart from her time here before she went to the Yukon. She gripped the sheet of paper in both hands as she pulled her gaze from the ocean. It swept up to the treetops and Maria felt as if she looked directly up to her hidden perch and saw her. In that instant, she knew. Recognized the look from dozens of soldiers when they understood what real sacrifice meant.

Maria was on her knees, scrambling back to the trunk, lowering to the next branch, even as Storm spoke into the microphone. Maria barely heard the words, but she didn't need to. She knew their meaning, if not the exact words.

"But it is killing people. And it needs to be stopped."

TWENTY-NINE

THE PAUSE WAS INFINITESIMAL. Between the time it took for her words to reach the audience and the time it took for them to register. There was a strange weightlessness to it, her hands on the podium the only thing keeping her grounded.

Fingers stopped tapping and cameras dipped ever so slightly. A young man about her age was already standing, a question forming on his lips, even as a soldier moved to push him back down in his seat.

A searing burn cut into her feet.

She looked down, trying to see where the pain was coming from. The laces on her boots were tied, her feet planted shoulder-width apart. She tried to step back, away from the pain, and it spread to her shins and knees, a field so pure and concise it went directly to her core.

She looked to the crowd. They were on their feet, shouting, trying to move towards her. Could they see this?

The pain reached her lower back and her spine arched, jerking her face up to the sky. The dark clouds were so close she could feel them on her face and then she was falling, their blackness receding as the trees rose and she hit the stage.

She tried to roll towards the crowd, to make sure they had understood they would have to stop the Gatherer. Be the messengers that got this out.

Her mother's face was above her, her clear blue eyes raw with fear. Her mother struggled to push hands away from her and then she was gone, replaced by the stern blank faces of men who lifted Storm. There was agony wherever they touched her.

She was jostled and pulled as the men carried her off the stage. There was the darkness of the sky again, pressing the pain into every cell. Her ears roared. Was there shouting?

She tried to twist towards the crowd again. Strong, brutal hands held her tight. Wesley was behind her, his tight face pinched and furious. There was a brief moment of victory, that she had slipped from his grasp, taken the escape route he never expected. The satisfaction of it almost dulled the fire that was stripping away her nerves. She wouldn't get to see the Gatherer put to rest, but it would happen, and this was the start.

Wesley forced the men to stop, to inject something into her vein, but it was too late. She was far from him now, in a place where he would never reach her. She turned towards the pain. Was this how it had been for Daniel? Not running from the pain but recognizing that it knew your name and you knew it.

She gave into it, the place where she ended and it began no longer existing. Daniel was with her, the long boniness of his hand encircling hers as he positioned himself between her and the men who carried her. He helped her up and the pain fell away as he pointed ahead of them to something he wanted to show her.

She curled around him. Breathed in his scent and his strength, feeling as light as she had when they first met.

Far below her, on the ground, someone called her name.

THIRTY

"**L**ET'S GO!"

Wesley's command was sharp and urgent, and Adams and the other men responded with a sudden surge towards the treatment facility. They carried Storm between them, her head fallen back, and she hadn't responded when Wesley had jammed the syringe into her vein.

Storm's collapse had been instant. She had looked at her feet and crumbled, taking with her all of Adams's hope for Valerie and Camille.

A tiny ball of blood formed where Wesley had extracted the needle from Storm's arm as the yelling of the crowd fell behind them.

Adams could barely feel her weight, four of them not necessary to carry her, but the procedure had been automatic. Four men for maximum speed to rush her to safety. Except the attack had come from below her. He had seen the look on her face when she looked at her feet. The same way Camille had looked at the refrigerator in the early days. Looking for something she could feel but couldn't see.

Wesley ran ahead to open the door at the treatment facility. The standing guard held the other side.

Their footsteps echoed in the high emptiness of the foyer, the quietness feeling wrong. He had to remind himself there were patients here, resting in their rooms.

"This way."

Wesley ushered them down the main corridor and Adams lifted his head. He counted six doors to the sound of the men's breathing. The first five were empty and he struggled to remember if they had been occupied when he had come to see Valerie and Camille. He hadn't noticed, had seen only the door where Valerie and Camille had waited.

At the sixth door, he stumbled, almost losing hold of Freeman.

The room was empty, the bed stripped bare. The men clanged through a set of doors, going deeper into the silent building. There were more empty rooms, some of them without furniture, and his confusion grew. The air was stagnant and the rooms absent of life.

People don't get better here.

And he had disagreed. Told Valerie she needed to be positive. So certain that he had brought them to the one place that would make them better.

The corridor ended at a blank wall, a rough door cut out of the adjacent wall. They slowed, none of them believing that dark stairway was where they needed to go.

"Adams, you'll need to carry her."

Wesley stood at the rough entrance, a long dark stairway leading down. Would Valerie and Camille be at the bottom of this darkness?

He easily took Freeman's weight and turned towards the stairway as the other men retreated. Wesley waited for him to go ahead, waving him in with a frantic urgency.

The stairwell was newly made, with rough seams, the few lights barely providing sufficient light. Freeman drooped like a rag doll in his arms and he pulled her closer, his hands slipping on the excess material of the suit, her thinness far beyond what it had appeared.

At the base of the stairs he stepped through a single door. There was no corridor of rooms, or an underground oasis for the patients. It was a single barren room, as rough cut as the stairwell, a single unmade bed against the wall, and a plastic patio chair beside it.

"Put her here."

Wesley indicated the bed, already striding to the empty IV stand.

Adams didn't move. Couldn't. He needed to turn around, try this again and enter into the clear, brightly lit corridor of a state-of-the-art medical facility. Nurses moving busily about. Relaxed, healing patients tucked in their rooms.

"What are you waiting for?"

He held Freeman closer. She was supposed to be better, the miracle that would lead them all out of this disaster. But she was barely alive, whatever illusion they had managed to create up on that stage stripped away as easily as it had been created.

Wesley came around the bed, each strike of his boot precise and controlled. He put his arm beneath Freeman's knees, the other under her shoulders. He was so close his smudged freckles showed beneath his bluish skin.

"The longer you wait, the less chance she has."

Adams let her go, his chest cooler when she was gone.

He followed Wesley to the bed. She lay twisted on her side, one foot hanging off the side. Her pale skin was gray against the white blouse, the bead of blood smeared down her arm. Someone this sick needed doctors and machines, a whole team to support her.

Wesley had removed her blazer and was unbuttoning her blouse. He freed her arm from the sleeve and jammed the IV needle into the back of her already-bruised hand. Freeman didn't flinch.

"Can you take off her boots?"

The boots were black, the kind that went to the ankle, with lace holes running up the front. He was caught in an image of Valerie doing up the thinnest strap on her high heels, her calf muscle taut as she reached down.

Wesley undid Freeman's belt and pulled it out from under her. His movements were different than the medics in the field. They had occasionally rested a hand on the arm of a patient, or tucked a blanket. Even when the patient had been unconscious there had been that recognition that they were human and would need reassurance. Wesley's care was abrupt and sterile, more suited to a piece of equipment than a living being.

Wesley moved to her feet and loosened her laces. With a brusque tug, the first boot was free.

"Will she live?" asked Adams.

Wesley paused with the heel of Freeman's boot cupped in his hand. He looked up along her sprawled body. She looked liked she had already gone, even if her pulse was still beating.

"If I want her to."

The air went out of Adams. He hadn't realized he had been holding his breath, using the pressure of it to keep his panic under control. "Where are the others?"

It had been a mistake to bring them here. Valerie had seen it. And he had been blind, telling her these people understood the plague better than anyone. That they would be the ones to cure her.

"That's classified."

Wesley had the cold, lifeless eyes of a reptile.

"They are my family."

Wesley lowered Freeman's bare foot onto the table and dropped the boot to the floor, like it didn't matter where it landed, that Freeman wouldn't be needing it.

"They're out of your hands now."

Adams stepped back, his body in motion even before he had understood the decision, bounding up the stairs three at a time, barely feeling the steps beneath him as his panic and terror forged into a single, blinding force.

THIRTY-ONE

MARIA'S FEET TOUCHED THE ground and she pressed her back flat against the tree. Shouts sounded from the open area, overridden by the clipped orders from the soldiers. She ran through the underbrush, staying close to the ground, and stopped at the edge of the grove, hidden behind the fronds of a large fern.

The stage was empty and the Prime Minister's cavalcade was speeding towards the gate. The soldiers had formed a tight circle around the journalists even as the crowd tried to snap photos and take video of a group of four men, hurrying towards Storm's building, carrying someone between them.

A flash of red hair before the door closed confirmed it was Storm being rushed away.

What the hell had happened?

In the few moments it had taken to descend the tree, Storm had gone from being surprisingly healthy to a complete collapse. A collapse likely triggered by that cable beneath the stage and whoever controlled it.

The doors clanged shut and on the green the soldiers moved quickly, cutting off any means of flight and pushing the journalists closer together. Two of the soldiers accompanied Alicia, though it looked more like escorting, along the curving path to the headquarters. Stanton had his back to her, conferring with the young soldier who had been in charge of the sound.

Maria ran crouched, back the way she had come, parallel to the path that ran through the grove, alert for the soldiers that would still be out there. She passed the tree and the curve where she had hid from the two women, the hum of the wind in the trees masking the sound of her footsteps and preventing her from hearing the patrols that would be nearby. She slowed, relying on her sight, the tree trunks creaking and swaying like an old ship gaining speed.

She stopped at the edge of the grove, concealed by tall grasses, the air and stalks damp from the spray kicked up by the frantic ocean.

The back of the building where they had taken Storm lay twenty paces to the northeast. A series of identical windows showed on the wall closest to her, any kind of entry through them completely exposed.

The first drops of rain struck her shoulders and the grass. Big, fat drops promising the deluge to come. She silently thanked whoever or whatever it was delivering this distraction. She wiped the dirt from her knees, set her shoulders, and stepped onto the grass.

As she moved beyond the cover of the grove, the soldiers positioned along the water came into view. Four of them. Two facing the ocean. Two facing her. They were far enough away she couldn't see their faces and they couldn't see hers, the growing rain adding to her cover. She didn't acknowledge them or turn her head. Kept moving forward. She lowered her chin slightly as if she were speaking into a mic and adjusted her gait to look like she was carrying. It was pathetic, the efforts not enough to fool anyone who was really looking. Her only hope was that they were distracted by the press conference and not on alert for a woman in uniform.

Twenty paces from the back corner there was a sudden repeated beeping from the direction of the stage. She didn't let it affect her stride, she didn't even acknowledge it. Instead, she let a small part of her brain identify it as the warning signal of a large vehicle backing up. The bus to come pick up the crowd – though it felt too soon. Stanton was not one to let that PR nightmare slip out of his control.

Two steps to the corner.

The open area behind the building was the width of a single road before it reached the underbrush that ran along the perimeter. The wall was long and blank, a single ventilation grate, several windows, and a handle-less door further down providing the few breaks in the uniformity.

The rain soaked her shoulders as she walked faster. Jogged. The possibility of having been seen grew more real now that she could no longer see their response. Halfway down the wall, a trench blocked her path. It was roughly dug, with the dirt piled beside it and water flowing through it.

The ditch ran into the building, flowing through a vertical mesh grate before it disappeared. Bits of leaves and sticks stuck on the mesh, moving in and out as the water swelled and receded. Maria leaned down and laced her fingers through the grate, but it wouldn't budge. The concrete lining was messy at the edges as if poured in a hurry, out of place beside the sleek practicality of the building.

Maria took several steps back and took a run at the ditch, clearing it by a good inch. Her foot slipped on the mud and she landed on her ass, her elbows in the muck, the rain hitting her face. She scrambled to her feet, checking again for soldiers and ran the remaining length of the wall. The wet grass gave way beneath her feet.

At the corner, she snuck a look, the red tail lights of the bus refracted through the rain. The number of soldiers and guards around the bus and gate seemed to have multiplied since she reached the ground.

Maria ran back to the window, but the ledge was too high, her fingers not even reaching the glass. She looked for a rock or fallen log to stand on, but the underbrush was low and made up of young trees. She moved to the door, running her fingers along the edge for a place to hold on, the solid gray metal, slick and wet, a blank plate where the handle should have been.

THIRTY-TWO

ADAMS RAN DOWN THE empty corridor, his pounding feet and raised breathing breaking the deathly silence. He slammed through the set of doors, the noise enough to wake the dead. Nothing moved. He crashed through the sixth door, needing the noise and disturbance as if it could wake Camille and Freeman and bring them all back. The beds were stripped, the bedside table empty, not even an indent in the pillow where Camille had rested her head.

He circled the beds, checking beneath the mattress and under the frame. On the far side of Camille's bed, glass crunched under his feet. A glass had shattered on the floor, crushed pieces in the shape of footprints showing where whoever had taken Camille, had lifted her weakened body from the bed. He put his hands on the mattress. Dug his fingers into its hardness.

A pattering at the window startled him and he moved to the small square. The sky had opened up, pounding the trees, the grass and the ocean in a relentless fury. He stepped between the beds and opened the curtain that separated the two areas. A long, black hair clung to the plastic, held there by static electricity. He pulled it off and laid it in his palm. He had found hundreds of them in the bathroom sink, picked them out of countless meals. He would recognize the thickness of it anywhere; the blue tint when he turned it in the light, the slightest of curls at its end.

He squeezed his fist around it, lifted his face to the ceiling, and felt the desperation threaten to overtake him. He couldn't fail them now, not when they needed him most. He breathed. Pushed his desperation away.

THE GATHERER

He slipped the hair into his breast pocket and searched further, checking the drawer beside Valerie's bed. It was empty but for a single packet of mints. When he opened the closet door, a single red cardigan stared out at him. The top button was shiny and clear, the second one missing. The sweater Camille had worn every day for months.

He slipped it from the hanger and gripped the material in his fists, holding it to his nose. It smelled of laundry soap and mints, as if even here Valerie was always watching, always taking care. Except where were they now? With the sweater held tight in his fist, he lunged for the hall, the stale, stagnant air too difficult to breathe.

The corridor was cooler, a draft running through it towards Freeman's room, the fate of her and Wesley taking the whole world with it. He turned away from it, to the room beside Valerie and Camille's.

This room was empty too, as were the rooms down the hall. All of them showed signs of a rushed departure. A forgotten bracelet, a single shoe in the closet, and in one room, a pair of glasses lying on the beside table. Who had owned them? Had they been alone? As scared and weak as Valerie and Camille?

He checked another corridor, this one showing signs of habitation. A few locked doors protected pristine labs with no one there. At the end of the corridor, light filled a single window, out of place after the dimness of the rest of the building.

He slowed. A cold draft seeped from the door, the metal cold to the touch. The room was bright, well lit, the kind of space where he had expected to find Valerie and Camille. An attendant was moving between tables, a tablet in her hand.

There were more than a dozen, his mind counted fourteen, laid out on the tables in shiny black bags. They took up the length of the tables, the tags dangling off the end of each, refusing to comprehend until his gaze fixed on the single small bag at the far corner.

No.

His entire consciousness wrapped around that one thought as if he could hold onto it and stay afloat, above the despair that swirled around him and threatened to take him alive.

That couldn't be his family. He wouldn't have brought them to a place like this. He would never have made that kind of mistake. He was sweating, thinking he might throw up. He watched the back of the attendant as she methodically scanned codes on the tags and made notes on her tablet.

She looked up, and he ducked out of sight. Her expression had been flat and deadened, as if she were no more alive than whoever was in those body bags. He wanted to stand back up, claw his way into that room.

Except his body had him retreating down the hall, pulling his pistol from his holster. He had misread the situation. Mistaken this for a safe haven. The biggest mistake of his life when it mattered most. The horror growing inside him was so deep he would never escape it. Yet his body kept running, recognizing the danger and ran from it at full speed.

At the end of the corridor, the rain slashed against the tall windows in the foyer. The back of the guard was visible at the door. These were not his people. Or his team. None of them were now. He came to a full stop, watched the rain hitting the window and the guard outside, head bent beneath the onslaught.

He turned, the pistol in his hand, and ran back into the silent building.

THIRTY-THREE

MARIA DUG HER FINGERNAILS along the edge of the door, though she knew it was futile. She pulled her knife from her leg holster and jammed it between the door and the frame.

It was hopeless, these things were designed not to be penetrable. If she had tools or explosives, there would be possibilities. She slid the knife where the lock should be and felt a vibration. She laid her palm flat against the door and felt the vibration again. A mechanism inside was moving. She stepped back, scanning the door for what she had triggered, the rain soaking her face.

The door swung open.

Friend or foe? She had no time to care. She stepped in the door and pulled it shut behind her. The sound of the rain stopped and the mechanics slid the bolt back in place.

The room was dry and quiet, an electrical panel on one wall and the blinking lights of a control system next to it. Otherwise the room was empty, the concrete floor bare.

She scanned for a lens but unless it was hidden inside a duct, this room wasn't important enough to monitor.

At the door, she paused. She was in a small corridor, lined with doors.

She tread quietly on the hard tiles, wondering if it was Amanda who had opened the door or someone else.

She noted the other offices, all of them empty except for the one at the end. The desk held a monitor, a coffee cup, and a few sheets of paper. The air had a strange combination of the smell of a new building but also the stuffiness of disuse. She opened the door at the end and peered into a larger, wider corridor. It was lit by natural light at the distant end, leaving everything in dusk.

Across the hall, a rough opening had been torn out of the wall—a poor job—as if it had been added after the fact. It could lead to a maintenance room or to the Gatherers that must feed all of the buildings. She bypassed it, having no time for how the compound fed its endless appetite for power.

She heard no voices or noises and would have thought the place was abandoned if she hadn't seen them bring Storm in. She moved carefully down the hall, checking the empty rooms as she moved towards the front.

She eased silently through a double set of doors, holding the latch until it slid soundlessly back into place. A door closest to the ones she had just come through hung open. She approached carefully, her pistol ready in her hands.

All was quiet, and it had the same feeling of abandonment. She peered around the corner. It held an empty bed, an open closet door, the same dim light from outside covering all of it.

She moved past quickly, checking the other rooms, confused by the blanket of silence and the ongoing sense that no one was there.

She stayed close to the wall before entering the foyer, the rain pummeling against the windows, the green outside empty but for the soaked stage, the sagging canopy of the sound tent, and the dripping curtain of metal. The rain was as good as any enemy fire at keeping them all pinned in place.

A staircase lead to the second floor and a separate corridor ran in the opposite direction. Outside the exit, a guard bent his head beneath the rain.

As soon as she entered the small corridor, she hugged the walls tighter, these offices showing signs of habitation. Light streamed out of an open door at the end and a cold draft wrapped around her ankles.

THE GATHERER

She took shelter at each door, checking behind and ahead, straining to hear anything from the lit room.

Beside the open door, she pressed her back against the wall. Voices would tell her how many there were, footsteps how athletic, yet she heard nothing. She waited, listening to her heartbeat. She was about to enter when she heard a catch of breath. It was faint, almost a sob, and she felt her fear harden.

Ever so carefully, she peered around the corner.

Body bags filled the room. A woman lay on the floor in a white lab coat, and a cracked tablet beside her. Her face held the gray of the dead.

She ducked back around the corner. Was Storm in there? Why the rush if it was only to zip her into a body bag?

She heard it again. A faint, shaking breath.

She moved further into the room this time, past the door, into the blazing light and the grid of black bags. There was the stench of death now, despite the coldness of the room.

The sound came from the corner, behind two empty tables.

She ran in a crouch, using the lab tables as cover, moving so carefully her feet barely touched the ground. Was Storm already dead and catalogued with the rest? Then why the dead woman and the empty tables?

The ragged breathing had stopped. Had they heard her?

She risked a look around the table. Ducking back so quickly she wasn't sure what she had seen. Or couldn't comprehend it. There were body bags on the floor, opened, the bodies partially pulled out and a soldier—no, Adams—sitting between them.

She forced herself to breathe. Then looked again, into the barrel of Adams' pistol, pointed right at her. She pulled back expecting a shot to ring against the table. It didn't come. She heard shuffling, and a low whisper.

When she looked again, Adams had laid his pistol on the floor beside him. His hands and arms were full with his dead wife and child.

Her nausea rose hard and fast, the bile already in her throat. She swallowed. Breathed. Didn't look into their faces.

"Adams."

He wasn't looking at her. He only had eyes for the woman and child in his lap. He was deadly pale, his skin not far off from Valerie and Camille's.

Maria said his name again.

This time he looked up, his eyes widened from his shock, the fractured look in them a reflection of what had broken inside him.

"People don't get better here," he said.

He tried to pull their bodies closer to him but they were heavy and cumbersome, falling back where they had originally been.

She had met Valerie and Camille, remembered how devoted Adams had been. He had been a different person when he was with them.

"You can't stay here," she said.

How long until someone came? Rain or not, this makeshift morgue couldn't be here. People would come to clear it out. Make it look like it was never there.

"I can't leave."

She crouched beside him, moving the pistol out of his reach. The smell of death was so strong it caught in her nose and throat.

His lips had turned a faint blue as had the fingernails that grasped Valerie and Camille. A gleam of sweat shone on his forehead and he didn't seem to understand her.

She slipped his pistol into her pocket.

She started searching at the closest bag. She held her breath and unzipped the bag only enough to see the top of the face. She would know Storm in an instant.

And what then? But she knew: She would take Storm with her. It was why she had come. She wouldn't leave her now.

The first bag was the short brown hair of a man. The second the gray part of an older woman. The stench was overpowering. These bodies weren't newly dead. After the fourth bag, she checked the hall and heard only the distant hum of the rain.

After three more bags the smell got worse. She retched next to the table. The people in the bags further into the room had been dead longer.

"Freeman isn't here."

Adams stood at the side of the empty tables, pale and unsteady.

She wiped her mouth.

"Then where is she?"

He bent down, out of sight behind the table. When he didn't reappear, she moved to where she could see.

He had laid out Valerie and Camille side by side. The bags were open, their faces at rest. Valerie still wore the pale blue of a hospital gown, while the bright red of Camille's sweater almost brought color to her cheeks. If you didn't look too close.

Adams' hand shook as he cupped each of their cheeks in turn. Maria looked away.

He stood slowly, using the table for leverage, struggling beneath his grief. He took a few unsteady steps and held out his hand.

"I can show you."

He looked leaner, his edges sharper. There was a ferocity in his eyes that frightened her, even as the energy from it fed into her tired muscles.

Maria drew his pistol from her pocket and handed it to him. He could kill her or take her to Stanton. But he wouldn't. His rawness matched hers now, both of them in a clearer, more vulnerable place.

He stepped over the dead woman and entered the corridor without looking forward or back. Maria followed, turning off the light behind them and closing the door. She made the sign of the cross before moving down the hall.

The first time she had done that in a very long time.

Maria stood at the end of the small corridor, looking back the way they had come, alert for any signs of movement. Adams jostled the lock on one of the offices, the faint grind of metal on metal reaching her. It had taken only a few brief words to recognize they would need help, and it would need to come from someone they could trust.

At the sound of the latch releasing, she moved back to the door to join him. He ushered her into the office ahead of him and she sat in the desk chair facing the terminal. After closing the door Adams knelt beside her to see the screen. She tapped a key, relieved when the winged symbol of the log-in window appeared.

Adams reached across her and tapped in the keys for *AFreeman*, the letters of the password appearing as tiny dots. People never knew how much they gave away while being protected.

It amazed her that Adams was still functioning. He was in full operation mode, his personality, his self, locked away where it couldn't be reached. He was the perfect soldier.

"Why are you helping me?"

She had asked the question when they reached the protection of the corridor. He had been slow to respond, the answer coming from a part of himself he had shut down.

"Because I am."

She had accepted his answer. Understood it. The why didn't matter.

The landing page appeared, showing the aerial view of the compound, the grasses green and a freshness to the image that spoke of newness and hope. Somewhere there would be a log showing that Alicia had logged in from a new terminal. They had to hope no one was watching.

Maria navigated to the search engine and typed in the web address for her email account.

She used the most recent address she had for Amanda and sent a message with three words in the subject line.

Are you there?

The wait was interminable.

"Are you sure she'll answer?"

If Amanda was online, she would answer. If something had changed, if she had had to flee her stronghold, they would get silence.

It's about time.

Maria smiled, almost giddy with the relief. Amanda had opened the door. She'd been there all the time. She started to type but before she got to the first letter, another email arrived with an embedded link.

"We don't have time for this," said Adams.

Maria held up her hand to calm Adams as she clicked on the link.

The video started with the CBC logo. She muted the sound and turned on close captioning, as it opened on a newscaster sitting behind a desk. He had salt and pepper hair and infinitely earnest eyes.

"Storm Freeman, the inventor of the Gatherer, came out of hiding today, speaking to the press for the first time since the allegations of the plague were launched against the corporation."

It moved to a clip of Storm standing below a cloudy sky, the microphone shield blocking the view below her chest. She looked healthier, her recovery more evident up close, especially when she smiled, the old Storm in full power.

"Hello."

The sound of the applause seemed louder, the shots of the journalists applauding more exuberant than Maria remembered.

"It's good to be back."

Her smile was disarming, the confidence in it, the genuine sentiment that she was glad to be there. And of course she would be. In the end, that had been Storm's strongest draw, that she wanted to help people, make their lives easier.

The clip stayed with Storm as she issued her apology and the slow pan of her gaze that took in the whole compound. Anyone watching her would see the mix of pride and regret that struggled for dominance.

Neither Maria nor Adams breathed. They had heard Storm's words, understood the implication, and this would be the moment when the world knew it too. The cover pulled back.

Except Storm was gone, replaced by the earnest newscaster.

"Ms. Freeman went on to announce that a cure has been found for the plague that has affected a minority of people in the Gatherer's distribution area. To explain the details, we go to Ari Chaudhary, one of the original team members that created the Gatherer, and the brainchild behind the cure. Good afternoon, Mr. Chaudhary."

"What the hell?"

Adam's words expressed Maria's disbelief.

"How did they do this so fast?"

"They did it ahead of time," said Adams.

Ari sat at the desk next to the announcer, his hair smoothed back and a well-cut blazer sitting easily on his shoulders.

"Congratulations, Mr. Chaudhary. You seem to have a knack for ingenious solutions for saving the world."

Ari smiled and nodded, accepting the compliment with grace. He was almost as smooth as Storm – except not quite, his self-importance slipping through at the edges.

"The little shit," Maria said.

"He lied to us." There was a lethal flatness to Adam's voice.

"I doubt it."

Ari didn't lie. Not that she had seen. His perception got skewed by his ego but he always told the truth as he saw it.

Maria scanned forward through the video to Ari leaning forward, his hands clasped in front of him. "—Treatment reverses the damage caused by the earlier models and will allow us to continue to produce and enhance the newer versions without causing harm."

"How soon can we expect it to be available?"

Ari was nodding, a slight frown on his forehead. As earnest as the damn announcer.

"That's what many people will want to know. I can say that we will get it out as fast as we can. The same way the Gatherer was made available to the world, so will the cure. The Gatherer belongs to all of us. It's our future."

Adams exhaled in disgust.

Maria felt the distaste of the blatant pandering.

The video had moved back to the stage with Storm at the mic.

"It is a revolutionary device and it has brought our world great things."

It then switched to her shaking hands with the Prime Minister, abundant goodwill oozing off all of them like honey. Somehow they had made it look like Storm was leaving instead of arriving.

It wasn't what they would have wanted: Storm standing in front of the world, saying there was a cure. But it might work, the power of both Ari and Storm on the screen enough to make it look like they were together. Had Stanton managed to control this disaster?

We need your help, she typed.

Adams moved to the door and checked the corridor. The silence was absolute but for the distant sound of rain.

A link to another video arrived.

She ignored it and typed.

To get out of here.

Watch it.

Maria's anxiety was rising. Sooner or later they would be found, and they needed to be gone before that happened.

She clicked on the link as Adams came back beside her.

"Another one? Christ, we need to get going."

The image was grainier, taken from a longer distance and at an odd angle, but it showed Storm at the mic, her chin lifted to the sky before she had said her final words.

"She has access to the cameras too?" said Adams.

"I guess so"

Storm looked up into the tree, the moment when it had felt she had looked right at her.

"But it's killing people, and it needs to be stopped."

Even the world seemed to stop in that moment. A pause before it started up again on a different track. One of those moments that changes everything, before Storm looked at her feet.

Storm's collapse had been instant, like something had reached out of the ground and grabbed her. And, in a way, it had – the electromagnetic field from that cable was better than a physical blow.

The ensuing chaos was quick. The soldiers coming in around Storm, Adams's dark hair recognizable now that she knew he had been there. The crowd was on their feet, trying to take photos and film as the guards had circled them. Pushed them back. And Stanton was at the center of it, gripping Alicia's arm, as the Prime Minister's motorcade had sped away.

I'm releasing it now. Thirty news stations.

It would be the truth everyone was waiting for. The final piece that would destroy the illusion Stanton and the corporation had created.

No. Wait. Maria typed.

"Isn't this what we want?" Adams anger was quick with an edge to it that sent a warning.

Maria continued typing.

We'll need it as a distraction.

She could sense Amanda and Adams calming, recognizing what she wanted to do.

There was power in being that calming influence, her mind clear and sharp.

Explain. Amanda responded.

There was the distant sound of a door opening, followed by footsteps on tiles.

Maria met Adams' gaze.

Can you lock off this corridor?

On it.

Adams moved to the door as Maria typed. He slipped into the corridor and moved out of sight.

She had the briefest anxiety before she let it slide away. She was all in now. No matter what happened, there was no going back.

THIRTY-FOUR

MARIA AND ADAMS STOOD outside the closed door, their backs pressed to the wall. Maria took a quick look through the window at a large lab-type room, much like the makeshift morgue, except this one held a large flat basin at its center.

She lifted her shoulders, silently asking Adams where Storm had gone. He jerked his head towards the room, confirming she was in there, out of sight.

She laid her hand gently on the handle and tried to turn. Locked. She waited, not knowing if Amanda was still with them. She scanned the hall for cameras as the lock clicked.

They launched into the room. Adams first. Maria behind.

Storm floated in the tank and a soldier stood behind the glass of a control room. Adams' bullet shot through the glass and into the man's forehead while he was still reaching for his pistol. He wavered for an instant, his mild look of surprise making him look like a small boy before he toppled over.

She closed the door and pulled the blind as Adams moved to the control room. The rain wouldn't be enough to cover the sound of the shot that reverberated between the bare walls.

She circled the tub, the air in the room heavy with moisture. There were no windows except for the one to the control room, the only way out was the door they had come through. How long until someone arrived? A minute? Maybe two?

Maria reached the far side of the tub. A channel ran from the tub to the outer wall, murky restless water shifting through it. A barrier blocked where it reached the wall, but Maria knew the ditch it would meet on the other side.

She turned to the tank and leaned over. And there she was, Maria's relief so powerful that for a second she didn't move. Storm's skin was sallow and her white singlet clung to her wasted ribs and legs, but she was alive. Maria pressed her fingers into her neck, and felt the slow, distant pulse.

Storm's neck was supported on a head rest with five styrofoam bands floating her legs, arms and waist. Electrodes were attached to her forehead and ran over the edge of the tub, across the floor to the control room where Adams was dragging the soldier's body out of the way. The rest of Storm was free of attachments, the water rippling and lapping at the edges as if disturbed by the shot.

Maria peeled off the electrodes, leaving a series of red welts on Storm's forehead. Small bits of plant matter had discolored the white of her shirt and shorts, leaving smears of mustard green.

She plunged her arms into the water up to her elbows, the water warmer than she expected, and lifted Storm out of the tub. Water streamed down her front and onto the floor. Adams was beside her, removing the styrofoam floats before stepping back. His gaze lingered on Storm.

"Can you get us out?" Maria said.

She indicated the barrier that lead to the outside.

He didn't reply but moved back to the control room. Maria adjusted Storm's weight. She was at the edge of the channel, the bottom not visible through the murk. She heard Adams release the barrier mechanism as she stepped down into the ditch, the water from Storm running down her stomach to meet the water flooding her boots and reaching her hips. The cold shocked her even as she felt a surge of energy.

She looked to Adams, the reflection on the window of the control room preventing her from seeing anything more than his outline.

She lowered herself into the water, feeling its coolness steal the heat of her arm pits and chest. The barrier had slid back, revealing the dimness of an enclosed tunnel. She pushed off the bottom and floated towards the opening. She hadn't heard anyone arriving but that didn't mean they weren't there.

Adams reached the edge of the channel and she paused, the arch of the barrier overhead.

"Come on!"

They had rarely talked on maneuvers, had known the protocol and each other so well there had been no need. He was looking down at them, and more specifically Storm, unable to draw his attention from her face.

"Now."

She funneled all her anxiety, fear and urgency into the single word. He couldn't help but hear it. Yet he shouldn't need to.

The water lapped at the back of her neck. A new strike of cold.

"We have a better chance of getting out together. You know that."

He tore his gaze from Storm and lifted his frighteningly calm gaze to hers.

"Three of us are too easy to see. I'll find my own way out."

She shook her head, started to move back towards him, and thought she heard a noise outside the door.

"There is no other way."

He looked towards the door. He had heard it too.

"Go." He was already moving back to the control room "I'll close the door behind you."

She couldn't wait. Couldn't leave him behind. More waste laid at the feet of the Gatherer. She pushed off the bottom, the low ceiling of the tunnel closing around them. She wanted to call out, one last chance for him not to do this. She floated into the dimness as the barrier began to close. She turned to watch it, hoping for his sudden splash into the channel, a quick escape before it closed.

A dull thud marked the closing and she held Storm tighter against her. The water grew colder, her own panicked breathing echoing around them. She was in almost complete darkness, the barest outline of the tunnel and the slightest reflection on the water all she could see.

She turned away from the barrier and pushed forward, letting Storm float in the water, her head on her shoulder. There was no response from Storm, no fight in her muscles and Maria prayed they hadn't been too late.

Did she hear shouting? At the sound of a gunshot, she froze, turning to the darkness behind them as she held Storm against her. The water and tunnel vibrated with her heart beat, the darkness of that gunshot deeper than the tunnel.

When she heard nothing more, she pushed away from the sound and everything it might mean, moving fast, the light growing as they passed beneath the facility. Eventually she heard a low hum, that formed into the patter of rain, the vertical grate in the channel that she had seen from the outside taking shape ahead of them. She floated as close as she could without being seen, the rain and clouds making the day as dark as dusk.

When she was sure no one was waiting, she adjusted her grip on Storm and used one hand to test the grate. It didn't move any more than when she had tested it from the other side. She felt around the frame for a switch or release mechanism, her feet growing numb, her nose cold.

She backed up, tried to kick it, but could get no leverage, the grate too strong even if she were on dry land.

Her fingers detected no warmth where she held Storm, their heat no match for the insistence of the water. The tunnel behind them receded into darkness. The walls and roof were smooth and flat. Was this really how it would end? To get this far only to be left to slowly sink into hypothermia. Adams could be dead by now, or in custody. No one would know they were here.

There was a sudden screech above her, the sound of metal reluctant to move, and the grate slowly slid sideways, protesting every inch.

Drops struck her face, the water from the tub, the sky and the ditch combining. It was colder beyond the building and the buzz of the hammering rain surrounded them.

Maria didn't check for soldiers or patrols beyond the immediate edges of the ditch, focused instead on moving forward. They reached the section of the channel protected by the underbrush, a single branch dipping down to touch the water, and she ducked beneath it, the leaves scraping across her cheek.

At the junction with the main canal, she paused before entering the channel. She turned to face backwards, supporting Storm's shoulders and head and letting the rest float behind them. She thought she heard the sound of running feet and she pushed off the concrete base with her heels.

The water grew colder and she moved faster, Storm in her shorts and singlet more vulnerable than Maria was. But whether it was the cold or the outside light, Storm looked more alive, as if she had suddenly looked back towards Maria and the world.

Where the canal reached the ocean, she paused. She would need to swim beyond the perimeter fence that extended over ten metres beyond the shore, the waves large and rolling at its end. The cresting waves would make them harder to see, and Amanda would have released the video, but if anyone was watching from the compound, they would be seen.

Maria removed her boots and sunk them to the bottom, her feet even colder without their protection. She turned onto her back, floating Storm above her, her back resting on Maria's chest. She pushed off, feeling the bottom drop off beneath them as they entered the full breadth of the ocean.

The waves crashed over her shoulders, spraying water into her face, and she kicked harder, feeling the movement of the currents below the surface, the force of the ocean surrounding them. Wind slashed against the shoreline, the grounds of the compound hidden behind the gleaming algae-covered boulders that lined the shore. Between the rain and the waves, she could see nothing on land.

Maria had the impression that Storm was moving. Or it could be the ocean playing tricks. They made slow progress, each chain link of the fence passing slowly, the waves trying to push them into the metal links. She struggled to stay afloat, choked on the crashing waves, unable to tell whether Storm was swallowing water.

A long metal guiding wire ran out from the end of the fence to an anchor on the bottom of the ocean. She swam around it, waves cascading over the side of her head and then they were floating with the waves, rolling up and down. Storm's head rested close against Maria and she had the impression again of a tightening of muscles, the slightest kick to keep her afloat.

Maria floated as far as she could, rocks scraping against her feet, the waves trying to batter them against the boulders. The current had pushed them down the coast and she drifted into a small cove. She hoisted Storm onto a low-lying rock, flipping her onto her back away from the waves before she clambered out.

For the first time she had a clear view back towards the compound. Rain and wind lashed the open area, the shoreline empty.

She levered Storm to a sitting position and lifted her over her shoulder. She moved slowly on the rocks, climbing up and over the slippery mounds, until she reached the overgrown grasses of the empty lot, the roar of the wind and ocean buffered by the stones. A faint trail led along the base of rocks, veering away from the water after several paces. She followed it, feeling the blood return to her limbs, the distant warmth of Storm across her shoulders.

She followed the trail that lead along the back of the warehouses and at the last building looked for the low dumpster. She fell in behind it, lowering Storm to lean against it. Storm's lips were the faintest blue and tiny veins showed at her temple. Her hands and feet were a bloodless white.

Maria checked around the corner. An old camper van idled in the dirt parking lot, exactly as Amanda had promised.

Someone will be there.

Yet Maria couldn't help but feel fear.

She lifted Storm in her arms and ran to the vehicle's side door. It opened as she reached it, a blast of warm cigarette smoke greeting her along with a spotless compact kitchen, a bench along the back, and Amanda's shiny black hair in the driver's seat.

"Get in." Amanda's face was pale, a cigarette in the hand that gripped the wheel, the knuckles white.

Maria climbed in, lowered Storm onto the bench, and pulled shut the sliding door.

There was a small jerk and they were moving, the smell of diesel exhaust adding to the smoke.

Maria looked behind them, still expecting pursuit.

Rain pounded the broken pavement, the wind bent the faded grasses, and broken concrete barriers marked the end of the road where it butted against the compound.

"There are blankets under the seat."

Maria tore her eyes from the barriers and opened the drawers beneath the bench. Towels, blankets, pillows and instant heat packs were jammed into the drawer.

Amanda drove, and every part of Maria wanted to tell her to drive faster. Even now she could feel the force that would follow them gathering strength, knew the focus of the team that would pursue them.

She pulled off Storm's shorts and singlet and used one of the towels to dry her off.

At an intersection, Amanda tapped keys on a laptop on the passenger seat, wires and cables connecting it to a cell phone and several boxes.

"Did you release the video?"

Amanda nodded as she exhaled cigarette smoke.

She imagined it propagating out into the world, the illusion that the world would be saved cracked and broken on the ground.

Maria laid Storm out on the bench and wrapped her in several blankets. She activated several of the heating pads and slid them into the blanket one layer away from her skin. The blank stillness of Storm's feature frightened her, the movement she thought she had felt in the ocean, only her imagination.

"How is she?"

She met Amanda's gaze in the rear-view mirror. The clear space created by the wipers on the windshield showed low, industrial strip malls.

"I don't know."

She wished she had asked what was in the needles Storm had used in emergencies and knew what would help other than rest and sleep. Could she even come back from an attack like that? Or had that been Stanton's intention? To damage her so much, she would never again be a threat.

Maria dried Storm's hair and slipped a pillow under her head.

"Will the fields from the engine hurt her?" Amanda watched her in the mirror.

She looked down at Storm's still form – the fields could be attacking right now, Storm too weak to respond.

"Do you have an emergency blanket?"

They were stopped at an intersection, the large green signs for the freeway up ahead.

"In the cupboard behind me."

Amanda ground out her cigarette and tapped rapidly on the screen.

Maria found the first aid kit tucked under a flashlight.

"We can't take the highway," said Maria.

Amanda kept tapping. A car behind them honked when Amanda didn't move on the green light.

They crept forward and Amanda set her turn signal for the on ramp.

"They have the most extensive video network," said Amanda. "It's the easiest way for me to control what they see. Smaller roads would leave us open to random appearances on private networks."

The sound of the engine deepened as they climbed up the ramp. Several video images flashed on the laptop, before they began to go dark one by one.

"Should I drive?"

Amanda shook her head, fully focused on driving and managing the cameras.

THE GATHERER

"You're too recognizable."

Realizing how close she had crept to the front window, she pulled back, kneeling down to wrap the shiny emergency blanket around Storm. She leaned down close to her ear.

"Storm."

Had her eyelid flickered? Or was it the acceleration as they merged onto the highway?

Maria unfolded a second emergency blanket and made a rough hood to cover Storm's skull. Only the round circle of her face showed between the shiny material.

She laid her hand on Storm's forehead and felt the cold drawing the heat from her skin. She pressed both her palms to Storm's cheeks, willing her heat to feed into Storm. She wrapped her fingers behind Storm's neck, pushing back the cold, forcing warmth into her skin.

Storm's eyelids fluttered. An effort from a long way away.

Maria activated another heating pad, reheating her hands before pressing them to Storm.

Another flicker, Storm's eyes unfocussed.

Maria stripped off her wet clothes. They were cruising in the slow lane, people in the vehicles next to them taking no notice. She slid in beside Storm, keeping the blankets and emergency blankets in place. Storm was cold everywhere she touched.

She pressed her body against Storm's and felt her heat drawn away. But it was more than heat she was giving Storm. Their energies were merging, her own stable, solid energy providing the foundation for Storm's fragmented, damaged signal. She gave into it, imagining she could feel Storm drawing on her energy, using it to fill her depleted reserves, to come back and return to the world.

It was several minutes before she noticed a change, Storm's limp body tightening with the smallest of movement. Maria loosened her hold, drawing back the tiniest of fractions.

Storm's eyes opened, for longer this time, as if from a long sleep. She moved her head, lifted a shoulder in an attempt to rise.

"Stay where you are," said Maria.

Storm turned her head, her wild, panicked gaze finding Maria's.

She waited for Storm to see her, for the synapses in her brain to connect. How much damage had she sustained? Was she still in there?

Storm's mouth opened, her lips dry, the word barely above a whisper.

"Daniel."

Maria squeezed her tight.

"You're okay now. We got you out."

Storm seemed to relax, her fingers curling over Maria's arm as her gaze swept the roof of the camper, and the rush of trees and signposts past the window.

Maria met Amanda's gaze in the rearview mirror and nodded. It wasn't much, a few moments of consciousness, but it would have to do. Amanda nodded in return before looking forward to the looming bulk of the mountain range ahead.

Maria leaned back, her shoulder resting against the back of the bench, and tightened her hand around Storm's waist. She felt the slightest pressure on her arm in response.

ACKNOWLEDGEMENTS

THE LAST TWO YEARS have been a wild ride by any standards, and the path to get THE DISRUPTORS published has been no different. I am happy to be able to finally offer it to the world.

There are many people to thank for their on-going support and for occasionally allowing me to cling to their life raft while we navigated turbulent waters. First and foremost, I want to thank my writing coach and mentor Sherry Coman, for talking me back from the edge many times and for her unwavering belief. I also want to thank the people at Thrillerfest and in particular the Debut Authors program for their on-going support and outreach during the pandemic. I want to thank Chris Albanese, Shamus Bérubé, Philippa and Ben Campbell, and Chris Trower for their technical expertise, any errors are mine alone. Lori Twining, as always, is my irreplaceable advisor and sage companion on this writing journey. I want to thank Rebecca and Andrew at Design for Writers for providing potentially the largest life raft of all when I was reconstructing my writing career, and fellow author Mike Attebery for showing me the self-publishing ropes. I want to thank my agent, Gail Fortune of the Talbot Fortune Agency for her hard work and willingness to keep moving forward. Lastly, I couldn't have done this without the support from an overwhelming number of family and friends who continued to believe in this series even during the most challenging times. Thank you. And, of course, none of this would be possible without Ron, Bella and Elise.

ABOUT THE AUTHOR

Colleen Winter likes to explore. Books, ideas, and people. When she isn't writing, she spends her time climbing and hiking the beautiful places of the world with her family and her dog.

She was short-listed for the 2020 Rakuten Kobo Emerging Writer Prize in Speculative Fiction, received two Writer's Reserve grants from the Ontario Arts Council, won the Best First Sentence Contest at Thrillerfest 2018, won first prize in the CAA Leacock/Simcoe Erotic prose contest, received a SLS Fellowship from the Unified Literary Contest, and is an alumni of the Humber School of Writers. She is an electrical engineer, a former journalist, the past-President of the Writer's Community of Simcoe County and is currently an organizer of Word Up Barrie.

You can find her at:

Website: www.colleenwinter.ca
Instagram: winter_colleen
Twitter: @ColleenWinter3
Facebook: https://www.facebook.com/ColleenWinterAuthor
Goodreads: https://www.goodreads.com/colleenwinter

Manufactured by Amazon.ca
Bolton, ON